Die Laughing

by
Louis K Lowy

Die Laughing
All Rights Reserved
ISBN-13: 978-1-925148-46-6
Copyright ©2011, 2015 Louis K Lowy
V2.1 US

IFWG Publishing International
Melbourne, Australia
www.ifwgpublishing.com

Acknowledgements

Though writing is a solitary endeavor, it is never truly done alone. Many thanks to the following: John Dufresne for his generosity and guidance. The mighty Friday Night Writers for not allowing me to take the easy way out. Michael Gavaghen, Corey Ginsberg, and Melanie Mochan for being my support group. Aralis Bloise for helping me to utilize the Internet. Linda Couto for being my first reader. Kassandra Guzman for the cover mock-up. Debbie Orta, my eagle-eyed proofreader. Mark Goldberg and David Beaty for encouragement. Lynne Barrett for invaluable advice. Les Standiford for introducing me to *The Power of Myth*. Gerry Huntman for his stewardship, and IFWG Publishing for being so easy to work with.

Special thanks to my wife, Carol, and our children Christopher and Katie. Without your support it would have never happened.

For the real life Lois and Dick.

Chapter One
THE LUCKY LOUNGE 1956

"I couldn't trust my wife, that's why we got a divorce." Sam E. took a drag of his Pall Mall. He blew a heavy smoke cloud into the dark room. "She didn't come home one night. And the next day, when I asked her where she was, she said with her sister Phyllis. I knew she was lying." He sipped from his scotch just long enough for the room to hush. "Because *I spent the night with Phyllis.*"

The crowd burst into laughter. Syd Tate, the drummer of The Syd Tate Quartet hit double rim shots on his snare, ending it with a smash to his crash cymbal. Sam E. glanced to the side of the floor stage and winked at a busty blonde standing behind the curtain wings. She puckered her lips at him.

"Any of you folks encounter a spaceship yet?" he asked. "According to the newsreels they're all around us." He wiggled his fingers above his shoulders, and said in a spooky voice, "Waaaoooooh." The crowd chuckled. "A couple of spacemen went to a Mars nightclub, but they left because it had no atmosphere."

Syd Tate foot-thumped a *ba-dawp* on his bass drum.

"Seriously," Sam E. said. "If an athlete gets athlete's foot, what does an alien get? Missile toe?" He stepped from the floor stage center, to the front, where an elderly couple was seated. A cobalt spotlight trailed him like a coal car dogging a locomotive. "Where you folks from?"

"Texas," the man said.

"Texas," Sam E. repeated to the audience. "A Texas oil baron went to the dentist for a check-up. The dentist said, 'Everything's fine'. The baron said, 'Drill anyway, I feel lucky'." Laughter floated across the blue velvet walls.

"What brings you fine folks across the border to Las Vegas?" Sam E. puffed on his cigarette.

"We're newlyweds!" the old man said.

Sam E. bugged his eyes and acted as if he had choked on his cigarette smoke. A shriek of laughter echoed from the back of the crowded club. "I was in a bar the other day with a fellow of your vintage," he said to the man.

The elderly man smiled, as the spotlight lassoed the couple and settled back on Sam E.

"The old man was crying. I said, 'What's the matter, old timer?'" Sam E. glanced back at the busty blonde standing in the wings. She waved and licked her maraschino lips. His eyes widened briefly, and returned to the couple. "The man says, 'I married a beautiful woman'." Sam E. smiled at the elderly man's wife. She smiled and leaned into her husband. "'She's twenty-eight years my junior, built like Gina Lollabrigida, and wants to make whoopee every night'. 'Jeez', I says to the old guy, 'what are you crying for?'" Sam E. skimmed the crowded room, there was an electric hush, not even a rock glass was clinking. I got 'em, he thought. "And the old guy says to me, 'I'm crying because *I can't remember where I live!*'" The crowd crowed with laughter. The Syd Tate Quartet hit a soaring C chord. Sam E. thought, I hit it out of the park! He shook the elderly couple's hands, and said, "Thanks for being great sports." He grabbed a passing waiter. "Give these folks a drink, with my compliments."

A series of spotlights, like scattering UFOs, darted across the cheering crowd. "Ladies and gentlemen," a voice over a PA, said, "Mr. Sam E. Lakeside!"

The audience stood and the cheering renewed itself. Sam E. bowed and threw a kiss with his palm. He glanced one more time at the chesty blonde in the wings, but a diminutive, pointy-nosed man in a blue-satin suit and a small-brimmed fedora was standing where she had been. Sam E. saluted the exuberant crowd with his scotch. As he strutted off stage, the PA voice said, "On behalf of *The Lucky Lounge and Casino*, thank you and enjoy your stay."

He walked into the wings toward Syd Tate, who was packing his drumsticks. As he did, he passed the diminutive man, who doffed his hat and smiled at Sam E.

"Have you seen Mitzi? She was just here," Sam E. said to Syd.

"I wouldn't know," Syd replied. "Not since you took my dressing room."

"I had nothing to do with that."

"Sure you didn't." Syd brusquely walked away.

"Sore sport," Sam E. muttered to himself.

"Sam, it's your agent," a slim, thin-haired janitor, standing by the back-stage door, said. He handed Sam E. the receiver from a wall phone hanging next to him.

"Doc," he said, "I just finished the show. Yeah, I killed 'em…What do you mean I won't be here next week?…But I like this place. Did they dump me?…*The Steve Allen Show*? You're kidding me, right?…Yeeeaaaah!" He hopped in a small circle, tangling the cord around his shoulders. "Doc, I love you!" Unraveling the cord, he added, "Oh, and Marge too!" Before hanging up the receiver Sam E. grabbed the janitor by the shoulders and said, "I'm going to New York, Herkie, *The Steve Allen Show!*"

"I gathered that."

"Have you seen Mitzi? I want to give her the good news."

The janitor shrugged. "Maybe your dressing room."

Sam E. zipped down the hall and into his dressing room. The small, messy room was empty except for the diminutive man in the fedora. He was leaning against the wall filing his nails. He stopped briefly to again tip his hat.

"Who the hell are you?" Sam E. walked up to the man. "And where's Mitzi?"

"Sorry, friend, but I get to ask the questions." The man slipped a spit-polish black .45 from his shoulder holster and shoved it against Sam E.'s forehead. "And my first question is, 'Would you like to take a walk?'"

Chapter Two
HOT DIGGITY

Swhiiik. The shovel's stainless steel round-point blade sliced through the earth. It reflected the DeSoto's headlights as Sam E. forced chunks of mountain soil from their resting place.

Swhiiik. His back ached something awful. His heart was playing leap frog—not because of the physical work—but because the dirt pit was nearly large enough to fit a prone body, which in this case, he knew was going to be his. He stopped, removed his tuxedo jacket, and said, "The Lone Ranger and Tonto are searching for bad guys. Tonto gets off his horse and puts his ear to the ground, 'Hmmm', he says, 'Buffalo come'." The Lone Ranger looks around and says, 'How can you tell?'"

"Clam it," the diminutive man said, aiming the .45 at Sam E.'s damp skull.

"Don't be a party-pooper, Francis," Cricket said to him. "Let him finish, just for yucks. He's funny."

Sam E. studied Francis' slim, curvaceous girlfriend. He thought, if I can get her to like me, maybe I can buy some time. He traced upward Cricket's open-toe black-leather pumps, burnt-orange cigarette slacks, tight black v-neck cardigan, and her fleshy, red lips smiling dangerously at him. Sam E. focused on her emerald-gray eyes and shoulder cut golden-red hair, both made more sensual by the black beret shadowing her forehead. He purposely smiled back at her.

"It's not that funny," Francis said to Cricket. "Tonto answers, 'I can tell Buffalo cum, because ear sticky'."

Sam E. frowned. He leaned into the shovel, resting his clammy armpit over the shank; the DeSoto's headlights flooding his deep, ebony eyes.

"Yech, that's nowheresville," Cricket said, walking to the DeSoto. "I'm gonna play the rad-dio, dad-dyo."

Sam E. pushed his black, wavy-wet hair from his forehead. A ghostly breeze cut across the chilly Nevada mountainside. The comedian shivered as he saw himself lying in the dirt with a bullet in his head.

"Keep digging," Francis said.

"Um, look, Francis. Can I call you Francis?"

"I suppose."

"You seem like a nice guy. How about giving me a break? I'm going on *The Steve Allen Show*. I'll leave town, no one will know. I'll grow a beard and change my name."

"Do you know how many times I've heard that? Not the Steve Allen part; that's new."

"So how about it?" Sam E. flattened his hands together in a pitiful prayer.

"Keep digging." Francis inched the gun closer to Sam E.'s brain.

Swhiiik.

"Hey," Cricket called, poking her head out of the DeSoto's window. "Your engine's reading in the red again."

"There's oil under the back seat," Francis said. "Bring it here and turn off the motor."

"I thought the mob paid you guys better than that," Sam E. said.

"The bigwigs, not me."

"I have some cash saved," Sam E. said, "and my manager's a really good guy. He'll fork over more. How about it?"

"Can I level with you?"

"Sure, we're practically pals," Sam E. hoped.

"I don't pull the strings. If I do a good job, they leave me alone. If I do a bad job, my strings will be cut. I don't like it, but that's the way it is." Francis touched the 45's barrel to Sam E.'s skull. "Now, keep digging."

Swhiiik.

Between shovel strokes, Sam E. heard Cricket shuffling under the seat, the car's radio click on, and a distorted, loud Perry Como lazily crooning "Hot Diggity" through the automobile's tinny speaker.

Cricket stepped from the sedan. She handed Francis the oilcan. Sam E. said, "Oil veh."

Francis said, "Oil veh, isn't that Jewis—"

A low-pitched noise from above, like a bassoon, drowned him out.

The trio looked up. A turquoise streak flamed across the star-sprinkled night. It descended behind the tree-jagged horizon, causing a hoot owl to flutter in the firs.

"A shooting star!" Cricket said. "I wish for a brand-new '56 Thunderbird Roadster. Emerald green!"

Sam E. studied Cricket's bullet-bra bust line. She smiled seductively at him. She *does* like me, he thought. He mentally pleaded for her to save him.

"Keep shoveling," Francis said, watching him watching Cricket. "And do you have to look at my girl like that?" He pressed the gun's barrel tip into Sam E.'s chest.

Swiiik.

Francis said to Cricket, "You want to hear a funny joke? I've got one about a comedian."

Swiiik.

"There was this low-rent Sid Caesar. He was a horn-dog who couldn't keep his prick in his trousers. This Casanova pounds his pecker in the wrong place. Turns out he's humpin' Mr. Green-baum's new girl, Mitzi. When the boss finds out he's doing her, he has his number one hit man—me—pay the lousy comedian a visit. Now that's funny, right?"

Cricket nodded. She eyed Sam E.

He forced the sexiest smile his lips could muster, though his temples throbbed from fear. He knew women loved his dark eyes by the way they admired them and his firm nose and smooth, slightly chubby cheeks, which also served him well with onstage comic expressions. He lobbed a quick wink at her.

Francis raised the gun and crammed it into Sam E.'s ear. "Don't stop your shoveling, funny man. You're almost there."

Chapter Three
EXCAVATION

S am E. thought of the one time his mother tried to be funny. "Sammy, this is a good friend of mine. Leave us alone for a half-hour. Here's a nickel, buy a thirty-minute soda pop."

Sammy didn't come to terms with his mother being a whore until he was eleven, and Al Levin, the grocer's son, said, "Your mom sells pussy."

Sammy quipped, "So does Ted's Pet Store." He didn't hang out with Al much after that.

Swiiik.

Sammy watched his mother grow tiny, haggard, and lusterless. He never exploded, raged, screamed, battered, or spewed venom at her. He settled for a brick barricade mortared with one-liners.

Swiiik.

Sammy discovered his comedic flair as a teenager. As his mother dimmed, he brightened. He discovered his quick wit was a trolley car to parties, booze, and girls—especially girls. The more they laughed the more they adored him. Their adoration made him feel bright, like a stage light. People laughed, and he was someone who mattered. Females, especially, thought he was special. One girl, as she unzipped her skirt, said it had to do with, "Your funny jokes and sad eyes." He cracked a one-liner. She chuckled, nibbled his neck, and unbuttoned his fly. Though he never fell in love with them, Sam E. loved women. By the time he left home at sixteen, he had bedded several.

Swiiik.

Sammy Langstein evolved into comedian Sam E. Lakeside six years later, somewhere between scrounging as an aluminum siding salesman and his pathetic stab as a singing waiter. Jokes came easy to Sammy and even more easily to Sam E. As Sam E. Lakeside, he cracked one-liners through the toilet clubs of Chicago, across the wealthy Catskills, and eventually to the jangle of Las Vegas. This puffed his ego up so much he stuck his prick in the wrong place.

Swiiik.

He stopped digging. Against his better judgment, he wiped his brow as an excuse for time to think. He took in Cricket's daddy long legs and firm, round hips, swizzling to "Hot Diggity." She's my lifeline, without her I'm dead meat. He puffed his chest in the hopes his sweaty, fairly in-shape body would attract her attention.

Click.

He turned. The barrel of the .45 was locked between his eyes.

Francis glanced at the hole Sam E. was standing in. "Deep enough."

"Don't I get a last request?"

"This isn't Alcatraz."

"One last joke. It'll be funny, I promise."

"Come on, Francis," Cricket said. "Let's hear what he has to say. For giggles." She brushed the tip of her tongue ever-so-slightly outside and against Francis' ear, and at the same time winked at Sam E.

"Sure, doll baby." Francis dug the gun in Sam E.'s forehead and said to him, "Make it quick. Mr. Greenbaum gets upset if I take too long."

Sam E. smiled at Cricket. Her ripened lips turned slightly upward and steeled. Her green-gray eyes inured to a magnum-gray. Up until that moment he believed she wanted to help him; hoped she would smash Francis over the head and shove his diminutive body in the death hole. Watching her eyebrows arc in anticipation, he thought all she wanted was the thrill, the exhilaration, the sexual charge of seeing his life end in a soiled, point-blank heap. She wanted a giggle.

Sam E.'s pulse played duck-duck-goose. He groped for anything to prolong his breathing. "An escaped convict—a hit man—breaks into a house. He binds and gags a young married couple in their bedroom."

"Pick it up," Francis said.

"Relax, I haven't got to the funny part yet."

"He hasn't got to the funny part," Cricket repeated, widening her eyes.

"While the escaped hit man is ransacking the place downstairs the husband gets his gag loose. 'Honey', he says to his wife, 'this guy hasn't seen a woman in years. Just do what he says. If he wants sex, go along with it. Our lives depend on it'."

"Come on, come on." Francis checked his watch. "Mr. Greenbaum's waiting to hear from me."

"Shush," Cricket said, swaying her hips.

"After the guy tells his wife to go along with whatever the hit man wants, the wife spits out her gag." Sam E. watched Francis kneading his lip, knowing his patience had nearly succumbed to his trigger finger. "The wife says, 'Sweetie, I'm so glad you feel that way'." I don't want to die, Sam E. thought, I don't *deserve* to die. I want my shot on *Steve Allen. I earned the goddamn right.* He commanded his legs to run, but fear froze his kneecaps and ankles. He ordered his hands to choke Francis' bird neck but his fingers went AWOL. His humor was the thing that never deserted him. He said to Francis, "Here it comes, get ready." He thought again of *The Steve Allen Show,* his big break, the millions who would laugh at his jokes. His mark in the world. He blurted out, "The wife says, 'I'm so glad you feel that way because the hit man just told me what a nice tight ass he thought you had!" Sam E. leaped from his grave.

"Hey, that's funny," Cricket said.

"Son of a bitch!" Francis stuck his leg out and tripped Sam E. as he tried to run past him.

He tumbled to the ground.

Francis lowered the barrel to Sam E.'s face. He remained stone still; his close-set mahogany eyes contemplating the cowering comedian.

Sam E. stared into the black hole of the barrel, so close it looked like a hollowed log. He screamed, "No! No! *No!*" Sweat trickled from his eye corner, down his trembling cheek. He was about to squeeze his eyes shut when he saw a green-tinged platinum mist— like the devil-dancing mist bottoming Niagara Falls—surround him. His limbs chilled. He felt the haze thicken and girdle his body. The shiny green fog blinded his vision. He screamed but the sound was smothered. The fog stiffened like hardened cement. He struggled to breathe. Sam E. felt his body rise with the mist and float away.

Chapter Four
OVER THE RAINBOW

Sam E. opened his eyes. He was lying on a platform. Standing over him, as if he was confined to a hospital bed, were silver-haired cowboy Hopalong Cassidy, austere TV evangelist Fulton J. Sheen decked out in his full body cape and zucchetto, Jack Benny's bulbous-eyed black butler Rochester, flamboyant gossip columnist Hedda Hopper in a wide-brimmed mushroom cloud hat, and suave singer Nat King Cole. "Hot Diggity" weaved like a sidewinder through the room.

The group poked and prodded Sam E., each looking at the other curiously as they touched him. He shut his eyes and re-opened them to make sure they were in the open position. They were.

"Wire-draw stock-still," Hopalong said to him, as he pushed a spiky thing, like a fluorescent, twinkling knitting needle, into Sam E.'s nostril.

Sam E. tried to move but his body wouldn't budge. He felt a cold ache creep inside his nose and behind his forehead. He screamed.

The group stepped back. Hopalong removed the thick needle. Puzzled, he looked at Fulton J. Sheen.

Archbishop Sheen jiggled, blurred, re-jiggled, and became silky-haired Lassie. The collie stood on its haunches, wagged its tail, and said to Sam E., "Ameliorate?"

Sam E. fainted.

His body jerked. He coughed. Sam E. opened his eyes; his vision went from blur to soft-focus to focus. This time no one was standing over him. Sam E. was lying on an octagon shaped platform. Cricket, unconscious, was lying next to him. He looked around. They were in the center of a large, ring-shaped room with a tall concave ceiling.

The brightly lit room was empty except for a gray, refrigerator sized, egg shaped object near the wall. A steamy mist floated from its top. The oval object was held upright by a concave pedestal that reminded Sam E. of a hard-boiled egg cup.

He sat up. The platform he had been lying on, and now sitting, looked spiky hard, like a corrugated manhole cover, but his rump felt like it was resting on JELL-O. The platform was floating bed-high off the ground. Sam E. could plainly see the round, undecorated room he was in, but there were no lights, or light beams. No shadows. He shook Cricket. "Come on. Wake up."

Her eyes remained shut.

"Wake up," he repeated, patting her cheeks.

Her eyes jerked open. She screamed.

He pressed his palm over her mouth to stifle the sound. Her eyes searched frantically to make sense of her surroundings. When she calmed, he said, "I'm lifting my hand now, okay?"

Cricket nodded.

"Don't scream." He slowly removed his palm and helped her up.

Cricket scratched her beret. She again looked around.

Sam E. took a couple of steps. He stomped his foot a few times against the brass-like floor. "It feels marshmellowee, like the platform. Where are we?"

Cricket slowly spun her body, studying the hoop-shaped room. When she faced him again, she said, "In space."

"What kind of space?"

"'*Gort, Klatuu berata nik-toe*' space."

"Is that Russian? Are we in The Soviet Union?"

"Don't you go to the movies?" Cricket asked. "*The Day the Earth Stood Still?*"

"I work, remember?"

"It's what Patricia Neal said to Gort the robot. It's outer-space talk."

Sam E. stared at her for a minute. "Where's the punch line?" He burst out laughing. "There's always a punch line."

She shook her head. "I don't think so. In the movies the spaceships are always round, and this room is round."

"Do you want to know what I think? I think I'm having a bad dream."

"No, I don't think so," Cricket repeated.

"Sister, you're out of your gourd."

"Don't 'sister' me. My dad called me that, and I hate it."

"Fine, but we're not on a spaceship. We might've been picked up by Commies or something, but not bug-eyed monsters."

Cricket pointed to the egg shaped object standing upright near the wall. "How do you explain that?"

"You go to the movies, you tell me," Sam E. said, studying the steamy mist rising from the top of the egg shape. "It's probably a leaky pipe. We're in a Commie prison, and that's a leaky pipe."

"In Las Vegas?" Cricket asked.

"McCarthy says the Reds are everywhere."

"Go check it out."

"I will," he said, defiantly, "but I'm telling you we're in a gulag and the FBI's gonna save us." He approached the giant egg, Cricket walking behind him. Moving in close, he said to her, "It's just a leaky—"

The egg started spinning. Sam E. jumped back, bumping into Cricket. It stopped rotating.

"What the hell?" he exclaimed.

Cricket, beside him, said, "Get close to it again, and see if it starts turning."

"I don't think so. You do it."

"Let's both do it," she said.

"Not on your life."

"Are you afraid of the Commies?"

"No!"

Cricket shrugged. "Well?"

He smirked. "Okay. We'll both do it."

They looked at each other, nodded, and gingerly stepped forward. The egg object started spinning again. It became translucent.

"Look." Sam E. pointed inside the egg.

An image appeared inside the egg. It showed, from a viewpoint a few feet above it, the grave Sam E. had dug for himself.

"See?" he said. "We're still on the mountain."

The translucent egg jiggled, blurred, and re-jiggled, and the image inside changed to an ebony abyss sprinkled with sparkling red and gold pinpricks. Occasional brown-gray craggy slabs—some colossal, some miniscule—leisurely drifted by like mollies in a five-and-dime fish tank.

"That's outer space," Cricket said. "Those big things are asteroids and those tiny sparkly things are distant stars. Maybe it's where they come from."

"All that is, is a picture of the sky and the mountainside," Sam E. replied, walking around the egg. As he circled, he saw the same view from different angles. The thing reminded him of the crystal globe the Wicked Witch of the West watched Dorothy with. "It's three dimensional," he added. "I have to hand it to the Commies, they know how to build a television." He poked his finger in the egg but whipped it back.

"What happened?" Cricket asked.

"It was like a vacuum cleaner. It wanted to suck me in." He took a nickel from his pocket and held it next to the egg. He let go and the coin, as if drawn by a magnet, flew into it and disappeared.

"It was sucked into space," Cricket said.

"We're not in space. We're in a gulag somewhere on the mountain."

The image crackled as if lightning had interrupted the reception. The craggy slabs disappeared and the *I Love Lucy Show* appeared. Ricky was scolding Lucy for infiltrating his nightclub act.

"What the crap?" Sam E. asked.

Once more the object crackled. *I Love Lucy* disappeared, and inside the egg was a round, blue sphere floating in space.

"Look!" Cricket pointed to the globe-like object. "That's gotta be Earth. We're looking at our planet!"

Sam E. stared at the ball for a moment. Then he laughed hard. Not the 'Now this is funny' laugh, which he was making fun of Cricket with. This was a panicky, gut-wrenching noise that nearly caused him to vomit. He ran from the egg, banged his fists against the walls of the ring-shaped room, w h i c h felt like an inner tube against his skin. He circled the room until he couldn't catch his breath and his stomach hurt with exhaustion. He lay back on the floating platform he had woken up on and closed his eyes. He thought this would be a good time to wake up from his nightmare.

"You okay?" Cricket dabbed his face with a hanky slipped from inside her bra.

Chanel N°5 caressed his nostrils. He took a deep whiff. The perfume settled around him like a warm hug. He opened his eyes and said, softly, "How the hell did we get here? And what do they want with us?"

Cricket shook her head.

"Why didn't they take Francis?"

"You know as much as I do."

"Aren't you afraid?"

"Yeah," she said. "But in the movies it usually turns out okay."

"How?" he asked.

"A scientist figures out a way to kill the spacemen."

"Do you know any scientists?"

Cricket shook her head.

Sam E. groaned. "Neither do I." He rubbed his aching temples, and thought, this is a joke and there's got to be a punch line. There's always a punch line.

Wooouuush

Sam E. bolted upright, staring in the direction of the windy noise. Abruptly, as if someone had stuck a wedge in the top of a waterfall, the wall siphoned apart, and through the haze a shadowy figure appeared.

Chapter Five
SAY KIDS!
WHAT TIME IS IT?

Sam E. felt Cricket inching closer to him as the shadowy figure emerged into the light.

"Francis?" Sam E. watched the diminutive man in his fedora approach them.

"Say kids, what time is it?" Francis asked.

On Francis' shoulder was a freckle-faced wooden puppet with red hair, ears sticking out like open taxi doors and a brimming, gap-toothed smile so over-abundant it was more creepy than cheerful. He was dressed in tiny boots, dungarees, a plaid cowboy shirt and a neckerchief tied around his neck so that the flap was facing front. Sam E. recognized him immediately.

"It's fucking Howdy Doody time," Francis said, standing in front of Sam E. and Cricket.

"Fawking," the marionette repeated. It extended its hand-carved neck forward, and said to Sam E., "We ain't from this direction, Flippy. Ree-al gone. Fluttered from beyond. Cannon when feasting your loam. Spade what we blade. Keep. Ya dig?"

Sam E. kneaded the nape of his neck, hoping it would relieve his headache. He said to Francis, "You killed me, right? I'm not in space. I'm in hell."

"You're not dead," Francis said. "Meet my galactic friend." He motioned to the Howdy Doody puppet.

"Compeer, fidus Achates," Howdy Doody said.

"Howdy Doody's from outer space?" Sam E. asked.

"Don't be ridiculous, that's not the real Howdy Doody," Francis said. "When they fly over earth they pick up our television signals and they can make themselves look like anyone who's been on the airwaves. They get a kick out of it."

"They? Who are they?"

"The saucer-men," Francis said. "Don't ask me where they come from. They showed me a map, but I couldn't make sense of it."

"What do they really look like?" Cricket asked.

"You don't want to know," Francis replied.

Sam E. studied the alien. "How do they become television people?"

"I bet it's like in *It Came From Outer Space*," Cricket said. "The aliens slip inside the townspeople's bodies and take them over."

"You're not listening," Francis said. "They don't take over bodies, they copy them. The real people are still around."

Sam E. said to the puppet, "Can you look like someone who hasn't been on television? Can you look like me?"

"Hey, you talk to me!" Francis said, his voice filled with fury. "I'm in control."

"Sorry." Sam E. was taken aback by his anger. "Well, can they?"

Francis said to the puppet, "Can you look like someone who hasn't been on television?"

The puppet shook his head.

"They can only duplicate someone who's been on TV," Francis said to Sam E.

"It's kind of like the Metaluna spacemen in *This Island Earth*," Cricket said. "They had the Interositer, a weird contraption that allowed them to pick up airwaves."

Howdy Doody nodded.

Sam E. said to the alien, "You hear the one about the two antennas who met on the rooftop, fell in love and got married? The ceremony was lousy, but the reception was terrific."

Francis backhanded Sam E. across the mouth. "I told you to talk to me!" His hand thrust nearly caused the puppet to tumble from Francis' shoulder.

Sam E. doubled over.

Francis raised his fist and advanced on him.

Cricket grabbed his arm. "What's got into you? We need his help to fight the," she discreetly nodded toward the alien puppet, "ace-spay uppet-pay."

"Don't *ever* grab me like that again." Francis jerked her hand away. "I pull the strings, now. You got that?"

Cricket, stunned, nodded.

"Him and I are business partners." Francis cradled the puppet. "Aren't we?"

The puppet vigorously nodded his freckled face. "How-do, partner."

Sam E., wiping a blood trickle from his mouth, said to Francis, "How'd you guys become partners?"

"I owe it all to you."

"What does that mean?"

"Remember that shooting star?" Francis asked.

"The one Cricket wished on?"

"That was their saucer," Francis said. "They had mechanical problems and had to land. They heard the car radio and decided to check it out. We didn't know it, but they were watching us nearly the whole time."

"Okay, what does that have to do with me?"

"You remember when you fell on the ground and I pointed my gun at you?"

"How could I forget?"

"You won't believe this, but I almost let you go," Francis said.

"Why? Because I was funny?"

"You were pitiful. But I liked the twist about *The Steve Allen Show*. It was touching in a pathetic way."

"Oh," Sam E. said, disappointed.

"Anyway, before I had the chance to decide, you screamed 'No'. The sound scared the creatures and they shot that green mist at you. That's how you ended up on their ship."

"How did that make you partners with them?" Sam E. asked.

"Now, that's a good one. After they zapped you and Cricket, they came after me. That's when I saw how they really looked. I was haunted house scared. So scared, I dropped my pistol. There was only one thing I could do."

"Run like hell?" Sam E. asked.

Francis smiled. "I threw the oilcan I was still carrying at them. The oil splattered on their faces and they went fruity, like frogs on a hot-plate."

Howdy Doody bounced his pine-limbed body like he was trying not to pee in his pants. "Oy-yell, Oy-yell, Oy-yell!"

"You see?" Francis patted the puppet's shoulder. "After that, the spacemen and I had a committee meeting and they made me a partner."

"Just like that?"

"Sure. I'm a big shot like Al Capone and Baby Face Nelson. They know I pull the strings."

"Where'd they get that idea?" Cricket asked.

"From watching *Dragnet*. The syndicate bosses always wear fedoras and carry .45s." Francis waved his .45, and said to the puppet, "Don't they?"

"Executive, overseer, proprietor," Howdy Doody stated.

"That's right," Francis answered. "I'm the kingpin."

"Stick 'em up, partner," the puppet added.

Sam E. said, "So the punch line is, if I hadn't screamed none of this would've happened."

"That's right," Francis said.

"There's always a punch line," Sam E. said to Cricket. He turned to Francis. "How long have we been here?"

Francis shrugged, pushing back his fedora with his gun barrel. "Long enough for them to repair their space tub, I guess."

"Probably a day or so," Cricket said, rubbing Sam E.'s cheek, "because you guys have some stubble." She said to Francis, "They're gonna let us go before they split, right?"

"I'm not going anywhere. I told you, we're business partners."

The puppet clackety-clicked his wooden eyelids.

"What kind of business are you in?" Sam E. asked.

"Exportation."

"I'm gonna roll the dice here and say your friends are slave dealers who want to export the human race."

"They don't give a shit about us."

"They want our planet," Cricket said. "Like in *Earth Versus the Flying Saucers*?"

Francis shook his head.

Sam E. said, "Then the oil must be like acid to them and they want to use it as a weapon."

"They're not Attila the Hun," Francis said. "They're salesmen."

"They want to sell it?" Cricket asked.

"Queen for a day! They go for oil like Geronimo goes for hooch. It makes them gaga. They want to export it to wherever they're from and make a mint."

"What's *your* angle?" Sam E. asked.

"When we're done, the saucer-men get the oil and I get the planet."

"What are you gonna rule if there's no oil left?" Sam E. glanced at the Howdy Doody alien. "Doodyville?"

Francis punted his wingtip into Sam E.'s groin. A yellow, spear-like pain seared through him. He fell to his knees.

"You just don't know when to quit, do you?"

"Francis, we have to stick together!" Cricket said.

"No, we don't. I pull the strings now."

"No! We need to fight back."

"Who are you? Captain Video?" Francis stood toe-to-toe with her, angry eyed.

"I'm a human. In the movies the humans always fight back."

"You're a human B-girl, and I'm Gus Greenbaum's human lackey. Not anymore. The saucer-men are gonna make me king of the earth."

"It's not right."

Francis clamped his hand around her cheeks. "I didn't ask you if it was right."

"Veracious, comme il faut, okee-dokee," Howdy Doody said.

"Lemme gow, Franchis," Cricket said, from her clenched jaws.

He squeezed harder.

Cricket moaned.

"Let her go." Sam E. struggled to his feet.

Ignoring him, Francis said to her, "Don't you get it? This is my chance to be the big boss. Nothing's taking it from me, not even you, party doll." He squeezed harder.

Sam E. body-slammed him. Francis, with Howdy Doody perched on his shoulder, tumbled.

The puppet twirled his head in a 360. He made a noise similar to ice skates scratching across a frozen pond—"*Skiiiisshhh!*" He jiggled, blurred, re-jiggled and soared in height: towering over Sam E.'s head. At the same time, he changed from the little boy puppet into his true self; a bony, locust shaped thing with barnacled, dark-green hide. Its scaly head rumpled outward and into a mangled, snout-faced creature with a lipless razor slice mouth. It reminded Sam E.

of a Rottweiler he had once seen that had its face crushed by a pick-up truck. The alien flashed its twin rows of tiny scalpel-like teeth. Its eyes became beacons of brilliant purple. Its legs—like desiccated limbs of an Egyptian mummy—shuffled forward. Branchy, claw-hands crunched loudly as they reached for Sam E.'s neck.

Sam E. jumped back, grabbed Cricket and ran toward the wall opening Francis and the puppet had come through. As if exiting a dark cavern, other barnacled creatures appeared from the opening. All screamed *"Skiiiisshhh!"* and pointed their talon-like fingers at the two of them. The green-tinged platinum mist—more like a shower this time—sprayed from their tips, sprinkling above the pair.

"What'll we do?" Cricket screamed.

His heart galloping in his chest, Sam E. seized her arm and ran to the giant egg. It started spinning and became translucent. Once again they saw inside it the image of the grave he had dug for himself.

Francis grabbed his gun and fired. A bullet winged past Sam E.'s shoulder and disappeared into the egg.

"What'll we do?" Cricket repeated.

The deadly shower sprinkled closer to them.

"Close your eyes," Sam E. said. "And hold your breath!"

She clenched her eyes shut and pinched her nostrils as if she was diving feet first off a pier.

He pushed her into the egg. She disappeared. Sam E. felt the first drops of the creatures' green shower trickle on him. He heard another bullet whiz past his ear. The shower lowered, circled and squeezed him. He thought it whispered something, something just beyond his fingertips. He shut his eyes and leaped into the translucent mass.

Sam E. tumbled over Cricket, who was lying in the burial pit he had dug. Dazed, he stared at the quiet morning clouds, tinged pumpkin from the sun's early rays. "What the heck just happened?"

"The egg wasn't a television monitor. It was a monitor *and* a transporter. A *transmonitor*! It's even better than the gadget Dr. Anderson invented to pick up the Venusian's voice in *It Conquered the World*."

"Shut up with the sci-fi flicks, already. Let's get out of here." He stepped from the pit, helped her out, and wiped dirt from his soiled clothes. "At least we still have the DeSoto."

"I left the keys in the ignition," Cricket said, walking with Sam E. to the car.

He peeped in the driver door window. "They're still there." Opening the door, Sam E. heard the repeated short warble of what he thought was a bluebird circling overhead. He glanced up. An enormous brass colored object, not flat-round like a coin, but more like the shape of a baseball cap—flat-round with a visor—hovered overhead. "Shit!" He jumped into the chrome-grilled sedan's driver seat as Cricket scrambled to the passenger side.

The object lowered and hovered a few feet from the ground in front of them.

"It's a flying ball cap!" Cricket said, now able to see the saucer's domed ceiling.

Sam E. cranked the engine. The car grumbled as if shaken from a drunken slumber.

A triangular opening appeared in the saucer's dome. A trio of aliens, now back to television clones Hopalong Cassidy, Hedda Hopper and Rochester, stepped out on the ship's visor, which was facing the DeSoto. Behind them came Francis with Howdy Doody on his shoulder.

Sam E. cranked the engine again. Black, beefy smoke popgunned from the tail pipe. The car stuttered and stalled.

"Hurry," Cricket said.

The aliens leapt off the visor and approached the car. They pointed their fingers at the two as they neared the vehicle.

"God *damn* it!" Sam E. watched them approach. "Not the green spray again." He pumped the gas pedal frantically.

Hedda Hopper thrust her hand in Sam E.'s window and reached for his neck. He yanked his head away.

Rochester ripped Cricket's door open. Hopalong Cassidy tore the back door open.

Francis, kneeling on the ship's visor, fired his .45 at the car. A whirly-noised bullet zipped through the car's ceiling and burrowed into the back seat.

The engine cranked but refused to turn over. Sam E. stopped pumping the gas. "The motor's flooded!"

Hedda Hopper's green spray showered from her finger into the car. Sam E. held his breath and counted three, to give the motor time to settle.

One.

Hedda Hopper again reached for him. The green spray choked him.

Two.

He felt her fingers scrape his ear. His skin chilled and his head buzzed from the platinum-green falling over him.

Three.

He cranked the ignition. It wheezed. "I think I can," he mumbled. "I think I can. I think I can."

A bullet shot cracked the windshield. The rearview mirror tumbled to the dash, and as if the jolt awakened the DeSoto, it blew another smoke ball and sprang to life.

Sam E. rammed the car in reverse. He felt his lungs tighten from the remnants of the alien's green spray as he spun the car around and hot-rodded it down a foliage lined rocky trail.

Francis fired several times.

Pwopa! Pwopa! Pwopa! echoed through the underbrush. The De-Soto's back windshield crumbled. Sam E., ducking, slammed his head against the steering wheel. He saw sparks but kept the car moving until the shots faded and they approached the mountain base, where the trail siphoned into a two-lane highway. He slowed the vehicle.

"You don't look so good," Cricket said.

"I'm okay," he said, not sure if he was woozy from banging the steering wheel, or the after-effects of the green cloud. As he was about to enter the highway, an eighteen-wheeler that said *Shrieber Trucking* on the side zoomed by; blasting its air horn at the DeSoto. Sam E. slammed on the brakes, barely avoiding the diesel. "Maybe you better drive." Sliding over, he added, "The engine's running hot."

Chapter Six
DREAM A LITTLE DREAM

"You awake, Sammy?"

Sammy smelled talcum powder. He opened his eyes and saw the wrinkled, powdery armpits of his chemise-draped mother. She tucked his rodeo themed blanket around his small, chilly body. Smiling, she asked, "You hungry?" He stared at the bruise on her jaw. "I won't be long, sweetkins, and then we'll go to Muncie's for a pizza. Extra crispy the way you like it. Okay?"

Sammy nodded.

"Hey Judy, where-for the hell art thou?" a husky voice rattled outside Sammy's bedroom door.

His mother closed her eyes, stiffened, opened them, and said to Sammy, "We don't choose our destiny, only how we handle it. Will you remember that?"

Sammy nodded, but he forgot the words as soon as she left the bedroom and he heard grunts coming from his mother's room. He squeezed his ears with his palms to squelch the sound, which smelled to him like musty brown.

"You awake, Sam E.?"

He smelled Chanel N° 5. His eyes opened. He watched Cricket's long, peach-skinned fingers swiping a washcloth along his brow. He rubbed his damp forehead. His body trembled. His stomach cannonballed. He vomited.

"**B**etter?" Cricket asked, sometime later. "You don't stink anymore."

Like an addict coming down, Sam E. shook a heavy, lethargic grogginess off his being. He dragged his eyes around the familiar, dingy dwelling: the uncomfortable wool and teak-arm couch he was lying on, the pocked walnut desk holding the seventeen inch Raytheon table top TV that the couch faced, the Kit Cat Clock with its bulging eyes and J-black tail swaying to the ticking seconds. The speckled Formica table in the palm-green kitchenette below where the cat clock hung. Room 27a. His room at the El Atomico Inn off of Stewart and 4th Street, two blocks from the main drag, Fremont Street. It had never looked so good, he thought.

"Open up." Cricket slipped a warm mug between his lips. He sipped and nearly retched again.

"Bosco and hot water. Couldn't find milk. You don't like?"

"There's Seagram's under the sink, next to the Maypo."

Cricket took the seven steps from the living room to the kitchenette.

"Glasses on the top shelf below the Kitty Clock," he said.

"Ice?" she asked.

"Straight."

She filled two rock glasses with healthy portions. Returning, she handed one to him, and said, "Cheers."

Sam E. took a second to let the slightly sweet, oak-charred odor comfort his nostrils before taking a deep slug of the whiskey.

"You were in a bad way last night."

"Last night?" He realized he was out of his suit, in a clean muscle tee, and yellow-with-red-squares boxers. "I threw up."

"Big time. I usually get extra for clean up." Cricket took a drink, observing him.

He saw their original clothes, dirt-caked, heaped in a pile by the bathroom. Cricket was wearing a clean pair of his slacks and one of his white tux shirts. "What happened?" he asked.

"You don't remember?"

"It's foggy."

"The spaceship?"

"Foggy," he repeated. He felt nauseated and had a brief memory of bad pepperoni from a Muncie's pizza.

"We went through the transmonitor," she said, "and landed on the grave you dug. Do you remember that?"

"Not really. How'd we end up here?"

"We jumped in the DeSoto and you drove us."

"They didn't come after us?" he asked.

"They tried to kill us; but, no, they didn't follow. The ship looks like a giant baseball cap."

"Why?" he asked.

"Maybe they like baseball."

"I mean, why didn't they come after us?"

"Maybe we're not important enough, or maybe once we got on the highway they didn't want to take the chance that they'd be seen."

"Or maybe they don't exist." He cricked his neck to clear his head.

"What does that mean?"

"That I'm beginning to think it was all a crazy nightmare." Sam E. took another slug of his whiskey.

"It was real," Cricket said. "We were picked up by beings from outer space. Just like Peter Graves was in *Killers From Outer Space*."

"What do the space people look like?"

"You know."

"Maybe I do and maybe I don't. Tell me."

She cleared her throat. "Sort of like grasshoppers with squirmy legs and crushed heads." She paused. "And they look like Howdy Doody and Rochester."

"How many movies have you seen where they look like that?"

"None."

"Someone slipped a Mickey in my Scotch," he said, more to himself than to her. "I bet it was Syd Tate. He's pissed because I took his dressing room."

"It was real." Cricket grabbed the pile of dirty clothes and shoved them in his face. "How do you explain these, or me, for that matter?"

"I smoked tea with a cigarette girl once in Palisades Park, we ended up in the bearded lady's tent covered in candy apples. As for you, well?" He winked smugly.

"Don't be an asshole," Cricket said. "I'm way out of your league."

"Sorry, sister, but it was all a goofy dream."

"Don't 'sister' me. I'll prove it. Do you get the paper?"

Sam E. sat up. Now that he figured it out, he was feeling better. "Yeah," he said, walking to the kitchen and pouring another Seagram's. "It should be outside the doorstep. So what?"

"Francis brought you up the mountain on the twenty-third. We had to be gone at least a couple of days." She opened the front door, brought the paper in and unfolded it.

"What's it say?" He plopped back down on the couch, with his refilled drink.

Cricket hesitated. "Sunday June 24th 1956—hot and sunny."

"You're welcome to keep my clothes," Sam E. said. "Thanks for a fascinating evening."

"This is serious. They want our oil!"

"If it's true, which it's not, how would we stop them?"

"I don't know, but we have to try," Cricket said.

"You try. I've got a date on *The Steve Allen Show*. You need a taxi?"

"You're an asshole!"

"You already said that. Where do you want the cab to take you?" He dialed the telephone.

Chapter Seven
WHAT'S UP, DOC?

The receptionist, a cheery, dyed-blonde with wing-flare eyeglasses, who looked younger than her forty-two years, picked up her desk phone and said, "Doc, Stu's here." The woman, attractive in a down-home manner, led a dour, pencil-thin mustached man from her reception room to the office behind it.

She motioned him in and closed the door behind him, as the man took a seat in front of a cluttered olive green metal desk.

On the other side of the desk Doc Ronco—a hefty, bulldog jowled man with a mischievous glint in his eye like a gold-bearing leprechaun—leaned back in his leather chair. He fanned himself with a handled cardboard fan picturing a pintsized bellhop and the words *Call for Phillip Morris!* printed below. Doc fanned and waited.

Finally, Stu said, "Three hundred a week is all I can afford for Lakeside. Take it or leave it."

Doc, fluttering his fan, said, "Stu, I love you, but Sam's packing your place tighter than a Marciano-Louis rematch. We gotta have five hunj a week."

"Who do you think he is? Phil Silvers?"

"No," Doc said. "He's the guy that's gonna be on Steve Allen's show next week."

"Bah!" Stu shushed his hand at Doc. "He's not worth it. I'll hire that new guy, Dangerfield."

"That's your prerogative." Doc's desk phone rang. He picked it up and said, "Hey, Artie! Yeah, Sam E. will be available next week. That's right, six hundred a week." Doc put his hand over the phone.

He said, hush-hush to Stu, "Sam likes you, he wanted to give you a break." Doc spoke back into the phone, "He'll be there first thing, Artie, after *The Allen Show.* Did you hear Presley's gonna be on it? Yeah, and Imogene Coca, too. They expect a record audience."

Stu grabbed the receiver and plunged it in the cradle. "All right, Doc, five hundred, but not a fucking penny more!"

"Whatever you say." Doc pulled a contract from his desk drawer. "Read it and sign."

Stu signed, shook his head, and left Doc's small office. As he passed the receptionist, he said, "Marge, your husband's a mother."

Marge, pushing her glasses up her nose, gathered papers from a file cabinet. She smiled. "I'll tell him you said so."

"Please do!" He exited heavily from the room.

Marge walked into Doc's office. "Stu says you're a mother."

Doc fluttered his fan. "And you're one hell of an Artie. Remind me to give you a raise."

She laid the papers on his desk, and said quite sincerely, "I'm proud of you."

"What's that about?"

She shrugged. "I know how much *The Allen Show* means to Sam, and I know how hard you worked to make it happen."

"It was nothing." Doc's jowls flushed red. "He's the funny one, I'm just his agent."

"Sure, Doc, sure," Marge said. "You know you two will have been together six years next month?"

"Has it been that long, already? It seems like yesterday we were both so broke I was giving him haircuts. Remember about four years ago when he got in trouble in Ohio?"

"For telling those jokes about J. Edgar Hoover," Marge said.

"Do you remember what he said to us after we bailed him out of the pokey? 'You're the first people who ever cared about me'."

"I think we're the first people he's ever cared about," Marge said.

"I know." Doc stood. "Maybe we could have a little six-year anniversary party next month."

Marge pecked his cheek. "I packed your trench coat in case the weather dampens in New York."

Doc squeezed her hand. "Let's go get him; I promised we'd all have a good meal before me and him take off tomorrow."

Chapter Eight
HONEYMOONERS

Sam E., whistling "Whistle While You Work", snapped shut the leather valise lying on his bed. He took a pee, washed, and slapped Old Spice on his cheeks. Carrying the valise to the door, he thought of Doc and Marge, and that hokey saying about real friends being the ones with you before you make it. *Hokey, but true.* He glanced at the Kit Cat Clock: 5:57. He clicked on the Raytheon, adjusted the bunny ears and watched the news. *No alien Howdy Doodys, no giant baseball caps, no delusional females.* He stretched his arms and yawned.

Knock ka-knock knock.

"Coming, Doc." He turned off the television.

Knock ka-knock knock.

"Okay." Sam E. went to the door. As he reached for the knob, the door swung open.

"How are you, funny man?" Francis barged in. Howdy Doody was perched on his shoulder, smiling his thick-lipped, heebie-jeebie smile. Following behind them were Alice Kramden in a powder-blue housedress with oversize pockets, and Trixie Norton in a button-down lavender blouse and tartan slacks. Shutting the door, Francis said, "Sit down." He pushed the stunned comedian onto the couch.

Sam E. felt out-of-bounds as if he was being pulled outward and inward all at once.

Francis said, amusing himself, "What's the matter? Jester lose his tongue?"

"What do you want?"

"Nothing." Francis sat next to him. "Nothing at all."

Alice Kramden and Trixie Norton stood in front of Sam E. and frowned.

Francis slipped his .45 from the shoulder holster beneath his sport coat. "We just came by to wish you luck on *The Steve Allen Show*."

"What kind of luck?"

"You see?" Francis said to the aliens. "That's what a comedian does, he turns things around in an unexpected manner to make us laugh."

The aliens tilted their heads curiously at Sam E.

"You might say that's what I'm going to do," Francis said. "I'm going to flip things around in an unexpected manner. I've done some research on Steve Allen and I know he's—"

Ka-nock knock knock.

Francis put his finger to his lips, motioning for Sam E. to keep silent.

Knocka-knock "Hey Sam, it's Doc."

"Tell him to go away," Francis whispered.

"Go away," Sam E. said loud enough for Doc to hear.

"Quit buffaloing around. Marge and I are starving. Let's go," Doc said through the door.

"Get rid of them," Francis said.

"Okay, but put the gun away." Sam E. walked to the door.

"No funny business." Francis slipped the pistol in his holster.

Sam E. opened the door. "I'm not feeling well," he said to the couple. "Come back tomorrow."

"It's just nerves," Doc said. "Where's your bag? Let's put it in the car now."

"Go away. Marge, tell him to go away."

"Doc, maybe we should come back," Marge said.

"I'm starving." Doc forced his beefy body past Sam E. "Where's your suitca—" He froze, staring at the figures in the living room. Finally, Doc rushed forward. "Sam never mentioned he knew you. We're big fans of *The Honeymooners*. Marge, look who's here!" Doc extended his hand toward Alice and Trixie.

Marge looked at Sam E., confused.

Sam E. said, "Get him out of here, I'll explain later."

"Marge!" Doc said. "Get in here."

"Hurry," Sam E. said, "take him away."

"Why?" she asked, anxiety in her voice.

"Please, Marge. Just do it."

Marge entered the apartment and tugged on Doc's arm. "Doc, let's go."

Sam E. followed, and tried to push Doc out.

Doc shrugged him off, re-extending his hand to Alice Kramden. "I'm Doc Ronco, Sam's manager, and this is my missus, Marge. We'd love to do your show, wouldn't we Sam?"

Sam E. continued trying to push Doc toward the door.

"That's enough." Francis stood up from the couch. "All of you, sit down."

"Who are you?" Doc asked. "And what the hell is *he* doing on your shoulder?" Doc motioned to Howdy Doody.

Francis reached in his jacket.

"I'll handle this," Sam E. said to Francis. "Sit down, Doc. I'll explain later."

Marge grabbed her husband's arm and pulled him down on the couch with her.

"That's better." Francis removed his grip on the pistol. "If you want to keep managing, button your trap. Got it?"

Doc eyed him.

Marge's brown eyes, always mischievous, were large and frightened. The look scared Sam E.

"No more pussy footing around. You're going to *The Allen Show*, and you're going to introduce us to him," Francis said to Sam E. "Got it?"

"Sure," he said. "But why do you want to meet Steve Allen?"

Francis smiled. "None of your business."

Howdy Doody whispered in Francis' ear. Francis shook his head. The puppet nodded.

Francis turned to Sam E. "He says, if you say something funny we'll tell you."

"Did you hear about the cannibal who was late for dinner?" Sam E. said. "He got the cold shoulder."

Doc smiled. The aliens looked inquisitively at him, imitating his smile.

Francis looked at Howdy. The spaceman nodded. Francis said to Sam E., "We need you to get us backstage and alone with Steve Allen."

"Why?"

"We're gonna kill him and then we're gonna copy him. We don't want it to be messy."

Marge gasped. Doc started to stand, but Sam E. jerked him back down again.

"Why?" Sam E. repeated.

Francis glanced at Howdy Doody. The space marionette shook his head. "None of your business," Francis said.

"Why do you need *me*? Can't you just go somewhere else and kill him?"

Francis glanced at the puppet. The puppet nodded. Francis said to Sam E., "Say another joke and we'll tell you."

"Jesus went to Mount Olive and Popeye beat the crap out of him," Sam E. said.

Doc chuckled. The aliens imitated the noise.

Francis shook his head in disgust. He said to Sam E., "We don't want to kill him until after the show. If we do it before, and the fake Steve Allen goes on the air, people will know something's wrong. Just because they can look like Allen doesn't mean they can act like him. You hear how they talk. I'm teaching 'em to speak better, but it takes time. We want to kill him in private, that's why you're gonna get him alone in your dressing room."

"Why can't you just knock him out? You don't have to kill him."

"Yes I do, Lakeside. I don't want to take a chance of him making trouble while the spaceman copy is walking around."

"Spaceman?" Marge asked. "What does that mean?"

"Shut up!" Francis said. "Or I'll rip your tongue out."

Marge leaned hard into Doc, who flung his fist at him. Sam E. snagged it before it hit its target.

"Let them go," Sam E. said to Francis. "They don't know anything. I'll do whatever you want."

"Sure," Francis said. "We don't care about them, we care about you."

"I know this is probably not in my best interest," Sam E. replied, "but why don't you copy me and then have my lookalike get Steve Allen alone?"

Francis glanced at the space marionette. The creature nodded. "Tell another one of your crappy jokes," Francis said.

"What do you do with an elephant that has three balls?" Sam E. said. "You walk him, and pitch to the giraffe."

The aliens tilted their hands side to side. Howdy whispered in Francis' ear. Francis said to Sam E, "They thought that one was iffy, but they'll give you one more shot."

"Jesus," Sam E. said, "you guys are worse than the club owners."

Doc laughed.

The aliens imitated his laughter. They nodded to Francis. "They liked your manager's laughter so I'll continue, even though I told you this one before," Francis said. "They can only mimeograph anyone who's been on television. It has something to do with broadcast signals. They can't duplicate you because you've never been over the airwaves."

"Okay. I'll do it under one condition. I get to do my act."

Francis glanced at the extra-terrestrials. "I told ya," he said to them. "All actors and comics ever care about is their career." He said to Doc, "Ain't that right, pudgy?"

"Is it a deal?" Sam E. asked.

Francis glanced at the puppets. They nodded.

"Let them go," Sam E. said. "You promised."

"We didn't promise anything. But as a gesture of magnamity, we'll let one go, and keep the other as insurance."

"That's it!" Doc sprung up. "This buffoonery has gone too far."

"Sit down!" Sam E. grabbed his shoulder.

Doc pushed his hand away.

"Now, look here," Doc said to Alice and Trixie. "I don't care if you know Gleason or not. You don't threaten my wife or my friend."

The aliens arched their eyebrows.

Marge, tugging on his arm, said, "Please, Doc, sit down."

"And as for this creep," Doc said, waving his thumb over his shoulder at Francis, who was standing behind him, "if you think having a ventriloquist around is any way to conduct business, then Sam doesn't want to be on *The Honeymooners* anyway." He turned to Sam E. and Marge. "Let's go."

Francis reached into his shoulder holster.

Sam E. put his arm around Doc's shoulder. "He's just kidding," he said to Francis. "Doc and I'll go to New York, and Marge will stay back here, at home. That's where their office is."

"What the hell's going on?" Doc asked.

"Nothing, Doc. Nothing. Let's go." Sam E. motioned to Marge. "Come on, Marge, we'll drop you off."

The trio made their way to the door. Francis, stone cold, eyed them. As Sam E. picked up his bag, he said to the aliens, "Let Marge stay at the office while we're in New York; she won't go anywhere, she's a working girl."

Trixie said, "Working girl: prostitute, floozie, whore."

"What did you call my wife?" Doc rushed to the aliens.

Sam E. ran to him. "It's a misunderstanding. Let's go!" He grabbed Doc's bicep. "We'll do whatever you want, I promise," he said to the aliens.

"You talk to me, Lakeside!" Francis said.

"The hell we will!" Doc brushed Sam E.'s hand from his arm with such force it thumped into Alice's gut. The alien, startled, glared at Doc, and said, "*Skiiiisshhh!*" Trixie eyed him, and repeated the harsh sound.

"Doc!" Marge scrambled to him.

The aliens pointed their fingers at Doc. They sprayed the platinum-green shower on him.

"No!" Sam E. shouted, as the spray intensified and engulfed Doc until only his thick hands, reaching out in desperation, showed through the green mist. Quickly, the spray dissipated and Doc's lumbering body crumbled to the floor, wiggled, and fell still, blood foaming from his ears. Marge screamed.

Sam E. grabbed Francis by the neck. He grunted and squeezed until his fingertips hurt. He held tight until he heard "*Skiiiisshhh!*" and the platinum-green cloud, lighter than when it hit Doc, squeezed Sam E. harder than his hands squeezed Francis. His body shivered, and as he drifted into darkness, he heard Francis say, "It doesn't pay to mess with me."

"It doesn't pay to mess with me," a broad-shouldered man said. "That's all I have, Tony. I swear."

"Ya know I try to be nice. Don't I, Judy? I even put up with that seven-year-old rat of yours, and this is how you treat me," Tony said, his canoe-littered Hawaiian shirt heaving with his shoulders.

"Leave Sammy out of this."

"You think because your daredevil flyboy crashed over the Pacific and left you with a bun in the oven and no wedding ring, you can get uppity with me? I pulled you and your bastard kid outta the stinkin' rotten alley and gave you a job. Remember?"

"Go to hell."

"No, you go to hell!"

Sammy watched the broad-shouldered man's fist pound his mother's jawbone. "Now get me my money and get back to fuc—"

Sammy lunged from behind his bedroom door, pumping his fists against the man's lower back.

"*Figghu di buttana!*" Tony pushed back his flailing chestnut hair, spun around and clamped Sammy's neck. Tony cocked his fist at him. Sammy stared at the boulder-sized meat hook squared between his eyes. He felt as if he was falling. He saw in minute detail the blood-red creases in the man's knuckles, the sparse hair on his digits, the grease spot lodged beneath his thumbnail. Sammy fixated on a yellow, stamp-sized scar on the man's quivering forearm.

"Stop it!" Sammy's mother opened the icebox and threw out a small wad of bills onto the aluminum-legged kitchen table. "That's all of it."

"Much better, ducky." Tony released Sammy.

Sammy's mother huddled him in her arms, and whispered, "We don't choose our destiny, only how we handle it."

Tony thumbed the bill wad. "Take a hike, kid."

His mother nodded at Sammy. He stared at her blackened, pulpy jaw, and the blood trickling from her nose. His mother wiped the red fluid from her ashen white skin, smiled, and said, "I'll be right here when you get back."

"That's my girl," Tony said, as Sammy left the apartment.

"What's black and white and red all over?" Sammy said to himself in the narrow hall. "My mother," he answered, crying.

S am E. felt something wipe his tears. He opened his eyes. Standing over him was Alice Kramden. She lifted her tear-wet thumb from his cheek and stuck it in her mouth. She puckered as if she had tasted fresh lemon, and spit out the fluid. Next to her sat Francis, spread legged on a kitchen chair turned backwards. He was eyeing him as he cleaned his nails with a switchblade.

Sam E.'s mind lifted softly like a mid-morning fog. He was lying on his couch. Along with Alice, Trixie stood on the other side of Francis. The space puppet was on Trixie's shoulder. Francis stood, moved the vinyl-bottomed seat aside and jammed his knee in Sam E.'s ribs.

A hurled-bowling-ball-like pain rammed into Sam E.'s chest.

He gurgle-groaned and curled up like wood shavings.

"That's for the neck bruises." Francis rubbed his jugular vein. He took his place on the backward chair, and said "Let's get back to business."

"How do, partner," Howdy Doody said to Francis.

Sam E., struggling, sat up. "Where's Doc and Marge?"

"They were pushy. It's not smart to be pushy."

His stomach sank. He breathed hard and looked around for signs of them. Nothing. Not even blood stains.

Francis slipped an envelope from his coat pocket and handed it to Sam E. "Your manager left this for you."

Sam E. unfolded the flap. Inside were the airline tickets Doc had purchased for them. He pinched back tears, not wanting to give Francis the satisfaction of gloating over Doc and Marge's death. *They deserved better.* "Wouldn't it be easier for me to ride in the saucer?"

"A spaceship landing at LaGuardia isn't exactly hush-hush. Besides, we have other things to take care of while you're in the air."

"What happens when I get to New York?"

"Don't worry about it," Francis said. "You just get there. Got it?"

He nodded. "I get to do the show, right?" Sam E. asked the Howdy Doody-alien.

"Hey!" Francis said, waving his knife. "You talk to me."

"I get to do the show, right?" he asked Francis.

"Yeah, our word's as good as oil."

"Oy-yell, oy-yell, oy-yell," the aliens chanted.

Francis walked over to him. "Don't try anything stupid, or you'll end up like pudgy and his wife." He jabbed the blade into Sam E.'s shirt, below the collarbone. Sam E. screamed, feeling a line of warm blood soak through the yellow cotton. "That's how close you are to dying. Remember that, if you get any funny ideas." To the aliens, he added, "We're done here."

Howdy Doody waved his wooden finger, the platinum-green mist sprinkled over himself, Francis, Trixie, and Alice.

As they vanished, Francis said to Sam E., "Later, Alligator."

Sam E. unbuttoned his red-stained shirt. He imagined Marge and Doc lying in a crumpled heap on his apartment floor. *They were good friends. You don't often find good friends in show business.* The thought no longer felt corny. It felt like something else. He didn't know what, but it squashed his fear, squashed it like Doc and Marge were squashed. It hardened his resolve. It clenched his fists. The vengeful, angry feeling pulsed through his veins. "Go to hell, Francis. I'm not your puppet." He removed the bloody garment from his chest.

Chapter Nine
CRAPS

"Sweetie," the man at the crap table said, "I asked for an extra olive."

"Sorry, I'll take care of it," Cricket said.

"You do that." The man smiled at the fleshy crevice in her low-cut bustier.

As she walked to the bar, he rubbed the dice cupped in his hand across his thick, blonde brow, and said, "Go, daddy, go!" before heaving the dice on the craps table. As they tumbled over the pass line and stopped on the come box, he lurched from his seat and shouted, "Eeeuuuu, it's a lucky seven!"

"Extra olive for Mr. Lucky," Cricket said to the bartender, a thin man with widow-peaked silver hair, gaunt cheeks, and a perpetually unflustered expression.

The bartender toothpicked a pair of olives, cramped with others, from a large jar. He handed the skewered garnish to her. "Another fun night in paradise."

"Jack, do you like working here?"

"What does that mean?"

"I was just thinking, you're always here. Why don't you go on vacation or something, enjoy yourself while you still have time."

"Are you okay?" Jack said. "Did Francis take a swing at you again?"

"We broke up."

"Good. He was a pissant."

"Hey, Tootsie!" the crapshooter said to Cricket, from the crap table. "Extra olive?" He rolled the dice. It tumbled across the green felt and stopped. "Eleven!" he screamed.

"Jack, do you believe in UFOs?"

Jack shrugged. "Right after Santa Claus."

"Yeah, I thought you'd say that."

"What else would I say?"

Cricket nervously tapped her long, blood-red nails on the bar. "What if I told you I was inside one? What would you say?"

For a brief second Jack's eyebrows rose, momentarily changing his unflustered face. "I'd say 'You've been working too hard'."

"Yeah, that's what I keep hearing."

"What does a guy have to do to get an olive!" the crapshooter yelled.

Jack glanced at the indignant man. "Pissant."

"It sounds crazy, I know," Cricket said to Jack, "but I'm not a liar."

Jack, studying her, pinched the droopy skin beneath his chin. He blew an air puff. "No, you're not a liar." Jack reached into his vest pocket and pulled out a business card. "Get in touch with this man. He can help."

"God damn it," the crapshooter said, leaving the crap table. "I want my damn olive."

Cricket read the card. She sunk. "He's a psychoanalyst."

Jack nodded. "He came in the bar last week. I hear he's real good." Jack put his hand on her shoulder. "I'll talk to Sal. I'm sure he'll give you some time off."

"Forget it. I was only kidding."

Jack removed his hand. "I'll talk to Sal, anyway."

"Maybe Lakeside was right, it was just a dream," Cricket said to herself, as Jack walked to a steamy sink and began rinsing glasses in and out of it.

The crapshooter stomped toward the bar and grabbed the skewered olives from Cricket's hand. "You did that on purpose, to

throw off my timing, didn't you? I know how you casinos work."
He slipped the olives in his mouth, sucking them off the toothpick.

"Sure," she said. "That's what I live for, to screw with your
timing."

"Hey," the crapshooter said, smiling. "You're feisty, I like that.
What do you cost for a night?"

"I'm not your type. You're way too classy for me."

"You're a piece of shit," the crapshooter said. "That's what you
are."

"You got your olives, go back to the crap table."

"Piece of shit," he repeated.

Cricket swung her hand at the man. Before she could smack his
face, another hand grabbed her wrist.

"Why don't graveyards have locks?" Sam E. asked the crapshooter.

The man looked at him, bewildered.

"Because people are dying to get in." He released Cricket's arm
and stuck his hand in his sport coat pocket. "You get my drift?" he
asked, a gun-barrel protrusion forming inside the pocket.

The crapshooter glanced at the jacket-covered pistol, and
gulped. "Sorry, pal, it was a misunderstanding."

"Scram!" Sam E. inched his pocket forward. The man scurried
back to the crap table.

"Let's go," Sam E. said to Cricket. "We've got space goons to
fight."

"But you didn't believe me."

"Well, now I do."

"Why?"

"We haven't got time for it, now. Are you with me or not?" He
looked into her eyes. They seemed gloomier than he remembered
them.

She nodded. "Let me change first."

"Don't take long. I need to get a gun."

"How about the one in your jacket?"

He pulled his hand out, shaped like a pistol. "It doesn't fire bullets."

He clasped her arm, and as he led her past the man at the crap table, the dealer said, "Twelve. That's Craps."

The crapshooter elbowed his arms on the baize table, dropped his chin in his hands and groaned.

Chapter Ten
The Atomic City

Cricket, wearing her black beret, black pedal-pushers, and a pink sleeveless blouse tied at the waist, waved to Vegas Vic, the Pioneer Club's perpetually smoking, perpetually waving, perpetually cocky mammoth neon cowboy, as she and Sam E. passed beneath Vic's glowing blue jeans. Strolling along the crowded, nightly hubbub of Fremont Street, they passed the open-walled El Dorado Club. A beehive-haired woman inside yelled, "Holy bejesus!" as the *cha-cling-cling-cling* of tumbling coins fluttered from the one-armed bandit into her wax-paper cup.

"It's gonna be a lot quieter here if Francis and his oil-guzzling aliens get their way," Sam E. said, as they crossed Fremont Street's car heavy, four lane drag. "At night it's atomic. Like horses around the track, you know?"

"Yeah," Cricket said. "Around and around going nowhere."

They entered the Golden Nugget, walking beneath its fifty-foot sign of radiant promises.

Sam E. said, "During the day, the sun shines too bright. It dims everything good about Vegas."

"Or shows it for what it is. A sucker's game."

"You're cynical enough to be a comic," he said.

Inside the gaggle of avocado-colored poker tables, revolving red roulette wheels, and bell buzzing silver slot machines, he spread his arms beneath the blazing fluorescents of the gambling hall as if it was sanitizing his body. He felt human again. Vibrant. "Now this is a casino." He pilfered a drink from a passing waitress. "Not like that dingy place you work at."

"Used to work at."

Sam E. glanced at his Timex. "God, I want to play one last game of Blackjack. Just so I can pretend nothing's changed."

"What time does the plane leave?"

"Noon. We've got nearly fourteen hours." He gulped down his drink.

"I still need to pack, but that's plenty of time. And you said you were already packed when your manager—" She stopped herself.

The casino's sparkle and noise drummed in his head as if it was daytime and he had a hangover. He felt dirty again, ashamed that he even thought about pretending. "Come on." They walked to a red door near a dim corner of the bright lobby. Sam E. knocked twice on the door, paused, and knocked three more times.

"I have this in case we need it." Cricket flashed a switchblade from inside her snap purse.

"Put that thing away. We need to get real fire power." The door opened. She quickly shoved the knife back in.

A tall, slender man with large lobed ears, little eyes, thin lips perched above a recessed chin, and a soft trilby hat tipped sideways over his narrow face, stood in the entranceway.

"How are you, Mousey?" Sam E. asked. "This is Cricket."

"Hello," Mousey said to her. "How are you, Mr. Lakeside?"

"Fine, fine."

Mousey said, "Mousey heard you was leaving us."

"I am. You see, Mousey, I'm flying to New York and I need a gun."

"A gun? How's come?"

"Well, there's these spacemen and they—"

"Spacemen?" Mousey asked.

"Tell him the truth," Cricket said. "You see, Mr. Mousey, I got in a little money trouble and Sam is helping me get to New York, but the loan shark, he's not very nice."

Sam E. added, "It's a bit embarrassing."

Mousey kneaded his slender hands together, "You always been nice to Mousey, Mr. Lakeside." He turned to Cricket. "Mr. Lakeside let me stay at his apartment once when my place was being tented."

"That's nice," she said.

"We watched *Rin Tin Tin* and we played pick-up sticks." Mousey turned to Sam E. "Mousey beat you twice, remember?"

"I sure do. So, um, Mousey, can you get me the gun? This is important."

"Well, Mousey shouldn't be doing this, but. . ." Mousey chewed his lower lip. His squinty eyes widened briefly. Peeping his head around, he said, "Hurry up," and ushered them inside the doorway, which he quickly closed. They were in a narrow, dull yellow hallway evenly lined with matching green metal doors. Rosemary Clooney's jaunty "Come On-A My House" echoed down the long passage.

"Mousey'll get you the gun," Mousey said, walking them down the corridor. At the fourth set of doors he stopped. "Don't tell anybody. Promise, Mr. Lakeside?"

"Sure, Mousey, and thanks."

"Wait inside. I'll be back in a jiffy," Mousey said, before leaving.

Sam E. and Cricket entered the fourth door. They stood in a thick, baby blue, windowless room with a metal desk and two metal chairs. Sam E. knocked on the concrete walls. The room was dead silent. "Okay, after we get the gat—"

"The *what?*"

"The gat. The gun. Just because I'm a stand-up doesn't mean I don't know about guns, sister."

"Don't *sister* me. I told you, I hate that."

There were two knocks on the door, a pause, and then three more. The door cracked open. "Mr. Lakeside?" Mousey said.

"Yeah, Mousey, we're here."

"Good." He cracked the door open. "I got the gat."

Sam E. smirked at Cricket, when he heard 'gat'.

A large pistol waved through the door opening.

Sam E. reached for the pistol. The door widened. Standing next to Mousey, waving the revolver, was a hefty, log-faced, bald man with an abundance of body hair.

The hefty man smiled. "How are you, comedian? I hear you're in a rush to get to New York."

"Mr. Greenbaum." Sam E. stepped back. "I didn't know Mitzi was your girlfriend. Honest."

Greenbaum aimed the gun at Sam E.'s balls.

"Mousey?" Sam E. said with astonishment. "We played pick-up sticks when your place was tented."

"Mr. Greenbaum paid to have Mousey's place tented," Mousey said, as the pair entered and shut the door.

Gus Greenbaum fired, singeing Sam E.'s left thigh.

"Fuck!" He grabbed the blood spot near his front pants pocket.

"That's what got you into trouble in the first place, jerk-off." Greenbaum aimed for another shot.

"Wait." Cricket stood in front of Sam E. "This is Francis' hit."

"Out of the way," Greenbaum said, "if you don't want to end up like Lakeside."

"My mistake." She scooted next to Greenbaum. "Fire away."

Sam E., hobbling on his good leg, said, "I *swear* I didn't know Mitzi was your girl. She said she was new in town, ask her."

"Mitzi's dead, just like you're gonna be." Greenbaum tightened his grip.

Sam E. fell to his knees. Closed his eyes. He imagined himself standing on stage, behind a black curtain, waiting for it to rise.

Steve Allen was in the wings, nodding at him. He heard *click*, a loud *tha-kump*, and a noise like a braying mule. He opened his eyes. Gus Greenbaum was crumpled against the wall massaging his groin. Mousey was taking a potshot at Cricket. She ducked. Mousey's bullet hit the desk and ricocheted into the ceiling. Cricket whipped the switchblade from her purse and flung it. It pierced the middle of Mousey's forehead. Red flowed between his squinty eyes. Mousey fell on his back, and his elbows and hands flopped back like the haunches of his namesake.

Sam E. hobbled up and grabbed Mousey's revolver. He took the dead man's hat to hide his wounded thigh. "Did you do that on purpose?" He motioned to the blade jutting between Mousey's brows.

"What do you *think*?"

"You and I have got to have a chat." He clutched her elbow and rushed her out of the room.

"**D**amn, that hurts!" Sam E. said, bunching his toes together. "Be grateful that Mr. Deskclerk was selling from his overpriced liquor cabinet." Cricket dabbed more Fleishmann's on Sam E.'s wounded thigh. "It wouldn't be hard for that to become infected in a dog pound like this."

He looked around and cringed at their new digs; a two-bit, two-bed, piss-stinking out-of-the-way dump called The Wampum Inn. "Maybe you know a better place two people with twenty-three dollars can lay low for the night, after one slams the syndicate boss' girl, and the other slams the syndicate boss' nuts?"

Cricket dropped a swig of liquor on the wound. He howled. "You did that on purpose!"

She smiled and slid into the other bed.

Sam E. turned off the lamplight, rubbed his thigh, and let the night fall on his leg pain like an itchy wool blanket. He drifted into a painful unconsciousness of different named stones pummeling against his body. Some names, like Mother and Marge, he recognized. Others, like bowties and bullets, he didn't. Each hurt equally. His temples clanged like a school bell. It stopped when Cricket shook him and turned off the ringing alarm clock.

Sam E. rinsed his tarnished face in the tarnished sink. He stuck his tongue out, and rubbed his fingers across his stubbed cheek. *Relax.* He closed his eyes, swept in the musty air and held it. He exhaled. *Better.* The doorknob clicked and he jumped.

"Here you go, crackerjack." Cricket tossed him a Gillette razor and shaving cream from a small paper sack. "Keep it clean, we have to share." She pulled out a toothbrush, toothpaste, and deodorant. "Same for the toothpaste and deodorant."

"From the desk clerk?" he asked.

"Twelve smackeroos, including coffee and two baloney sandwiches."

"He's all heart; a real Eleanor Roosevelt." He shook the can of Rapid-Shave.

Sam E. slipped his slacks over his boxers, wiggled his wounded thigh, and flinched. He grabbed his coffee and sandwich from the cigarette-scarred nightstand.

Cricket brushed her wrinkled bed sheet before sitting on it. She bit into her baloney sandwich. Her eyes followed him as he sat on the other bed.

"Can I ask you a question?" he said.

"As long as it's not 'What's a nice girl like you doing in a place like Vegas?'"

"Oh." He bit into the bread, thinking of something else to ask.

"Let me ask *you* something," Cricket said. "What is it with the Oedipus thing?"

"The what?"

"Last night you screamed about Mom again. Just like that night at your apartment after we escaped the saucer-men. What were you dreaming?"

"I wasn't dreaming, exactly. I was…I don't know what it was, but it feels different. Heavier." He shrugged. "The only thing I recall from last night was something about killing myself and waking up feeling like shit. Sort of like I felt after the outer space creatures hit me with their green cloud."

"Did you have those kinds of things before?"

"Before what?"

"This." She poked her index finger at him, imitating the aliens spraying their mist.

"No. But you got the spray that night on the mountain, too. Did it do anything to you?"

"I felt confused for a while, but that was it." She bit into her baloney. "Maybe they're giving you an extra dose, or maybe you're allergic to the zapping. Either way, it's kind of spooky."

"Do you get a lot of sugar-daddies with talk like that?"

"That's mean."

He closed his eyes. His head hurt.

Cricket walked to the window and looked over the brown desert. "I don't give a crap what you think of me. Got it?"

"I'm sorry." He rubbed his temples.

"You sure are." She closed the cactus-print curtain running along the ring pole. The room darkened.

A humpback, black '48 Chevy pulled into the sparse Las Vegas Airport parking lot. The driver—a pot-bellied, brown-haired man with a large front-combed wave, and a rubber ball nose— pressed the brakes. The back door opened. Sam E. and Cricket stepped out. The driver stuck his arm out of the window. He opened his hand and Sam E. pressed some bills in his palm. The man drove off in a dusty contrail.

"Zippity do-dah," Sam E. said to Cricket. "Mr. Deskclerk just got eight bucks for driving us less then ten miles. My condom's off to him."

"How much do we have left?"

"Three dollars," he said. "We better hurry, we're running late."

They scuttled toward the terminal.

Sam E. stood in the depot rubbing his wounded thigh. He looked around the empty terminal. He handed a smiling, bouffant-haired counter-girl the tickets. She looked at them and said, "Whew, the plane's about to depart." She pointed to a runway.

"Let's go," he said, motioning to Cricket, who was sitting near the counter.

The girl watched them hustling toward the tarmac. She smirked and dialed her desk phone. "They're here," she said.

A smiling stewardess, in white gloves and wearing a matching copper skirt-suit and pillbox hat, stood at the top of the boarding ramp, below the plane's arched doorway. She looked at the two passengers approaching the steps and checked her watch.

As Sam E. and Cricket approached the ramp, he said, "Hold on a second." He rubbed and wiggled his wounded thigh.

"Still hurting?" she asked.

He nodded as a tram rolled away from the plane's luggage department.

"Keep moving, please," the stewardess shouted down to them. "We're about to depart."

The tram, carrying two men—a slim driver and a bulky, goggled man on the tram's passenger side—approached the boarding steps.

The stewardess once more checked her watch. She again shouted to Sam E. and Cricket, "Hurry, they're going to remove the ramp." She stepped inside as the propeller engines started warming up.

"Shit!" Sam E. double-stepped up the stairs. The tram stopped near the side of the ramp. As he and Cricket, who was following behind, hustled up the steps, Sam E. heard a loud bang. For a second he thought it was the tram backfiring. He turned around. The bulky, goggled man was standing in the vehicle, pointing a smoking pistol at him. "Duck!" Sam E. pushed Cricket down. He pulled his gun from his coat pocket and fired; the bullet missed the man by several feet.

The bulky, goggled man fired again. Sam E. felt an air-whiz tickle his scalp. Sam E. fired again; the bullet nowhere closer to the goggled man. The tram driver whipped out his pistol, stood, and fired along with the bulky, goggled man. Sam E. ducked next to Cricket.

"Give me that." She grabbed his pistol, stood, and fired three shots. "Okay, let's go."

Sam E. listened. The only thing he heard were the propellers ramping up. He gingerly stood and looked below. Slumped in the tram were its two passengers. The driver had a bloody shoulder and chest wound. The bulky, goggled man had an expanding red dot below his left eye.

"I'm not nearly as good with a gun as I am with a knife, or I would have got them in two tries," Cricket said. "What do we do now?"

He glanced up at the plane's door. The stewardess was nervously peeping through it. He wiggled his fingers at her. The metal door slammed shut. "We haul ass." He nudged Cricket down the ramp, toward the tram.

"Do you know how to drive this thing?" he asked.

She shook her head.

"Neither do I." Grabbing the dead driver's gun, Sam E. yanked him from his blue cushioned seat, and hopped behind the steering wheel. He removed the bulky passenger's goggles. "Son of a *bitch*. It's Gus Greenbaum." He kicked Greenbaum out of the vehicle and said to Cricket, "Hop in." Sam E. slammed on the clutch. The tram lurched forward.

Chapter Eleven
MR. SANDMAN,
BRING ME A DREAM

The antsy turkey vulture do-si-do'd across the signpost. Its rumpled red face watched the tram sputter off the deserted two-lane into a craggy ditch, blow a final smoky hurrah and fall silent. Blinking once—slowly—the vulture tucked its neck into itself and went to sleep.

Sam E. stepped from the dead vehicle. He shaded his eyes from the white sun's reflection. He glared at the crown-head sign the sleepy bird was perched on. The sign said *US 93/446*. He didn't need the information to tell him they were in the center of a magnifying glass' heat spot called the Mojave Desert. Sam E. trampled through the shrub-dotted sand ripples, shushed the vulture away, and leaned against the signpost.

"What's next, Mr. Wizard?" Cricket asked.

"We hitch a ride." He shimmied his butt down the pole until it smacked against the cracked, dehydrated soil. He rubbed his wounded leg and looked around the tawny wasteland. "Being as there's so many cars to choose from, I say we wait for that spanking new green Thunderbird you wished for the night we were on the mountainside. Anything else we pass on."

Cricket hopped out of the vehicle. "Unbutton your shirt and take off your pants."

"It's too hot for that. I can't get it up."

"Don't be a twerp. I want to check your wounds."

"I knew that." He unbuttoned his shirt. "I was making a joke."

She yanked his pants down.

"Hey, that smarts."

"I knew that. I was making a joke." Cricket looked at the thin scab across his chest. "That one's coming along nicely." She unwrapped a cloth from his thigh and smelled the lesion. "You'll live."

"Yeah," he said, dressing, "but for how long past *The Allen Show*?" He walked to the middle of the empty blacktop and watched the slithering road wither into steam heat.

S am E. shivered. "Goddamn, how'd it get so cold?" He tossed Cricket a cushioned vest from the tram's storage.

Cricket wrapped the vest around her. "Sun sinks. It cools down."

"Not in the clubs where I hang out." He slipped into another vest, laid down and stared at the prickled indigo night. "Hey, saucer-men," he shouted to the cloudless sky, "we're hungry, how 'bout dropping some TV dinners and a couple bottles of Coca-Cola and Seagram's."

"You think they know where we're at?" Cricket asked.

"No. If they did they would have picked us up." A high-pitched yelp skimmed the dark. He jumped.

"You're a real country boy, aren't you?"

"From the most dangerous country in the world, sweetheart. Philly." He slipped his hands behind his head. "Is that where you learned to shoot? In the country?"

"No. My father was a sergeant. Marines. He taught me to handle a knife and gun."

"Military brat?"

"The worst."

"My manager, Doc, was in the army. That's where he learned to cut hair. He used to cut mine when we first started out." He stared at the heavens. "He'd probably be a barber somewhere in Chicago if he hadn't hooked up with me. He loved that town, the music and all." *If he hadn't hooked up with me.* The words made him feel tiny and at the same time large; like the boy who stuck his finger in the dike to keep it from flooding. The feeling tamped heavily upon him, like concrete sludge.

"I'm sorry about him and his wife. You must have been close."

His eyes welled up. "Yeah. Are you and your father close?"

"He's dead, too. But don't be sorry. We hated each other."

"Oh." He let the silence settle in. "How do you think Greenbaum knew we were at the airport?"

"Where would you be if you knew someone was in a hurry to get to New York?" Cricket picked up a pebble. "Do we have a plan?"

"We need to start by telling as many people as we can about the spacemen."

"I already tried that. The same thing happened to me that happened to Miles Bennell, the doctor from *Invasion of the Body Snatchers*, when he tried telling everyone about the pod people."

"What happened to him?"

"They thought he was loony and were ready to send him to the bug house."

"That won't happen to me. I know how to talk to audiences."

Cricket said, "Why don't you just not go on *The Steve Allen Show*?"

"Because as long as Francis and his space goons believe I'm cooperating, we have a chance to stop them."

"Is that the only reason?"

"What does that mean?" He sat up, staring at her face shadowed in darkness.

"I've been around enough entertainers to know all they care about is their career."

"Hey! That's unfair." He hoped she could see the anger in his face.

"Unfair or not, millions of lives are on the line."

"I know that." The concrete sludge weighed even heavier on him, only this time it felt like guilt.

"Why do they want you to kill Steve Allen?" she asked.

"They wouldn't tell me. Let's just get to New York," he said, frustrated. "Okay?"

"Okay."

A sandy wind circled them. He lay back down and again slipped his hands behind his head, listening to the wispy movement.

"Sam?"

"What?"

"Is your mother still alive?"

He closed his eyes. The wind seemed to yearn for something, he thought, something he couldn't quite grasp. Sam E. imagined, as he always did when he lay in the darkness, that the pitch black was a stage curtain struggling to open, but as always, the curtain never parted.

Sammy hated the pine tar scented stucco corridor; especially now in winter, with the heat turned up. Two nurses wheeled a gray-skinned man strapped to a squeaky bed, past him. The air-trail smelled brown, like the mothballed leather grip that belonged to the father he never met. The drab, white brick nursing home bore down and suffocated him until he felt like a brass-helmeted deep-sea diver untethered and sinking into bog water. He entered a room the same shade as his mother's nicotine-stained fingernails, smiled and said, in a cheery English accent, "I say, Mum. Buckingham Palace never looked spiffier!"

His mother didn't move her eyes from the drip bottle above her head. Sammy followed the rubber tube to the needle invading her scrawny wrist.

"You eatin', Mum?" he said in his English accent. His mother gurgle-hacked and shook her head.

"What'd the doctor say?" he asked, without an accent. She shook her head again.

Sammy heard a moan outside the room. "Doc booked me the Vegas job," he said, watching his mother's eyes, inflated and red rimmed, slide from the drip bottle to him. He almost made a joke about her sneezing, holding her mouth, and the air backing up from her face into her pupils. "I'll be leaving Tuesday."

"What day is it today?"

"Saturday."

"Saturday," she repeated, looking up at the bottle again.

"Do ya' need anything, Mater?" Sammy said in his English accent. "A few polo ponies? Wot, wot!"

She didn't respond. Sammy unbuckled her wrist, the one without the I.V., from the bed rail and held her curled hand. He squeezed it for a moment. This was the only time he could remember reaching out for her. "Mum," continuing his accent, "it's tea time and you know how perfectly dyspeptic the duchess gets if I'm tardy." He gently released his grip.

His mother again looked at him. "Sammy," she said. "We don't choose our destiny, we only choose how we handle it."

Sammy closed his eyes. "I don't understand," he said, feeling his body rock.

"We only choose how we handle it."

His body shook violently.

"**S**nap out of it!" he heard Cricket say, rocking his body harder. Sam E. opened his eyes, flinching from the morning light. He heard a purring motor wheeling their way. It rounded the corner, and for a second, he thought he was still dreaming. A goddamned Thunderbird. A goddamned green Thunderbird! He ran to the blacktop and flapped his arms like the wings of the antsy turkey vulture.

Cricket, scuttling behind, slung her beret on her head and joined in the turkey flapping.

The sleek, petite convertible nearly ran them over before gliding to a stop. "Looks like you need a lift," said a pleasant looking, stout man with round tortoiseshell glasses.

"You bet." Sam E. opened the passenger door, motioning for Cricket to slide in. He followed. It was a tight fit, Cricket nearly squeezing onto the man's lap. He figured the driver, who looked to be in his late twenties, didn't mind.

The man, dressed in a yellow-with-red plaid jacket, a white button down shirt and a black bowtie, glided the convertible forward. The hot wind blew through them like a radiator fan.

"Was that your tram back there?" the man asked.

"Not really. We were dropping it off for inspection when it conked out," Sam E. said.

"Really?"

Sam E. glanced in the front-view mirror at the man's bushy-topped hair swishing like a roto-rooter. It would have been comical, he thought, if not for a sad air around the man's full face, and lazy smile. He got the impression the man misplaced something precious. "Nah," Sam E. said, "we shot the driver and we're on our way to the east coast."

"That's funny."

"Thanks, Mr...?"

"Beaumont. Lee Beaumont." The man glanced at them, lingering a second on Cricket.

"Are you a scientist?" Sam E. asked, hopefully. "You look smart."

"I'm a dishwasher." Lee shifted into fourth and stepped on the gas.

Sam E. glanced at Cricket, asleep on Lee's shoulder. "Lee," he said, "can I ask you a question?"

"Shoot."

They passed a wooden sign staked in the barren landscape. It read, in over-sized turquoise letters: **INDIAN JOE SAYS "CORN, HAMBURGERS, SODA, WE GOTTEM!"**

Sam E. glanced at the morning sun. He asked, "What's a nice kid like you doin' in a buggy like this?" as they passed a second sign that read: **"FISH SO FRESH YOU'D SWEAR WE CAUGHTEM!"**

Lee said, "When nice kids have daddys with money, they get buggies like this."

"Then why is the kid a dishwasher?"

"Because the kid's not going to change his life for his dad."

"What does that mean?" Sam E. asked, as they passed a third placard.

"TRUCKERS WELCOME – WINTER, SPRING, SUMMER, AUTUMN!"

Lee shrugged. "The car's a bribe, but the kid's too proud, or too stupid, to cave in."

"The kid must really love washing dishes."

"I guess so." Lee raced the Thunderbird past a fourth sign that read: **"COME TO INDIAN JOE'S AND SIT YOUR BOTTOM! TWO MILES ON THE RIGHT"**

Chapter Twelve
HOW

The green convertible turned into a sandy parking lot next to a large, tee-pee shaped building. The white concrete structure was dotted with Indian stick-figures on horseback—some blue, some red—bowing their arrows at cowboys and buffalo. A stucco totem pole aligned one side of the building's screen-door entrance, and a phone booth aligned the other. Painted below the building's pointed peak, in bold letters: **You're here! Indian Joe's Cafe.**

As the three made their way inside, Sam E. pulled Cricket aside. "How much money do we have left?"

She skimmed through her handbag. "About ninety cents. Don't go crazy on food."

When they entered the cafe, a skinny white man wearing a red feathery Indian headdress, standing behind the register, raised his palm to them, and said, "How!"

"How, Dick," Lee said to the bony-cheeked, salt-and-pepper haired owner.

Behind Dick was a chrome trim counter fronted with single poled, backless leather-bottom stools. On the back side of the counter was a cigarette dribbling cook standing guard over a burger sizzling on the grill. On a shelf above the aproned cook, a shoebox-shaped radio crooned, "It Wasn't God Who Made Honky Tonk Angels." Next to the grill was a portal-windowed swinging door leading to the kitchen. Through it came a pretty, ponytailed waitress dressed in a fringed buckskin vest and skirt. Circling her head was an Indian headband with a yellow feather sticking up in the back. She handed a check to the only customers, an elderly couple sitting at the counter bar stools. They dropped some change and walked toward Dick.

Glancing at his watch, Dick said to Lee, "Early, aren't you?"

"Thought I'd grab a bite before shift. This is Cricket and this is Sam."

"How," Dick said.

"That's what I've been trying to figure out," Sam E. said. "You see, there're these saucer-men who want to take over the world for its oil. They want me to help them by going on *The Steve Allen Show*."

Dick took a step back. He said to Lee, "Is he?" Dick twirled his index finger around his temple.

"No, he's a comedian," Cricket said to Dick. "He's practicing a new act." She turned to Sam E. "I told you no one would believe that routine."

Dick shrugged. "Today's special is Sitting Bullabaisse."

As Lee led Sam E. and Cricket to a booth, the elderly couple approached Dick. He said to them, "How," as he rang up their bill.

Sam E. slid into the booth. "So this is where you work."

"'fraid so," Lee said.

"You are one crazy cat." Cricket slid into the other side.

"No B.S., what's your story?" Lee sat down next to her. "And don't give me that business about tram inspecting."

"Like I told Dick, these space guys flew down and zapped us into their flying saucer," Sam E. said, studying the placemat menu. "They tasted oil and—"

"Shut up." Cricket elbowed him.

"Let me guess," Lee said. "The oil is like Beluga caviar to the aliens. They want to suck us dry and they need you two to carry out their nefarious plan."

"How did you know that?" Sam E.'s eyes jumped to Lee.

"Hi, Lee. Coffee?" the ponytailed waitress asked.

"Hey, Lois. Sounds good, and Papoose pancakes, extra butter."

Sam E. eyed Lois. Angelic eyes, he thought, twenty-two, maybe. Nice smile; not bitter like Vegas women.

"Miss?" Lois said to Cricket.

"Coffee and toast. You have strawberry jam?"

"I'll check." Lois turned to Sam E. "For you, Mr. Lakeside?"

"Do I know you, angel?" He smiled at the auburn-haired waitress.

"I saw you at The Cascade a few weeks ago. You were a riot."

He beamed. "I'll have a Cheyenne shake, patty melt, and fries."

Cricket cleared her throat loudly.

"Make that coffee and toast."

"Sure thing, Mr. Lakeside."

"Sam," he said.

"Sam," she repeated. "My name's Lois, if you need anything."

"What's your name if I don't need anything?"

She laughed. He followed her curvy suede-covered sidestep as she walked behind the counter.

"Get back on your pony, Geronimo," Cricket said.

"You really are a comedian?" Lee asked.

"I told you. Now, what's your story? And I don't mean the dishwasher part."

"You want the long or short version?"

"Make it short. We haven't got the time."

"My father owns five car dealerships in Nevada. Straight-Shooter Shawn."

"I've seen his commercials on television." Sam E. shaped his hands like a pair of six-shooters. "Strait-Shooter's shootin' down the price!" he said, fanning his guns.

"I write comic books. Straight-Shooter thinks it's low rent; worthless."

"What's that got to do with working here? And how'd you know about the saucer-men?"

"Come on." Lee laughed. "That hooey about caviar and invasion is standard comic book fare. As for dishwashing, have either of you heard of Senator Estes Kefauver?"

Sam E. nodded.

"Uh oh," Cricket said.

"Exactly. I was brought before his sub-committee on the evils of comic books. Called un-American, branded a seducer of the innocent, and blackballed out of the business for indecency."

"What kind of funny books did you write?" Sam E. asked.

"*Interplanetary Terror, Weird Tales of the Unknown*, things like that."

"Well, no wonder."

"No wonder what?" Lee asked.

"Nothing," Sam E. facetiously replied. "Nothing at all."

"I suppose your act is pure as the day is long?"

"As a matter of fact I got arrested once for cracking a joke about J. Edgar Hoover."

"And you have the nerve to insinuate *I'm* indecent?"

"At least Hoover's an adult, not like the kids who read your stuff."

"The only thing indecent around here is you." Lee slid out of the booth.

Cricket grabbed his arm and pulled him back. "Don't go. He didn't mean anything."

The two men eyed each other. Sam E. said, "I don't like to hear about kids being mistreated." He smelled the lousy brown stink of the apartment he grew up in.

"My stories don't mistreat kids. That's the whole thing, I write up to them, not down to them, and it pisses off the senators. They want me to treat my readers like rosy conformists. Because I won't do that they want to shut me down."

"I don't get it, but I guess I'm willing to take your word."

"Thanks for nothing," Lee said, as Lois placed drinks on the table.

Handing Sam E. his coffee and toast, Lois said, "On the house," as she placed a Cheyenne shake next to him.

"Sixty-Minute Man" came over the radio. Lois snapped her fingers. "Hey, PJ," she said to the cook. "Turn that up." The music swelled. Lois looked at Sam E. "I just love rhythm and blues."

"Sugar, I have the LP version, 'Ninety-Minute Man.'" He winked at her. "Maybe you'd like to hear it sometime?"

Lois blushed and walked away.

"Don't you ever stop?" Cricket asked.

"It's a bad habit." His eyes lingered on the pretty waitress.

Cricket said to Lee, "So you were run out of business and you wash dishes because you don't want to go back to Straight-Shooter."

"Something like that. What about you two?"

"I don't think it's something we should share," she said.

"What she's trying to say," Sam E. said, wrapping his arm around Cricket's shoulder, "is what I've been telling you. We were stuck in the desert, and we have to get to New York City to jump start an alien takeover. Oh, and we have to kill Steve Allen."

Cricket shook her head.

"You're full of crap." Lee pulled out a small pencil and notepad from his shirt pocket. "But it'd make a great story. You mind if I use it?"

"Start scribbling," Sam E. said.

Lee licked the tip of his pencil point and motioned for him to begin.

"**O**kay, I'm changing the comedian to an insurance salesman and the dame to a divorcee. Better chemistry. The rest I like." Lee closed his notepad. He forked a pancake swatch from his plate, swabbed Log Cabin syrup with it, and stuck it in his mouth.

Sam E. asked, "Why don't the spacemen just kill us now and take the oil?"

Lee swallowed, and said, "Because they can't. You said they're merchants, not soldiers. They wouldn't have powerful enough weapons to take over an entire planet. They're also too greedy to get their government involved. They want to keep all the profits for themselves. Remember, oil's an exotic delicacy to them; they can charge a lot of whatever they use for money."

"Makes sense." Sam E. tapped his fingernails on his coffee mug. "Can they keep an eye on us from their space ship?" He snuck a look at Lois, wiping down the front counter, and waved quietly to her. She glanced at him and smiled.

"I don't think so or else they would have picked up the insurance salesman and the dame when they were stuck in the desert. That transmonitor thing the heroes escaped through isn't like radar. It's sort of like a tunnel. It takes you from one end to the other."

"And they can set where it's going to take them," Cricket said.

"That's right."

"You mean," Sam E. said, "if it was pointed at the asteroid instead of the mountainside, that's where it would have taken us?"

"I believe so. In my story that's the way it's going to be."

Sam E. looked at Cricket. "I'm glad it was pointing where it was."

"Physically, of course, the space creatures could follow anyone, but that's not practical." Lee forked another pancake bit into his mouth.

"When they landed, why did they walk out of the ship instead of using the transporter?" Cricket asked. "In the movies that would be an inconsistency."

"Why are you asking me these questions? It's your story."

"Because all we have is what we told you."

"And because you write about weird interplanetary stuff," Sam E. said. "That makes you an expert and the closest thing we have to a scientist."

"But I mistreat kids, remember?"

"Come on." Cricket touched Lee's arm. "He said he was sorry."

"No, he didn't." Lee eyed Sam E.

Sam E. hesitated. "Fine, I'm sorry."

Cricket arched her eyebrows at Lee as if to ask, "Okay?"

"I don't trust him," Lee said. "But, I'll answer it for you. They didn't use the transporter when they walked out of the saucer for the same reason you don't drive your car next door: convenience, cost, energy consumption. When they're in the air then they would have to use the transporter."

"How do the salesman and divorcee get to New York with no car and no money? Rob the cafe and steal a car?"

"That's one of two ways, but that would make them villains and according to the Kefauver subcommittee's newly mandated comic code, all criminals must get their just reward."

"They die?" Sam E. asked.

Lee nodded. "I'll make sure the insurance salesman dies."

Sam E. gulped.

"What's the second way?" Cricket asked.

"Convince the guy who picked them up to take them."

"Ever been to New York?" Sam E. asked. "You'd love it. There're tons of comic book publishers."

Lee wiped his napkin across his lips. "I've had it with big cities and their editors who turn you over to subcommittees to save their own skins." He stood up. "I'll handle the check. That lunatic story was worth it. You two ought to think about writing dime store novels." Before walking away, he added, "Don't get any flipped out ideas, Dick has a Luger under his register."

"Who wins, Beaumont?" Sam E. asked. "Us or them?"

"I haven't figured that out yet." Lee walked away.

Sam E. slid out of the booth.

"Where you going?" Cricket asked.

"To rob the cafe and steal Lee's car."

"That'd make us the villains. We'd have to die."

"That's only in comic books." He walked toward the register.

"Wait for me." Cricket slid out of the booth.

"How," Dick said, as they approached him.

Sam E. asked, "You have change for a dollar?"

"Lo, you want to trade tip-change for cash?" Dick said to Lois, who was standing near PJ the cook. They were listening to Carl Perkins' "Honey, Don't!" on his radio.

"Sure do." Lois approached them.

Through the kitchen door's portal-window Sam E. saw Lee's back bent over the sink, his arms, piston-like, bobbing in and out of the soapy water.

"Whatcha need?" Lois thumbed through her skirt pocket. She looked up at Sam E.; her almond shaped, sable eyes, gleaming at him. She smiled, a gentle gesture. The contours swept away his filthy world. In the benevolence of her upturned lips he saw the two of them, old, sitting on a pier over a rippled burgundy lake. He heard a fish, probably a bass, splish-splosh beneath the shadow of a droopy cypress over-hanging the bank. He felt her warm arm cup his shoulder and smelled her apricot scented hair as she leaned into his chest. It was the kindest smile he'd ever seen.

"What we need is the register open." Cricket plucked the switchblade from her purse. "And don't go for the Luger," she said to Dick. "You'll never make it."

"Is this a joke?" Lois asked Sam E.

"I'm sorry," he said to her, before pointing his gun at Dick.

"Buddy," Dick said to him. "You might want to reconsider."

"Don't make it difficult. I want this to end right."

Dick shook his head and opened the register.

"Your money, too," Cricket said to Lois.

Lois said to him, "This is my college money, Sam."

"No," he said to Cricket. "She needs it."

A voice came over the radio, *"This is Sandy Slusher your Rock and Roll Usher, here's a doozy for you."*

"Don't fret, Lois," Dick said. "Nobody's handing over anything."

The radio voice continued, *"There's been a string of robberies around the Las Vegas area. Filling stations are being plundered, and get this, the only thing they're taking is oil!"*

"Because," Dick continued, "PJ is pointing his shotgun at about the area where the little lady's beret is."

Sam E. glanced at the cook. PJ's dribbling cigarette had stopped bouncing. He had the twin barrels of a sawed-off shotgun aimed squarely at her skull.

The radio voice continued, *"Is that kooky? Jars and cans of oil!"*

Sam E. looked at Cricket and nodded. They lowered their weapons.

Dick grabbed the gun and knife. He folded the switchblade and stuck it in his pocket, all the while keeping the gun on Sam E. and Cricket. "Lois, call the police." Lois glanced at Sam E., hesitated, and ran outside to the phone booth.

The radio voice continued, *"Now here comes the wild part, kitties, the guy doing the robbing is Straight-Shooter Shawn Beaumont!"*

Sam E., hearing the name, elbowed Cricket.

As PJ slid his shotgun under the counter, the radio voice continued, *"That's right, every filling station attendant has identified the crook as car dealer Straight-Shooter Shawn. My theory is his jalopies are so leaky he can't keep oil in the crankcases."*

Dick turned to Sam E. and Cricket. "You two get back in your seats." He prodded them to the booth.

The radio voice continued, *"Enough facts, let's get back to the wax. Here's the rockin' Luella Jenkins with her real gone hit, 'Blue Jeans and Alligator Shoes!'"*

Just as Sam E. and Cricket were sliding in the pleated seat, the rock-a-billy song cut off.

"I'm sorry, Dick." Lee was standing behind PJ the cook, his arm slung over PJ's shoulder. His other hand pressed a sudsy butcher knife to the cook's neck. "Those two are going with me."

"I can't do that," Dick said. "They tried to rob me."

"They didn't take anything."

"Principle." Dick shoved the weapon into Sam E.'s back.

"I'll carve a sirloin out of PJ." Lee inched the knife into the cook's leathery neck. PJ's lips loosened. His cigarette tumbled to the floor.

Dick's eyes bounced from the cook, to Sam E. and Cricket.

"He's not bluffing," Sam E. said.

Dick went back to Lee, and to the knife threatening the cook's throat.

"He'll slice him," Sam E. said. "Like strips of raw bacon."

Dick hesitated. "Jesus H." He lowered the gun.

"Give it to me." Sam E. snagged his gun back from Dick. "Give her the knife back, too."

Dick pulled the knife from his pocket and handed it to Cricket.

"And your Luger," he added.

"But I got that in the Invasion of Normandy."

"Sorry."

Handing the gun to Sam E., Dick turned to Lee. "Were you? Bluffing?"

Lee shrugged. He lowered the butcher knife from the cook's neck. "Sorry, PJ, didn't mean to frighten you." Lee grabbed the shotgun from beneath the counter shelf.

"No harm, kid." PJ rubbed his throat. Picking up his cigarette, he added, "I figured it to be a put-on."

Sam E. motioned for Lee and Cricket to leave.

Lee grabbed his jacket from a clothes peg near the register. He said to Dick, "Straight-Shooter's a lot of things, but he's not an oil thief. These two know something and I've got to find out what it is."

"How?" Dick asked.

Sam E. raised his palm to Dick, and said, "How!" He, Lee and Cricket left the cafe.

As they exited, Lois stepped from the phone booth near the screen door, and said, "Hey! You better hurry. The cops are on the way."

Sam E. emptied the Luger and handed it to her. "Give this back to your boss, it's a souvenir from his combat days."

"Now, give me your gun." Lee pointed the confiscated shotgun at him. Sam E. handed over his pistol. Lee shoved it in his coat pocket. "You drive. Just because I'm going along doesn't mean I trust either of you."

"Is it okay if she drives?" Sam E. motioned to Cricket. Cricket beamed.

"It's jake by me."

Cricket hopped in the driver's seat.

As Sam E. slid in the passenger side, Lois grabbed his arm. "Here." She handed him her money and planted a kiss on his cheek.

He brushed his fingers along the wet spot. "No, that's for college. What are you studying?"

"Teaching."

"You're gonna make a great teacher." He kissed her hard on the lips.

Lois smiled. She slowly stepped away.

Sam E. took his place next to Cricket. As Lee slid into the Thunderbird, Sam E. shut his eyes to feel one more time Lois' lips pressing against his. The convertible roared away. He opened his eyes and stared at the fierce open highway.

Chapter Thirteen
PACKARD UP

Cricket removed her beret.

Sam E. studied her cat eyes soaking up the desert's sweeping turquoise and amber hues, as they raced along the blacktop. He smiled, watching her gleefully floor the convertible around a wide curve.

Over the wind rush, Lee asked Sam E., "How much money do you have?"

"We got about fourteen bucks from the till."

"I've got six dollars," Lee said.

"We need to ditch the car," Sam E. said.

"Why?" Cricket asked, disappointed.

"Dick called the cops. They'll be on our trail."

"We should be passing Chloride in a minute. That'll make us about a half-hour from Arizona, specifically Kingman. We're stopping there."

"What for?" Sam E. asked.

"You want another car, don't you?" Lee's voice was stern.

"You don't have to be so grumpy," Cricket said.

"Look, I just want to find out what's going on with Straight-Shooter and the oil."

"We told you," Sam E. said.

"You told me some cock-and-bull about space creatures. I want the truth."

"Trust me. That's the truth."

"I don't trust anybody. Not after the Kefauver hearings." Lee watched the vehicle zip past a crooked sign that read Chloride. "You want another car or not?"

"When you see Kingman," Sam E. said to Cricket, "turn in."

"That's no fair. I want to keep the Thunderbird."

"Nothing's fair, anymore." Sam E. thought of Doc and Marge murdered, and of never seeing Lois again. He stared at the shotgun on Lee's lap. He felt as cold as the twin barrels facing him.

"**Y**ou know who's from Kingman?" Lee asked, as Cricket drove the Thunderbird along a four-lane highway with western style storefronts on one side and a cashew colored, Pueblo motif railroad depot on the other. "Andy Devine."

"Who?" Cricket asked.

"Jingles Jones," Sam E. said. "The fat, gravelly voiced guy from the Wild Bill Hickok show. You should watch TV more and stay away from the movies. It's cheaper."

"Make a left at Mr. B's." Lee pointed to a green-on-pink burger stand with "Kingman's Best Cheeseburger!" written in block letters above the pick-up window.

Cricket cornered the vehicle.

"Next block turn right, you can't miss it."

"Miss what?" Sam E. asked.

Cricket made the right and they came head on to a gigantic pair of blinking neon six-shooters. A large silver-glittered sign, on the roof of a boxy white building centered in a sea of new and used cars, proclaimed, "Straight-Shooter Shawn is Gunning For Your Business."

"Dealership number three," Lee said. "Pull in."

The trio sat on a black and white cowhide couch in a small, dark-paneled office. A clunking metal fan tossed warm air on them.

The couch faced the front end of an oak desk. On the desktop there was a nameplate pointed toward them. It read, *District Deputy Darryl Crabtree.*

Lee laid the shotgun by his side. He studied his road atlas. "There's a small airport about twenty miles from here, maybe you can catch a flight to New York from there."

"We can't chance that," Sam E. said. "Greenbaum's men will have every airport in the region staked out."

"You said he was dead."

"Yeah, but whoever in charge now will probably want revenge. I don't want to take a chance."

Lee traced his finger along a map in the atlas. "In that case, if we take Route 66 through Albuquerque, past Oklahoma City, to Afton…At Afton we head north on 69 to Kansas City Municipal. That's the first major airport. I'll drop you off there."

"How long will that take?"

"A day or two."

"How about if we catch a train to New York?" Cricket asked.

"That's worse than a plane," Lee said. "A call to someone. The train stops at the next station, the door slides open and guess who's there with a tommy gun?"

"You wrote crime comics, too?" Sam E. asked.

Lee nodded.

The door burst open. A red-headed, bulky man wearing a tan three-piece suit, a ten-gallon hat, and stitched boots flooded the room. "Lee!" he said. "I heard you were here. How the hell you holdin' out, partner?"

"Okay, Uncle Darryl. What have you heard?"

"Just those radio bastards, excuse my Chickasaw, miss," he lobbed to Cricket, before turning back to Lee, "keep spoutin' off about Straight-Shooter pilfering oil."

"It's not him."

"Course not." Darryl tossed his hat on a corner rack. "Your daddy's rich, he don't need to steal." He plopped into a leather chair behind the desk. Nodding toward the shotgun, he added, "Since when are you a hunter?"

"I, ah, won it in a bet."

"Hmmph," Darryl said. "What kind of bet?"

"Who could tell the best whopper."

"You had an unfair advantage. You're a writer."

Lee glanced at Sam E. "You'd be surprised."

"Have you and your daddy palavered?"

"No."

"Straight-Shooter's stubborner than a starving mule with a feed sack," Darryl said, "but then again, the bloom don't fall far from the cactus, does it?"

Ignoring the last comment, Lee said, "You think he'll be okay?"

"Hell, yes! He's got more lawyers than Frankie Laine's got number one records. He'll end up suing them for defamation. What I don't understand is why anyone would want to go around imitatin' him and doin' something like that?"

"Uncle Darryl, I've business I want to discuss—"

"Whoa, buckaroo. First things, first." He walked over to Cricket and took her hand with his two beefy ones. "Missy, my rude nephew neglected to introduce us. I'm Uncle Darryl."

"Are you really a deputy?" Sam E. asked.

"Are you a bad guy?" Darryl reached along the side of his suit jacket and raised an imaginary gun.

Sam E. said nothing.

The two steely-eyed each other.

Darryl fanned his thumb. "Pow!" he said.

Sam E. jumped.

"I'm Straight-Shooter's district manager. We call 'em deputies at the dealership. Now then, two ranch hands were in the barn packing hay for the winter. The first one says, 'You hear ol' Roscoe's got a new car?' The second ranch hand says, 'Oh no! That cowboy's gonna start crowin' the minute he comes in'. The first ranch hand says, 'Naw, he's not the braggin' type'. 'You wait and see', the second one says, 'Roscoe'll figure out a way to boast about his new car'. The barn door opens, Roscoe looks at the boys storing hay and says—"

"Let's *Packard* up!" Sam E. said.

"Oh." Darryl's voice lost its luster. "You already know it."

"I love that joke," Sam E. said, catching his disappointment. "You've got a great ear."

Darryl slapped Sam E.'s knee, and said, "It'd make a great opening! I caught you at the Shriners' convention last month. You're a funny man, son."

"You ought to be sheriff with taste like that."

"Told ya he's funny," Darryl said to himself. Making his way back to his chair, he said to Lee, "Now, what can I do for you?"

"Uncle Darryl, I want to trade in my Thunderbird."

Cricket frowned.

"Looks like your sweetie's not happy with that," Darryl said.

"She's not my sweetie." Lee threw a quick look at Sam E.

Catching the look, Darryl said to himself, "Range war."

"I want to trade the convertible for something less expensive and less obtrusive," Lee said. "But dependable."

"Deputy Darryl's got the bargain you're looking for!"

"We don't want Deputy Darryl's bargain," Lee said. "We want Uncle Darryl's."

"Gotcha." Darryl nodded earnestly to the trio gazing at him from the cowhide couch.

Sam E. eyed Cricket eyeing the open-winged chrome swan attached to the front of the bloated, four door sedan's cream-colored hood. *She hates the car*, he thought with amusement, as Cricket slipped into the driver's seat. He entered the plaid-patterned back seat and stretched his legs on the long, cotton weave.

Lee opened the dented front passenger door and slid in.

"She don't look like much, but this 'ol pony'll get you where you're going," Darryl said. "Which, by the way is?"

Lee said, "Kan—"

"Hey!" Sam E. purposely cut him off. "Did you know Andy Devine's from here?"

Darryl inclined his rusty-haired head like a rooster. He said to Lee, "Is there something you want to tell me?"

Lee hesitated. "I've run into a bit of, well, a bit of legal trouble since the Kefauver hearings and I want to keep my whereabouts quiet for awhile."

"What about these two?" Darryl motioned to Sam E. and Cricket.

"Hitching a ride, nothing more."

"Uh huh." Darryl rubbed his double chin.

A voice over a loud-speaker said, *"Deputy Darryl, Straight-Shooter on line one."*

Darryl leaned into Lee's open window. "Ya mind if I throw in my two centavos?"

Lee said nothing.

"If I was laying low, last thing I'd do is pick up two hitchers. But if I did, I'd make damn sure they didn't look like hobos."

Sam E. tried to smooth his rumpled, sweat-stained shirt and Cricket fanned her dirty pedal pushers.

"Next thing I'd do is make my hitchers bathe." Darryl said to Sam E. and Cricket, "No offense, folks, but you're gamier than a chuckwalla in mating season."

The loud-speaker voice said, *"Deputy Darryl, Straight-Shooter waiting on line one."*

Darryl, eyeing them, said, "There's water in the trough you ain't spilling."

"Darryl," Sam E. said. "There's something going on. Something bad. We're trying to stop it. There're these space creatures—"

"*What* did he say?" Darryl asked Lee.

"Space creatures," Lee said, timorously.

"Are you back on the bennies?"

Sam E. and Cricket glanced at each other.

"I kicked that monkey," Lee said. "You know that."

Motioning to Sam E., Darryl said to Lee, "Is Lakeside a bit off the railroad track?"

"Probably," Lee said, "but it's important I find out."

"Why?"

"Because it might have something to do with Straight-Shooter and the stolen oil."

Darryl cocked his hat back, studying Sam E. and Cricket. He finally said to Lee, "Is that why you're totin' a shotgun?"

"No. I told you I won it."

"Wouldn't it be safer in the trunk?" Darryl asked, his voice full of suspicion. "That is, if your compadres aren't dangerous."

"Well…I suppose." Lee motioned for Cricket to hand him the keys. Lee went to the trunk and deposited the weapon. Lee slid back in the passenger side.

Darryl rested his hand on the window opening. "I'll give you twenty-four hours to get out of town. Then I got to let your pappy know you were here."

"Thanks." Lee touched Darryl's hand.

"You take care of my nephew," Darryl said to Sam E. "If anything happens to him, I'll come gunnin' for you."

Sam E. smiled even though he wasn't sure if Darryl was kidding or serious.

"Now get this pony out of here!" Darryl slapped the door as if it were a horse's buttock.

Cricket cranked the ignition.

"Packard up." Sam E. said.

"Told ya he's funny," Darryl said to himself, watching the fifty-one Packard blow a hearty cloud, and roll away.

Chapter Fourteen
CRINKLE FRIES

S am E. took a greasy, brown bag from Mr. B's pick-up window. He sat at an outdoor white tile concrete table with Lee and Cricket. "Your uncle's right," he said to Lee, who was between burger bites. "We need a change of clothes."

"What about money?" Cricket sipped a bottle of grape Nehi.

"With what Uncle Darryl gave me for the trade-in, we've got enough to get things done," Lee said. "There's a Ben Franklin around the corner. You can grab new clothes and then we'll get a room at the Beale for a quick clean up."

"Ben Franklin?" Cricket said. "They're practically a five and dime. I don't like their clothes."

"I don't like a lot of things," Lee said, "but we have to make do with what we have."

Cricket smirked. "Says who?"

"Says me," Lee tapped his coat pocket, "and Sam's revolver."

Sam E. removed a handful of crinkle fries from the bag and plopped one into his mouth. He wasn't sure whether he liked Lee or not, but there was something about the stocky man that made him uneasy, as if Lee's presence had altered the path they were on. He just didn't know if it was for better or worse.

S am E. swiped a comb through his damp hair. *I look like a hayseed!* He stared at his green flannel shirt and Oshkosh bib overalls reflected in the dresser mirror. He shook his head and lay on the lumpy hotel bed, watching a small television that was resting on the dresser. Behind the bathroom door, near the room's entrance, the shower sizzled like chicken cooking in a deep fryer.

"Wasn't she the one in the hurry?" Lee sat on the other bed.

"Hold on." Sam E. scooted to the television and turned it up.

"Apparently Straight-Shooter isn't the only Beaumont in trouble," said a newscaster who could have been mistaken for an accountant. *"Lee Beaumont, son of Straight-Shooter Beaumont, is wanted for robbery."*

"Great," Lee said.

"Dick Howzer, owner of Indian Joe's Cafe, west of Chloride, called police two hours ago and..."

Cricket, in an untucked, black-checkered red button-down shirt, cuffed dungarees, and PF Flyers, stepped out of the bathroom. Both men's eyes bobbed between the television and the svelte woman towel-drying her hair. The homespun clothes, contrary to expectations, had the same effect that a schoolgirl's outfit has on a pin-up girl.

"Did I hear Indian Joe's?" She ran her fingers through her silky-wet golden locks.

"Shhh." Lee motioned to the screen.

"He's driving a brand spanking new green Thunderbird," the newsman said, *"and is with two people; one, a dyed red-head—"*

"Bull*shit!*" Cricket hurled the towel at the TV.

"...other person, funny-fellow Sam E. Lakeside, was, according to waitress and eye-witness Lois Sokel, an unwilling participant." A film clip of Lois appeared on the screen. "He's too nice to be involved. I know he was forced into it," Lois said into the camera.

"Lois." Sam E. tasted her lips against his.

The newscaster appeared on the screen, and said, *"The trio were last seen heading east on US 93/446. They are armed and danger—"*

Sam E. clicked the television off. "Let's get the hell out of here."

In the motel lobby Sam E. stopped at a phone booth. "Lee, do you know the number to Indian Joe's?"

"The cafe only has the phone out front," Lee said. "The one by the entrance."

"Will they answer it?"

"If they're not busy, but the lunch crowd sometimes gets pretty hectic."

"Give me the number." Sam E. pulled coins from his pocket.

"Cactus 7491."

Sam E. stepped in the oak and glass enclosure. "I'll only be a minute." He slid the bi-fold door shut. Pressing the receiver to his ear, he slipped the change in the phone's coin slot, each time causing an internal bell to ping. He dialed, waited, said in a gruff voice, "Is this Indian Joe's? I'd like to speak with Lois, this is her, ah, father. Thank-you." Sam E. watched Cricket and Lee staring at him through the outside of the glass. He put his hand over the receiver, opened the door partially, and said, "Wait in the car, I'll be right there." He slid the door shut and turned away.

"Daddy?" a tinny voice said to him, through the receiver.

"Lois?" he said, "I didn't know if Dick would put you on, so I told him I was your father."

"Oh my God!" Lois said. "The police came looking for you, but I told them you didn't do anything wrong."

"I saw you on television, you were beautiful."

"I was?"

"Yes."

"Stop it. You'll make me cry," Lois said.

He looked up. Lee and Cricket were still gazing at him. Cricket was smiling. He smirked and turned his back to them. "Lois, I know this is crazy. But," Sam E. took a big breath, "I want to let you know how much I really like you." He heard Lois cry. "Don't be upset. I just wanted to say it because, well, I may never get the chance again."

"I'm not upset," Lois said, sniffling. "I——"

The phone went dead. "Lois?" he said. "Lois?" he tapped the cradle button several times.

"I'm sorry, sir, the line went dead," the operator said. "Would you like me to try again?"

"Yes." Sam E. waited, heard a few buzzes and one clack.

"Sorry, sir. It happens in that area once in a while. Try back later."

"Sure," Sam E. said, glumly. "Thanks." He plunked the receiver in the cradle harder than necessary. I *what?* he thought. I like you, too? I *love* you? I want to spend my life with you? I, I, I? He stepped from the booth, the unanswered question like a noose around his heart. Sam E. walked toward the car, Lee and Cricket trailing him.

At nearly the same moment, at Indian Joe's Cafe, Dick stuck his head out the screen door and said, "Hey, Lois, table four is wait——" He noticed the receiver was hanging off the cradle. He put it in place, saying to himself, "I guess she must've gone back in," rubbed his nose, and re-entered the diner.

Cricket motored the heavy Packard east on a two-lane extension of Route 66, the narrow blacktop cutting through a landscape resembling a horned toad's parched, mottled hide. Sam E. stretched out in the back seat. The sun-hot breeze settled inside him like a tranquilizer. He raised his hand over his eyes, closed them, and imagined the black curtain that never parted. Paddling into a wave of sleep, he heard Cricket say to Lee, "You think Uncle Darryl will still give us twenty-four hours when he hears about the robbery?"

"I don't know," Lee said.

"Lee," Cricket said. "The spacemen need to see someone on television to photostat them, right?"

"That's the way you explained it to me."

"How did they copy your dad? He doesn't have a TV show?"

"Straight-Shooter does commercials."

Cricket nodded. "So if Sam is on *The Steve Allen Show*, they can copy him, too. Is that part of their plan?"

"This is your BS, remember? Why don't you tell me?"

"What's your problem?"

"There's no problem. I just don't trust you two," Lee said.

"How long are you gonna keep spinning that record? It's not very becoming."

"Do you really expect me to believe spacemen who look like marionettes?"

"I guess not, but can you at least pretend? We need answers." She glared at him.

"What was the question?"

"If Sam goes on *The Steve Allen Show*, then they can copy him, right?"

"Once he's been on TV, they can duplicate him, like they supposedly did with Straight-Shooter."

"So their plan's to copy Sam?"

"Maybe," Lee said, "but it doesn't explain why they would also want Allen dead."

The road curved into a long stretch of roadway, paralleling a railroad track running along an open field.

"Why don't you call him Dad?" Cricket asked.

"Because his name is Steve Allen."

"You know what I mean."

"He wants to be called Straight-Shooter. If I call him anything else, he ignores me."

"Did you ever want to call him Dad?"

"Are you writing my biography?"

"No," Cricket said. "Sorry."

Lee watched a kit fox scurry across the tracks. "When I was younger I wanted to, but I grew out of it."

"Are you close?"

"What do *you* think?"

"I think I'm not writing your bio," Cricket replied, "and it's none of my business."

Lee nodded. "What'd you call your dad? Daddy-o?"

"My father was a Marine sergeant. He'd have whupped my behind."

"Sam said you're good with a knife. Did your father teach you?"

She nodded. "And a gun. He figured that would make up for me not being a boy."

"You guys didn't get along?"

Cricket threw a hard look at him. "He said I was a mistake."

"Oh," Lee responded, his voice sounding uncomfortable. He glanced in the back seat at Sam E., sprawled out, sleeping. "You two aren't an item?"

"Sam's not my type."

Lee hesitated. "Who is?"

"You writing a story?"

"Always," Lee said. "What do you do for a living?"

"I play nice."

"What does that mean?"

"I stroke egos. I coddle. I fawn; whatever it takes to move up a rung."

Lee sucked his cheeks. He watched an approaching freight train, the heat wavering its image like a breezy sheet on a clothesline.

"You think I should be ashamed?" Cricket asked.

"I didn't say that."

"No, but I heard it. I'm not ashamed of anything."

"You heard your own misgivings." Lee looked at her. "I know, because I hear mine all the time."

She looked at the hefty writer's strong-set face. His eyes, black and brooding, also seemed comforting. Without her consent, her cheeks blushed and her eyes demurely lowered. She clicked on the radio. A raspy-voiced Big Joe Turner, accompanied by an amoral backbeat, implored his missus to get outta bed and wash herself up.

"You dig rock and roll?" She tapped her hand to the bulldozing piano riffs.

"More the jazz type."

"Thought so."

"What's wrong with Parker and Gillespie?"

"Nothing." Cricket smiled.

Big Joe and his band bellowed the chorus to "Shake, Rattle and Roll."

"You think I'm a square, don't you?" Lee asked.

"I didn't say that."

"Is it the bow tie?" He brought his hand to the black neckpiece.

"Could be."

"How's this?" Lee tossed it on the dash.

Big Joe wailed about his resemblance to a one-eyed cat that was peeking into a sea-food store.

"Better." She pitched it out the window. "Much better."

The chorus came around again. Cricket turned up the music and wailed along with Big Joe and his band. She glimpsed at Lee and adjusted the front view mirror, determined to keep the sun's platinum reflection from blinding her vision.

Lee smiled at her. "You better turn that down, you'll wake Sam up."

"So, you're worried about your career?" the judge asked.

The courtroom was chilly. Sam E. tightened his brown leather aviator jacket and wiggled his freshly polished, high-laced boots. He knew he was standing on the stage floor though it was too dark to see.

Sam E. focused on the black robed judge, who was sitting behind a raised desk. Sam E. said to him, "The judge says to the defendant, 'All your answers must be loud and clear? Do you hear me? Loud and clear! What is your name?' The defendant hesitates. He finally says, *'Loud and Clear'*."

"Come closer," the judge said. "Approach the bench."

Sam E. felt his boots march forward. The judge smells brown, he thought, just like Father's mothballed leather grip.

"Your big career break is coming." The judge leaned forward and his head entered a scarlet colored spotlight. "Seize it like there's no tomorrow!" He smacked his gavel against the desktop, and added, *"Because you won't do right to save your doggone soul!"*

"Stop!" Sam E. screamed. His eyes shot open.

"Hey," Lee said. "You okay?" He clicked off the radio.

Sam E. breathed erratically.

"Calm down." Lee flicked the car's roof light on. "You're pale as hell."

In a cold sweat, Sam E. said, "I don't want to sleep anymore."

"That must have been a hell of a nightmare. What was it about?"

"My career."

"Your career?" Cricket's voice was laced with suspicion. Sam E., too shook up to fight it, nodded.

"Stay away from crinkle fries," Lee said. "They don't agree with you."

"It's not the fries," Sam E. said.

Lee shut off the roof light. He studied the trembling comedian. Sam E. slouched against the back door. He stared out the window, listening to the hollow rumble of the blackwalls. He felt as gloomy as the moonless night they were driving through. "Something happened when the spacemen took me in their saucer," he said, softly. "It opened something, like a hole in the Hoover Dam."

"Do things flood in, or flood out?" Lee asked.

"I don't know."

Lee reached into his slacks for his notepad. As he did, his hand brushed against Cricket's thigh. She glanced at him and blushed.

"This is beyond comic books," Lee said.

"What does that mean?" Sam E. asked.

"That if it was true, which I don't think it is, I'd be frightened as hell."

"Of what?" Cricket asked.

"Of there being something we have no control over. That augurs badly for the end of the story."

Sam E. watched the headlights dissolve into the unknown. *There's gotta be a punch line*, he repeated in his head. *There's always a punch line*. He studied the Packard's twin-pyramid beams—like dim heralds to the future—losing themselves in the black, uncertain night.

Chapter Fifteen
HAPPY TRAILS

Roy hosed the gas blot near the ethylene pump. The purple-green rainbow it produced as it mixed with the water made him think of Toto poking out of Judy Garland's wicker basket. "Hey, Roger," he said to the lanky man inside the garage who was fixing a flat. "What do you think of Trudy?"

Roger, a pensive, leather-skinned fellow who looked older than his thirty years, said, "She's too sophisticated for a young fella like you, Roy. Stick with the teeny-boppers." Roger liked Roy. He thought of Roy, ten years his junior, as an impetuous younger brother. Roger also thought of Trudy as trouble. The wife of a Baptist minister is always trouble.

"I heard she knows how to kiss twenty-eight different ways," Roy said, feeling an itch crawl down from his chest to his crotch. He figured he better not tell Roger she already showed him at least twelve of those kisses, and half of them were below his waist.

"What happened to that big-tomatoed girl?" Roger asked.

"Suzette? She wants a husband."

Roger, wiping his hands on a rag, walked over to Roy. "Listen, don't get your pecker trapped in any girl's undies. The minute you hear from Henderson State you hop ship and get the hell outta here, you hear, Roy?"

Roy smiled that goofy smile he knew people liked, and said, "Thanks, Rog." He stuck out his hand and the two shook. The strawberry sun's final pink rays rippling across the Oklahoma plain added a warmth to the gesture that would have been lost in the earlier, blazing-white afternoon heat.

Roger walked into the station as the sky fell into gray. As he did, Roy glanced at the Sinclair Dinosaur clock near the entrance. He thought of Trudy's eraser-head nipples and how he'd be sucking on them a few hours from now.

Roger, feeling good about his big brother role, bent over the soda-pop cooler and pulled out a Pepsi-Cola. He felt a tap on his shoulder.

"Hey, buddy," Francis said.

Roger nearly dropped the cold bottle. "Scared me, mister. I didn't hear you come in."

"Yeah," Francis said. "Here's the thing. I'm waiting on some friends. They'll be stopping here."

"Well, we'll be closing in about thirty minutes."

"They're an hour or two away."

Roger puckered and unpuckered his lips. "Maybe you can meet them somewheres else."

Francis shook his head. "Nope, this is the place." He tipped his fedora back. "They're gonna need a new tire, and I'm gonna need oil."

"Oil's no problem. The tire I can change if they get here in the next half hou—"

"You'll change it," Francis said, sliding his pistol from beneath his suit jacket, "when they get here."

"Whoa," Roger said. "I'll be happy to. No charge."

"That's nice," Francis said. "Drink your soda."

Roger suckled the bottle.

Roy entered and said, "Hey, Rog, where's the detergent?"

Francis spun and fired his pistol in Roy's gut. Twice.

Roger dropped his soda.

Roy balled into a bloody heap.

"I don't like surprises," Francis said, nudging Roy's dead body with his wingtip. "You," he said to Roger. "Be still."

Roger bobbed his head. He stared at the brown cola-fizz mingling with Roy's rose-red blood.

Francis walked outside and waved his pistol toward the sky.

Roger heard a low hum. The soda cooler rattled. He looked through the pane at Francis. A brass-colored baseball-cap-shaped object, the size of an eighteen-wheeler, landed next to him. Roger figured he was dreaming and decided to go with it. He'd tell Roy all about it the next day. Roger watched the front of the elephantine baseball cap open—and now he *knew* he was dreaming—because Lucille Ball and Ed Sullivan stepped out and onto the visor.

"Ha, *Ha!*" Roger said. He didn't laugh. He just smiled, and said "Ha, *Ha!*" He repeated it over and over as Lucy and Ed entered the station and tore through the oil containers, guzzling the gooey brown liquid down their throats, licking the overflow from each other's jaws. He said "Ha, *Ha!*" when they made a ferocious sound like tires screeching. He said it until the man, the one Lucy and Ed called Fer-an-sus, told Roger to shut the fuck up and get rid of the body. Roger shut up but continued saying, "Ha, *Ha!*" inside his head as he dragged Roy away. He continued saying it as he threw a box of nails on the road. He continued it for the rest of his short life as he was shuffled from institute to institute.

S am E. closed his eyes and pictured Lois: her vivacious dark eyes, soft auburn ponytail, friendly smile. She was one of those women who were beautiful in an unassuming way, whose beauty lasts beyond the aging of her features. He opened his eyelids and stared at the Packard's headlights slicing through the dark sludge. He pretended that the ferocious lamps protected him from harm, from the next shitty club on the circuit, from black stage curtains that never opened, from a world that soon may not exist. Sam E. pretended that he and Lois were being swept on the twin car beams away from that misery to *The Steve Allen Show*. "How we doing on gas?" he asked Cricket.

"About three-quarters of a tank."

"Where are we?"

"How're you feeling?" Lee asked.

"Where are we?" he repeated.

"Outside of Amarillo, heading towards Oklahoma."

In the black distance, a hazy white building appeared to their left. Sam E. thought it looked as if it was standing below an overhead spotlight. Driving closer to the building, he saw Dino, the lawn-green Sinclair Apatosaurus, painted on the wall.

"Gas still good?" Sam E. asked, as they approached the station.

"Still good," Cricket said.

"Anybody need a bathroom break?" Sam E. asked.

"I'm okay," Lee said.

"Same," Cricket added.

"Then we keep moving." Though his throat was dry, and he half thought about stopping for a soda.

As they passed the friendly dinosaur, they heard a *poo-oof* and then another one. The car, like a deflating volleyball, floated downward. Cricket wobbled it to a stop. "Now what?" she asked.

"Turn around and pull into the station," Sam E. said.

*C*awwwaunk! *Caunk! Caunk!* Cricket released the car's horn. She glanced at the clock radio. "You think they're here this late?"

"I don't see any lights on inside," Lee said.

"Try it again," Sam E. said.

Cawwwaunk!

"Look." Lee pointed to a lanky, leather-skinned attendant shuffling out of the office toward them. Lee shoved the shotgun under the seat. He said to Sam E., "Don't try anything funny, I've still got your gun in my coat."

The man poked his head in the car window, smiled, and said, "Ha, *Ha!*"

Sam E. noticed the name 'Roger' stitched on his shirt. "We have a couple of flats, Roger. We're in a big hurry."

Roger motioned for Cricket to pull the car into the garage. He lifted the overhead door and guided the vehicle through.

"How long is this going to take?" Sam E. asked.

Roger smiled and shrugged.

"What does that mean?" Cricket asked.

"It means we go get a soda," Sam E. said. "Hey, pop, where's the soda pop?"

Roger smiled at him, pointed to a doorway leading from the garage to the office, and said, "Ha, *Ha!*"

Cricket and Lee headed to the office door, Sam E. trailing.

As the trio entered the dark office, a pair of arms tightened around Cricket. Sam E. heard a man say, "Baby doll."

The light flicked on.

Standing in the disheveled room, with her oil-soaked hand on the light switch, was Lucille Ball. Next to her was Ed Sullivan. Both aliens were drenched in petroleum. They stared with fascination at Francis French kissing Cricket.

Stunned, Lee stared at the spacemen.

Sam E., watching Francis violate the struggling girl, made him think of Doc and Marge. His anger flared. He swiped the revolver from Lee's coat pocket. "That's enough."

Francis, hearing him speak, broke his lip-lock on Cricket. He smiled at Sam E.'s bib overalls. "Heard any good outer space jokes, lately, Lil' Abner?"

The aliens aimed their fingers at Sam E.

"Tell them to knock it off." Sam E. jerked the gun closer to Francis. "Or you're gonna be the first to go."

"Sure." Francis nodded to the Lucy and Ed aliens. They lowered their fingers. "How's the chest and the leg?"

"As good as new." Sam E. patted his near-healed wounds.

"How'd you know about the leg?" Cricket asked.

"Baby, when you kill Gus Greenbaum, everybody knows about it."

"You're not angry?"

"The hell with him. He's small potatoes. Everybody's small potatoes, but me." Francis glanced at Lee, who was still wide-eyed, staring at the aliens. "This square's gotta be Beaumont."

"You know him?" Sam E. asked.

"I heard about him on the news. How do you think we hunted you down?"

Sam E. pulled the gun holstered in Francis' shoulder strap. He handed it to Cricket. "Keep this locked on the spacemen."

Cricket pointed the revolver at them.

Lucy and Ed canted their heads curiously at her.

"Be careful baby doll, or you'll end up like Pudgy and his wife." Francis cocked his fedora back, puffed his right cheek, and nonchalantly released an air puff.

His indifference inflamed a jumpy, virulent, hatred inside Sam E. He slammed Francis hard across the mouth. "That's for Doc." He lifted his fist and swung hard again. "And that's for Marge."

Francis fell to his knees.

The aliens screamed, "*Skiiiisshhh!*"

Cricket clicked her gun's trigger. Sam E. clicked his. Francis held his hand in the air. The Aliens relaxed.

"The game's over," Sam E. said. "Tell your outer space thugs to pack it up."

"Naw." Francis wiped blood from his lips. "It's not even close to ending."

Sam E. said to Cricket, "What was the name of that movie where no one believed that the space creatures were here?"

"*Invasion of the Body Snatchers.*"

"This time they're gonna believe it," Sam E. said. "Lee, call the cops and the FBI and anyone else you can think of. They're gonna want to see what we've got."

"I wouldn't do that," Francis said. "You might regret it."

"Regret what?"

"Let me stick my head out the door and you'll see."

"I'm not that stupid."

"You'll be real sorry." Francis stood. "Trust me."

Sam E. jerked Francis around and flung his arm across the front of his neck. He jammed the pistol's barrel into Francis' temple. "Take it slow."

They eased their way to the door. Francis said, "I need to wave, okay?" He stuck his head out and waved.

"I knee to wave," Ed Sullivan said, more to himself than anyone else.

Lee reached for his notepad. Lucille Ball raised her finger at him. He stopped.

"You notice they're talking better?" Francis asked. "That's part of the plan."

"The only plan is you're going to the big house, the spacemen are going to Roswell, and I'm going to *The Steve Allen Show*," Sam E. said.

Francis smiled. "Watch." He looked skyward.

The giant baseball cap lowered itself near the filling station pumps. As it did, a twisting finger of sand raised itself from the ground toward the object, and a sound like an approaching tugboat deluged the office Sam E. and the rest were standing in. As the saucer touched ground the sand twister fell apart and the noise faded into silence.

"Son of a batch of cookies," Lee said, poking his head out the door.

"You haven't seen the best part." Francis glanced at Sam E.

The domed ship's triangular door separated.

"This better not be a trick," Sam E. said, "or you won't make it to prison."

"It's not." Francis whistled the Davy Crockett theme song. From the darkness of the ship came two aliens in their true, over-towering, gnarly form.

Sam E.'s heart lurched. His throat clutched. Lois was locked between the alien's barnacled arms. She was trembling, fragile, a cracked vase. The yellow feather in her headband was bent and soiled.

"You want to let me go, now?" Francis asked.

He watched Lois mouth what looked like "Sam." He felt like retching.

"When I saw her on the news," Francis said, "it sure looked to me like you made quite an impression on her. That's why we picked her up."

"Let her go," Sam E. said.

"Give me the gun first, funny man."

"Don't do it," Lee said. "There are bigger things at stake."

"Oil," Ed Sullivan said to no one in particular.

Cricket jabbed her gun forward. "Quiet," she said to the alien.

"He's right," Francis said. "You kill me it's all over. I lose, the world wins. Of course the waitress dies and you'll miss your TV appearance because you'll be tied up with the authorities. But that's fair enough, right?"

Sam E., watching Lois whimpering, screamed. He clamped the trigger. Francis shut his eyes. Sam E. squeezed. *Ka-pawph!* Cricket jumped. Francis numbed. Lee gasped. The aliens eyed each other inquisitively.

The Sinclair Dinosaur clock, its face shattered by the bullet Sam E. shot at it, sputtered to the ground and settled over the dry-blood spot left by Roy's body.

Sam E. dropped the pistol. It fell to the concrete floor with a sharp *clack*.

"I told you," Francis said to the aliens as he picked up the weapon. "All actors and comedians care about is their career."

"Let her go," Sam E. said.

"Sure, just as soon as my baby doll drops her weapon."

"No, Sam," Cricket said. "He's lying."

"She's right," Lee added. "It's the oldest comic book ruse in the trade."

Sam E. went to Cricket, jerked the gun from her hand and gave it to Francis. "Now release her."

"As soon as you get us alone with Steve Allen," Francis said.

"I told you not to trust him," Lee said.

Francis smiled. "You should have listened." He nodded to the aliens holding Lois. They dragged her back in the spaceship. He turned to Sam E. again, stuffing a wad of bills down his overalls. "I don't care how you do it, but get to the Waldorf-Astoria by day after tomorrow. Got it?"

Sam E. said nothing.

"Oh, and one other thing." Francis sucker-punched him in the gut. "That's for hitting me the first time."

The wallop propelled the wind out of him. He fell in a tangle to the floor, gasping for air in large, wheezy, chunks.

Cricket and Lee lunged toward Francis. He swung his pistol at them. "Don't do it, or Lakeside's gonna lose two of his traveling companions."

They froze.

He said to Sam E., "This is for hitting me the second time." He nodded to Ed and Lucy. They waggled their fingers. The mist sprinkled from their fingertips and settled over Sam E. like a platinum-green veil.

Sam E. went frigid; his twisted torso felt as if ice fists were crushing it. He blanked out. In the cold ephemeral moment he saw a gun barrel aimed at Lee's skull. He watched the trigger tighten and the bullet enter Lee's head. The vision terrified him so much he forced himself back onto the chilly concrete floor he was sprawled on.

"Oil," Lucy said.

"Oil," Ed Sullivan said.

"Oil," they said together. "Oil."

"Relax," Francis said. "When we get to New York, I'll get you enough oil to flood Radio City Music Hall."

"Oy-yell! Oy-yell! Oy-yell!" the two said, locking hands and circling as if they were playing ring-around-the-rosy.

"You see the shit I gotta deal with?" Francis said to Sam E., who was still crumbled on the floor, struggling to breathe. Francis turned to Cricket and Lee. "You two make sure he gets to the Waldorf, or you'll be in the spaceship along with Pocahontas."

The two remained motionless.

"Well, help him up," he added.

They rushed to Sam E., wrapped his arms around their shoulders and stood him on his feet.

Francis watched the spinning aliens, shook his head in disgust, and fired his .45 into the ceiling. The aliens stopped twirling.

"Let's go get the oy-yell," Francis said. He and the space creatures made their way out of the filling station and into the space ship.

Sam E. watched the colossal baseball cap ascend and disappear into the star-dappled night. His eyes filled with quiet, unflinching hate.

Chapter Sixteen
PARKER'S MOOD

Sam E. watched the Packard's open-winged swan forge its beak through the nocturnal plains of Oklahoma and into a sun-sheet of Kansas City ice cream stands, station wagons, and drive-in theaters.

"According to the road atlas Kansas City Airport is about twenty miles from here. It should be a three hour flight to New York from there," Lee said, driving the car through a light drizzle.

Sam E., sitting in the front passenger seat, crooked his neck to beat back sleep. Other than what Lee had just said, neither he nor Cricket had spoken to him since they left the Sinclair Station. Sam E. said, "A woman goes into a doctor's office and says, 'Doc, my husband thinks he's Moses reincarnated'. The doctor says, 'Don't worry, it's a delusion of grandeur, it'll pass'. The wife says, 'Okay, but how do I get him to quit parting the bathtub water?'"

"Is that part of your act?" Lee asked.

"No."

"Good."

Sam E. glanced in the rearview mirror at Cricket, who was sitting in the back, on the passenger side, puffing an Old Gold. "What'd you think of the joke?" he asked her.

"Trashy," she said, without looking up.

"I'm going after them when the time is right," Sam E. said. "Why don't you believe me?"

"The time was right last night," Lee said. "You shouldn't have trusted them."

"The plan is for Sam to go on television first," Cricket said.

"Go to hell," Sam E. said. "If it was you or Lee they captured, what would you have wanted me to do?"

"It's not what we wanted; it's what was needed," Lee replied. "Nobody wants to see Lois harmed, but Francis was right. If you had taken him out it would have been over. The creatures would have let her go, and their plan would have been shot to hell."

"You don't know that for a fact and I wasn't going to risk it."

"Or blow your chance to be on TV," Cricket said.

Sam E. spun around and glared at her. She blew a defiant smoke ring in his direction.

"Fine," he said, turning back around. "Take the shotgun out of the trunk and blow my head off if that's what's needed."

"Is that supposed to be funny?" Lee asked.

"They need me to carry out their scheme, right?"

"I suppose."

"Do you suppose?" Sam E. asked Cricket.

She shrugged.

"Why do you think they haven't killed me? The game's over if I die."

"They'd find another way," Lee said.

"How do you know?"

Lee ignored the question.

"That's what I thought. Go ahead and kill me. Right now."

"All right, I get it," Lee said.

"In *Cat Women of the Moon*, Sonny Tufts did the same thing for Marie Windsor that you did for Lois," Cricket said. "I guess I see your point."

Sam E. said, "All I want is to get Lois out of there. Doc and Marge are dead because of me. I don't want the same thing to happen to her."

"That's not true," Lee said. "No one died because of you."

"If anything happens to her. I'll use the shotgun on myself to stop them."

"Stop it," Cricket said. "That doesn't happen in sci-fi flicks."

"If I don't have the courage," he said. "I want one of you to do it for me."

Both of them shook their heads.

"You'll do it. Like Lee said, there are bigger things at stake."

"That's not going to happen," Lee said, "because we're writing a comic book about an insurance salesman who *defeats* the alien's scheme to take the earth's oil."

Sam E. said, "He's a comedian, not an insurance salesman, and it has to involve Steve Allen."

"Regardless, first we have to figure out how the spacemen are planning to get the oil."

"How would they do it in the movies?" Sam E. asked Cricket.

"Force the earth to hand it over, I guess. Like in *Earth vs. the Flying Saucers*, where an army of UFOs destroys everything in sight."

"Our guys aren't that powerful. They've only got one spacecraft, and remember, they're merchants not warriors," Lee said. "They have something else up their sleeve."

They passed a large billboard with identical twin ponytailed teens in wide-belted, plaid circular skirts and sleeveless white blouses, holding a green pack of gum below their beaming, virgin-white smiles. Above them was printed *Double your pleasure! Double your fun!*

Sam E. glanced at the sign, and said, "They can look like other people."

"As long as they've been on television," Cricket added.

"How would we use that ability to write our comic book?" Lee asked, mostly to himself.

"Mimeograph Steve Allen, have him go on TV and hypnotize everyone into giving up their oil," Cricket said.

"You can't hypnotize anyone through a television screen."

"Why not?" Sam E. asked.

"It requires extreme concentration from the person being hypnotized. You might be able to get it from a few people, but not many. Most people watch TV flopped on the couch, drinking beer or eating potato chips."

"Maybe the fake Steve Allen says something over the screen that makes everyone give up their oil," Cricket said.

"Like what?" Sam E. said. "Attention inhabitants of earth give us your oil?"

"Have you got a better idea?"

"No." He rubbed his eyes, burning from tiredness, with the heel of his hands. Up all night, he was fighting sleep and impatience. Straightening his back, he said to Cricket, "Didn't you tell me that a scientist always saves the day in space movies?"

"In *The Day the Earth Stood Still*, Michael Rennie got all the scientists together and told them to tell mankind to make peace, or he would destroy the planet."

"That's a possibility," Lee said, grinning at Cricket's reflection in the rearview mirror.

Sam E. caught Lee's disappointment when her eyes at first seemed to welcome the sentiment, but then turned away.

Lee said, "The aliens would have to get all the oil owners together and force them to hand the stuff over."

"You mean like filling station owners?" Sam E. asked.

"Way bigger than that. How many of the aliens are there?"

"I've only seen five or six."

"Me, too," Cricket said.

"Okay, let's say there are half-a-dozen and they can all clone other people."

"Clone?" Sam E. asked.

"Duplicate. If you can only duplicate six people to get the earth's oil, who would they be?"

"That's easy. The most powerful," Sam E. said. "Because they control everyone else."

"Exactly. Now who are they?"

"Not Steve Allen," Cricket said. "He's funny, but he's just a comedian."

"Hey!" Sam E. eye-balled her.

"I didn't mean it like that," she said.

"Concentrate," Lee said. "In our story the aliens take over the six most powerful people on the planet and use them to hand over the oil."

Sam E. said, "Oil comes from Saudi Arabia, right?"

"A lot of it does."

"So the saucer-men duplicate King whatever-his-name-is and have him fork over the stuff," Cricket said.

"Something like that," Lee said. "And his name's King Saud."

"Even if they copied Saud, the aliens speak really weird. Wouldn't that be a dead giveaway that something was kookie?" Cricket asked.

"And wouldn't the king have to have been on television?" Sam E. asked. "And what about Steve Allen?"

"Beats me." Exasperated, Lee turned on the radio, rotating the dial until he was satisfied with what came through the speaker: a slow, wispy piano swinging above a jazzy-blues rhythm section. A few bars later a lugubrious sax tapped the piano on the shoulder and cut in. "This song is called 'Parker's Mood'. That's Parker on the alto."

"He sounds so lonely," Cricket said.

Sam E. glanced at Cricket staring at Lee's image in the rearview mirror. The saxophone's smooth covetous tone seemed to reflect her dread of Francis and her desire for Lee.

"Don't worry about Francis. He's a jerk." Sam E.'s own words caught him by surprise. Their eyes met in the mirror.

Cricket blushed and turned away.

"Let's keep working," he said to Lee.

"Huh, un. It's too confusing. We need to think about it."

"Fine, but step on it. The sooner we get to the airport the sooner we get to New York."

Lee pressed the accelerator. The Packard's engine thrummed at a higher pitch.

Sam E. closed his eyes, listening to what he thought was the saddest, most uplifting alto sax solo he'd ever heard. He leaned against the door until the heaviness drifted away, replaced with the smell of peaches. Peaches or apricots. *Parker's Mood*, he thought, feeling Lois part her fleshy, scarlet lips and nibble his earlobe. He tingled. Her slender fingers toyed with his nipples, lowered to his stomach, and her nails brushed his crotch. Her high round cheekbones glided to his brow. Her ponytail fanned his bare shoulders. His hands whispered along the naked wavelets of her ribs, down the curve of her waist to the widening of her hips. She moved over him and he pictured himself on a stage, behind a black velvet curtain. He felt their bodies unite in gentle, moistening, comforting, breezy, lifting exuberance. He...heard sirens.

Chapter Seventeen
SMILE

"License."

Sleep retreated from Sam E. like water from a draining tub.

He opened his eyes. The world was again sprayed indigo. Sam E. watched Lee shuffling in his pocket. Outside Lee's window was a motorcycle-helmeted policeman. He had a thin, sporty mustache similar to the one the star of *Sergeant Preston of the Yukon* wore. Sam E. saw the cop's motorcycle parked behind their car.

"I purchased the vehicle in Arizona," Lee said. "I have papers."

"I didn't ask you," the tall, leather-jacketed policeman said. He skimmed a flashlight across their faces.

Cars and trucks zipped past the Packard, which was parked along the side of the busy highway they had been on. Overhead, the dim rumble of an airplane drifted by. Close to the airport, Sam E. thought.

The policeman aimed his light at Lee's license. "Are you aware you were ten miles over the speed limit?"

"No," Lee said.

"Un, huh," the policeman said. "What do you do for a living, Mr. Beaumont?" He flashed the beam at Cricket.

"I'm a dishwasher."

"A what?"

"He's a writer," Sam E. said.

"Un, huh," the policeman repeated, pointing the light in Sam E.'s eyes.

"A policeman stops a guy for speeding," Sam E. said, shading his vision from the light. "The cop says, 'where's your license?' The speeder says, 'I left it in the trunk with the man I killed'. The cop radios his lieutenant for back-up. The lieutenant races over with his men and surrounds the guy—"

"He doesn't want to hear this," Lee said.

"Let him finish," the policeman replied. "I could use a smile."

"The lieutenant, who just arrived, says to the speeder, 'You're under arrest. You killed a man, stuffed him in the trunk and left your license there'. The speeder says, 'Are you nuts?' The man hands the lieutenant his license. He opens the trunk, which is empty. 'I don't get it?' the lieutenant says, 'the officer said you killed a man'. 'Really?' the man says, 'Next the liar will probably say I was speeding'."

"Hey, that's good," the policeman said. "You should be a comedian."

"I am."

"Yeah?"

"Sam E. Lakeside."

"I thought so." The policeman unholstered his revolver and pointed it at them. "Hands up, all of you. Now!"

"What for?" Sam E. asked.

"Armed robbery. Leave your belongings where they are." The policeman yanked the keys from the ignition. "Everyone out, slowly, spread eagle against the car." He gave them a quick frisk.

A passing Edsel, with a silver Airstream attached to its rear, honked loudly. The driver stuck his hand out and gave the policeman a thumbs-up. Annoyed, the cop puckered his lips, causing his moustache to prune.

Sam E. said, "I know this is gonna sound crazy, but we're fighting off a group of spacemen who want to take over the world."

"What's the punch line?" the policeman asked.

"If we don't stop them," Sam E. continued, "they're going to take away the earth's oil."

The policeman looked at both Cricket and Lee. They nodded, as if to say, 'He's telling the truth'.

The policeman raised his chin and studied Sam E. for a moment. "That wasn't as funny as the first joke." He waved his gun at the trio, and added, "If any of you so much as wiggle your toes, I'll shoot." Keeping his eye on them, the cop walked to the motorcycle. He uncradled his radio mouthpiece from its cabled receiver.

"Officer," Sam E. said, "we *do* have a body in the trunk. The waitress from the cafe."

"The missing girl?" the policeman asked.

"Lois Sokel."

The policeman replaced the mouthpiece and came back. "You just told me that gag." He shoved Sam E. against the car. "You think I'm gonna radio it in?" A pick-up truck honked, and a kid with long sideburns and a greasy D.A. leaned out and said, "Go, cat, go!" The cop smirked at the kid's remark. "Do you think I'm an idiot, Lakeside?" the policeman asked.

"No," Sam E. said.

"Good. Lie down on your belly." Sam E. lowered himself. The policeman said to Cricket and Lee, "One of you get in the front passenger seat and the other in the back. Shut the doors, roll down the windows, and stick your right arms out."

Cricket got in the front, Lee in the back. Both stuck their arms out. The cop handcuffed them together. "Get up," he said to Sam E.

Sam E. stood. The policeman jabbed his gun in Sam E.'s back, and ordered, "Open the trunk."

Sam E. cracked the trunk lid open. He reached inside, skimming his fingers along the shotgun they took from Indian Joe's Cafe.

"That's enough," the policeman said. "I'll do the looking."

A humpbacked Mercury slowed down and two pretty black

girls stuck their heads out, smacked their hands against the car door and yelled, "Come back, Shane, come back! Mama la-oooves you!" They let out a peal of laughter. As they skidded off, the vexed policeman glanced at their license plate. Sam E. grabbed the shotgun and shoved the twin barrels in the policeman's neck. "Give me your revolver. Handle first."

The policeman smirked. He flipped his weapon and handed it to him. Sam E. hid the gun in his overall pocket but kept it aimed at the policeman. He shut the shotgun in the trunk.

"Smile," Sam E. said, "like you want to more than anything in the world."

The policeman smiled.

"Now, let's walk casually back."

"Maybe I *am* an idiot," the policeman said, as they made their way to Lee and Cricket.

"Unlock them," Sam E. said.

The policeman took out his keys and fumbled with the lock. The keys slipped from his hand. He bent down. Sam E. stepped closer. The policeman lunged up at him and smashed the top of his head violently against Sam E.'s forehead. Sam E. screamed crimson shards. He lost control of the gun, but couldn't get his hand out of his pocket. The policeman grabbed Sam E.'s neck and squeezed until he grunted from the strain. Sam E. felt his Adam's apple push against his throat.

"I guess," the cop growled, digging his nails in, "I'm not the idiot." He bent his elbows and Sam E. was drawn to the angry man's ruddy, trembling face.

Sam E.'s eyes chuffed. His breath congealed and he tasted castor oil. His breathing stopped. He slammed his knee upward in a move reminiscent of a drum major high stepping past the judge's stand.

The policeman gasped. He grabbed his groin and tipped over.

Sam E. struggled for air. His vision smeared and his eyes stung like he had stayed too long in a chlorine-rich pool.

"You okay?" Lee asked. Handcuffed, he and Cricket could only hear what was going on.

Sam E. spit blood. "Yeah." His voice was raspy.

"What happened?" Cricket asked.

"I got him with a move I learned from you," Sam E. said, remembering how she made mincemeat of Gus Greenbaum's testicles.

"Hey," she said. "Our arms hurt."

He took the keys from the prone cop and unlocked her and Lee. They went back to the policeman. "Help me with Sergeant Preston," Sam E. said to Lee. They lifted the dazed man, dragged him to the motorcycle and straddled him on the leather seat. Sam E. slipped the pistol from his pocket and pointed it at the cop. He said to Lee, "Lock his wrists around the handlebars."

A beat up Rambler honked as it passed. The groggy policeman opened his eyes.

"Smile." Sam E. patted his cheek. "Remember?"

The policeman smiled as Lee wrapped the chain over the bar and locked the cuffs to the man's wrists.

"Rip out the radio," Sam E said. "And flatten the tires."

Cricket jerked the mouthpiece from the cable. Lee released the air.

Sam E. pulled the sparkplug, and said, "That should give us time. We're skippin' KC and going straight to *Memphis*," loud enough for the policeman to hear.

They scrambled to the Packard. Sam E. hopped behind the wheel. Cricket slid in the middle and Lee next to her. Sam E. stuck his head out the window and shouted to the policeman, "Keep smiling!"

The cop smiled. Sam E. flicked on the headlights and jerked

the car into drive. As he screeched onto the highway, the policeman flipped him a bird from his handcuffed wrist.

Chapter Eighteen
12TH STREET AND VINE

Sam E. cruised slowly along downtown Kansas City, passing old-fashioned brick sky-scrapers, dark-suited men and long-skirted women with Mamie Eisenhower bangs, hopping off and on green-and-white trolleys; black-skinned and white-skinned kids clustered around storefront windows watching flickering televisions; people going about their lives. He smiled, not sure why, but he thought it had something to do with movement and hope.

Near a corner marked 12th Street and Vine, he pulled into a parking space close to a large storefront window with *Weaver's Clothing* painted in gold cursive letters on it. Inside the display glass was a sleek manikin couple: a faint-smiling female, looking at nothing in particular, who was attired in a check wool pinafore dress over a white polo neck jumper, and a stoic male in a gray three-button jacket, white shirt, dark tie, and pleat front pants.

"This'll do," Sam E. said to Lee and Cricket. The trio entered the store.

Sam E. picked out an outfit similar to the storefront manikin's, but with a navy jacket, a powder-blue shirt, and a black tie with red slanted bars. Stepping out of the men's dressing room, he said to Lee, "How do I look?"

"Sharp."

Cricket stepped out of the ladies dressing room. "What do you think?" she said, tilting a black leather beret toward her left eyebrow. The men turned around and their eyes widened. Cricket's emerald-gray eyes and golden-red, silky straight, shoulder length hair was offset in oozing black: a figure-hugging black turtleneck pullover, knee length black pencil skirt over black leotards, and glossy, high-heel ebony boots.

As beautiful as she was, what pulled Sam E.'s attention was the look between Lee and her. Lee was dumbfounded. Little kid dumbfounded, like he had seen Santa drop from the chimney. Cricket's eyes burnished, as if the hustle and the tin-glitter of Las Vegas, and Francis, and the aliens had been stripped off and re-buffed with possibility. She glanced at Sam E. and he got the impression that she was seeking his approval to leap into the deep end of the pool. He nodded. She looked back at Lee and smiled.

Sam E. felt melancholy. He was envious, jealous—not because of their feelings for each other—but because he wanted to feel, with someone, what they felt. He thought of Doc and Marge and how they were gone because of him. And of Lois, whose only crime was waitressing the day he stopped in the cafe. His spirit fell. "Come on. Let's get to the airport." He walked out of the clothing store, and without looking up, thought the sky appeared as if it would stay forever gray.

Chapter Nineteen
F**KING

F rancis, looking at a *Life Magazine* article headlined 'D-Day Speech', said, "Okay, try this." He read aloud, "'Soldiers, sailors, and airmen of the allied expeditionary force, you are about to embark upon the great crusade toward which we have striven these many months.'"

A shadowed alien, sitting at a grand desk, just beyond the soft glow of the table lamp, said, "Solders, saylors, and airmen of the allied exdibitchonary force—"

"No!" Francis smacked the magazine against the desk. "Expeditionary, expe*dish*onary," he said. "Goddamn mother-fucker," he mumbled.

"Goddamn mother-fucker," the shadowed alien repeated, perfectly.

"Why does everybody get the goddamn curse words?" Francis said to an alien who was standing next to him. The creature was a Richard Nixon look-alike.

Nixon shrugged, licking oil from his 5-o'clock shadowed philtrum.

The alien behind the desk leaned forward into the lamp's wreath, exposing a nearly bald, white-haired grandfatherly man with deep blue eyes and thin lips.

Francis looked at the alien in wonderment. "If you're not a god-damn perfect Eisenhower, I don't know who is."

The Eisenhower alien removed silver-framed spectacles from the upper pocket of his gray suit jacket, put them on, and said, "Expeditionary."

"Good. And make your voice smooth and melodic, like a trombone." Francis said, melodiously, "Like a trommmbone." He added, "Try this," again reading from *Life*. "You will bring about the destruction of the German war machine. The elimination of the Nazi tyranny over the oppressed people of Europe."

Eisenhower said, "You will bring about the destruction of the German war machine."

Francis said, in his melodious voice, "Like a trommmbone—"

Eisenhower slowed his speaking, and continued, "The emilination of the Nazi—'"

"E-*lim*-ination," Francis said. "E-*lim*-ination."

"E-*mil*-ination," Eisenhower said. "E-*mil*-ination."

"Cunnilingus licker!" Francis once again swiped the magazine against the desktop.

"Cunnilingus licker!" Eisenhower said.

Francis rolled his eyes at the perfect pronunciation. "Forget it," he said, bunching the magazine. "In a few days we'll have the real thing and you can listen to him until you're blue in the face."

"Oil," Eisenhower said.

"Oil," Nixon repeated, hopping around like an unsuccessful fire-walker.

"Yeah, okay," Francis said, looking out of the spaceship's window. "When we get over Kansas City, we'll hit another station for a re-fill."

Eisenhower jiggled-blurred and rejiggled into Howdy Doody.

He hopped on the desk. "Stick-em-up! Oil."

"Jesus Christ," Francis said to himself, "the things I have to go through to rule the fucking world."

"Fucking," the aliens said, as they danced around the desk.

Chapter Twenty
FIRST CLASS

Sam E. guided the Packard along the desolate Kansas City Municipal Airport; a lengthy, four-story granite building.

It was checkered with rows of squared windows evenly spaced from one end to the other. If it wasn't for the tall terminal building jammed in the center of the structure, Sam E. thought, the airport would look like a giant harmonica. "I guess everyone's either sobering up or in church." He turned the vehicle into the near-empty, open-air parking lot.

"I forgot today's Sunday," Lee said, as the car inched to a stop.

The trio hopped out. The iron-gray morning hung over them like a damp blanket, dulling their shadows on the pavement. Sam E. wasn't sure why, but the dreariness seemed as if it was meant to be.

"What about PJ's shotgun?" Lee asked.

"Leave it with the car. At least we have this," Sam E. patted his inside jacket pocket, where the policeman's revolver was resting.

As they walked to the terminal, Lee added, "I wish we could get the shotgun back to Indian Joe's."

"I wish we could get back on the ship and get Lois back to Indian Joe's." Sam E. swung the terminal's plate glass door open.

Standing at the long, speckle-topped counter, Sam E. glanced behind him at rows of stainless-steel limbed, vinyl-bottomed chairs—some teal, some olive, others maroon. Lee was sitting in the front row next to Cricket. She was thumping her boot on the ink-blue rug. The carpet swept the largely empty, multi-hall terminal. Behind them, the rows of seats were empty except for a heavy woman who reminded him of Kate Smith, and a small group of Negro sailors.

"Welcome to Trans World Airlines," a smiling girl in a pink skirt-suit with gold wings embroidered on the lapel, said to him. "May I help you?"

"Give me three of your most expensive tickets to LaGuardia."

"Plane leaves in thirty minutes. I booked us first class on the Super Constellation." Sam E. handed Cricket and Lee their tickets. "Let's use all of Francis' money that we can." The group made their way down a long, beige concourse to gate nine, leading to the tarmac.

The Kansas City sun's morning gray, polished into an early afternoon marigold, buffed the backbone of the Super Constellation's porpoise-shaped fuselage. The trio stood in front of the boarding ramp, admiring the airline's marvel of modern science.

Sam E. counted the fourteen steps leading from the concrete tarmac up to the ticket taking stewardess. He squinted at the four propeller, triple-tail, ivory-white behemoth, and murmured, "You'll wonder where the yellow went when you brush your teeth with Pepsodent."

A tram chugged toward them. He and Cricket braced.

The driver nodded. The tram rolled past.

Cricket looked at Sam E. He asked her, "Are you ready?"

"As ready as I'll ever be."

He looked at Lee. Lee nodded.

Sam E. wanted to say something to Lee and Cricket that would give them an inkling of what he felt inside. The fear, the determination, the longing, the darkness of his mother, the guilty thrill of being on *The Steve Allen Show*, the heaviness of Doc and Marge's death—and Lois trapped with the space creatures. He let it all sludge through his veins, and said, "Let's do it." He took the first step up the steep ramp.

Chapter Twenty-One
THE VASTNESS OF THE SKY

"**P**illow? Blanket? *Kansas City Star? New York Times?*" a curvaceous stewardess in a teal skirt-suit and matching pillbox hat repeated, as they entered the tubular, gold-and-satinwood paneled cabin.

Lee took a *New York Times.*

Sam E. eyed the stewardess' nametag and blue eyes. "When does happy hour start, Doreen?"

"As soon as we're in the air," Doreen, a honey-blonde who looked as if she was the template for a *Frolic* cover, said. "May I see your tickets?"

He handed them to her. She glanced at them. "Drinks are complimentary for first class, Mr. Lakeside."

"Sam."

Doreen smiled. "It's a slow flight, Sam. Your group'll have the entire first class section to yourselves. There's also a lounge, if you prefer."

"Welcome aboard Trans World Airlines, folks, I'm Captain Kravit," said a brisk man with a dark widow peak and a slope nose. He was standing outside the cockpit, dressed in a black double-breasted jacket ratified with brass buttons and gold-striped epaulettes. He motioned to a stoic man with a crew-cut, and gold wings pinned to his starchy white shirt. Captain Kravit said, "This is our navigator, Mr. Duhamel."

Mr. Duhamel nodded.

"You hear the one about the pilot who pulled out a .38, laid it on the control panel and said to the navigator, 'This is for navigators who get me lost'," Sam E. said to the men.

"Sounds like a ripsnorter," Captain Kravit said, grinning.

"After the pilot pulls out his .38, the navigator pulls out a .45. The pilot says to him, 'What's that for?'"

Captain Kravit nudged Mr. Duhamel. Mr. Duhamel blinked stoically.

"The navigator says to the pilot, 'The .45's here because if we get lost, I'll know it first'."

"Hey, I like that!" Mr. Duhamel said, laughing so hard his chest jiggled, causing his gold wings to wave. "I gotta tell Les!"

Captain Kravit cleared his throat and motioned for Mr. Duhamel to return to the cockpit. "Hey, Les," Mr. Duhamel said, as he entered the cockpit. "Wait till you hear this one!"

"You're funny." Doreen smiled at Sam E. "Follow me." She walked them down the tubular aisle.

"You really can't stop, can you?" Cricket said to him.

"It's therapy." He followed Doreen to first class; a capacious area with four pairs of tall, beige leather seats. Each chair was garnished with white broadcloth headrests neatly flapped over the top. Two pairs of seats faced each other. They were separated by a rosewood coffee table. Across the aisle, the other two pairs of seats were lined in traditional rows. Each side had a portal window framed with gold-thread brocade curtains. The section was separated from the rest of the plane by blue curtains.

S am E. lazily licked a glass swizzle stick before re-inserting it in his whisky and soda. He stared through the portal window over his right shoulder and took another drink.

Cricket and Lee sat facing him, on the other side of the coffee table. Cricket was smoking. A glass of strawberry soda was resting in front of her on the coffee table. Lee was sipping a beer and studying the sports page of his complementary *New York Times.* "Maglie's pitching the World Series opener for Brooklyn tomorrow night."

Sam E. scrutinized a ruffled cloud coasting below the far propeller. "Who cares?"

"Ford's on the mound for the Yanks."

He turned to Lee. "How can you talk about baseball for Christ's sake?"

"I have to talk about something."

"How about talking about saucer-men sucking up oil and screwing up *The Steve Allen Show?*"

Lee lowered the paper. He and Cricket stared suspiciously at Sam E.

"I didn't mean it like that," he said.

"Just because I believe the aliens exist doesn't mean that I trust you," Lee said, tucking the paper in his coat pocket.

"What do you think? We're all spies dying to turn you over to an anti-commie committee? I got news for you, you're not that important."

"I got news for *you.* You're a prick."

"A prick with a career." Sam E. stood. "Not like a dishwasher who couldn't cut it as a funny book writer." He flung the partition curtains apart and tramped out of first class.

Cricket raised her eyebrows at Lee.

"Screw him." Lee closed his eyes and rubbed his temples. "We'll figure it out without his help."

Cricket continued gazing at him.

Sam E. stomped down the aisle. *He's a jerk! We should have left him at the cafe.* He barely noticed the others on the near empty flight: a mother holding a sleeping toddler, a snoring sailor sprawled across two seats and a leathery old man in the last row wearing wire-frame glasses. The man was reading *Sports Illustrated*. Sam E. passed the man, nodding briefly to him as he entered the Starflight Lounge. It was a peppy, petite room decked in earth colors: greens, browns, and ocean blue. It had a large, globe trekker themed brown panel above the portal windows. The panel curved to the ceiling and contained maps and sketches of exotic travel locations. For some reason it reminded Sam E. of Disneyland, though he'd never been there.

He plopped on a palm green sofa facing the portal windows. The room was empty. He bent his elbow on the armrest, cupped his chin in his hand, and stared out at the boundless sky. He tried to suppress the shameful thought, but here—intertwined with the heavens and his anger—he couldn't do it. *All actors and comedians care about is their career.* He remembered the terrible looks on Doc and Marge's face when Francis said it. Sam E. wanted to do *The Steve Allen Show* even if it meant the start of the invasion. *Even if it meant sacrificing Lois?* "It's not fair," he said. "I didn't ask for any of this." The sky made him feel small. No, he thought, not small, petty. Shame rose inside him. He took a deep, heaving breath and laid down on the sofa. Squeezing his eyelids shut, he tried to lose himself in the mournful grumble of the propellers, trying to smell apricots. Apricots or peaches. The smell of Lois' hair.

"Sam?"

"Sam?" Doreen repeated.

"What?" Sam E. opened his eyes. Doreen was holding a tray with a fresh whisky and soda on it.

"Are you okay?"

"No."

"There's a sleeping quarter in the back. If you'd like to use it, I'll tell them you're not feeling well."

He sat up and looked at the drink on her tray. "Is that for me?"

"Yes." Doreen's jacketed breast brushed against him as she bent down to give him the glass.

He took a long swallow. "Do you ever think of dying?"

Doreen side-tilted her head. "That's a morbid pick-up line."

"I'm sorry. I didn't mean anything by it."

"Really, are you okay?"

"Did you hear Donald Duck wanted to divorce Daisy? His lawyer was talking strategy with him. 'I don't understand', Donald said to the lawyer. 'Daisy's not insane!' The lawyer said, 'I didn't say she was insane. I said she was fucking Goofy'."

Doreen smiled. "You're funny." She sat beside him.

"I'm a comic."

"I know. I go to Las Vegas all the time. I fly for free." Doreen paused. "Have you been to New York before?"

"Not really."

She sucked her cheeks a moment and added, "Are you married?"

He held out his ring-less fingers.

"I've got a studio apartment in Greenwich Village, and a few days layover."

"If you had said that to me a week ago."

"Is it the pretty red head?"

"Cricket? No. She likes the other guy."

Doreen thought a moment. "Sam, what's it like being a comedian?"

"I'm not a comedian. I'm a stand-up comic." He swirled his glass, his thoughts whirling with the liquid. "It can be good. Other times, not so much."

"Is the comedy business mean?"

"Life is mean."

"Yes." She sat next to him, and added, "What's she like?"

"We only met once, last week." He knew exactly whom she was talking about.

"Do you love her?"

"I think so, but I've never been in love before."

"But you're not sure?"

Sam E. studied her sky-blue eyes. They were breezy, carefree; as vast and boundless as the heavens they were flying through. She moved her mouth closer to his. He wanted with all his being to taste the comfort in her gently unfurled lips. He wanted, in her honey-blonde hair, to stroke away the heavy weight of contempt and guilt and terror that was pulling him down. He moved closer, smelling her light, burden-less cinnamon scented perfume. Her open collar and hint of alabaster-skin cleavage promised something he hadn't dared think of: life. He closed his eyes and for one brief moment felt the thrill of being on stage. "I'm sorry," he said, drawing back.

Doreen looked at him, confused.

"It wouldn't be fair. I'm sorry."

"It's okay." Doreen stood. "Whoever she is, she's a lucky girl to have someone like you."

He watched Doreen walk out of the lounge. "Yeah," he said to himself. "Lois is about as lucky as a turkey at a Thanksgiving feast." Sam E. stared at the whisky glass in his hand. He had the vague notion that if he concentrated on it hard enough, it would dull his gloominess.

"Once things start cooking," Lee said to Cricket, "it'll be like Humpty Dumpty after his fall."

"Suppose we do nothing and let the spacemen take the oil. We go back to horse and buggy. The end."

"It's more than that. Toothbrushes and Tupperware are gone; plastics are petroleum by-products. No more rock 'n roll records, they're plastic. Hospitals as we know them are gone. Disease would flourish."

"Are you sure you're not a scientist?" Cricket asked.

"I grew up in the car business. I know all about oil."

Cricket took a drag of her cigarette, blew smoke sideways and studied the red lipstick ring around the filter. "It's like *War of the Worlds.*"

"It's worse. We'd have no refrigeration or gas-powered farm equipment. Insecticides are oil by-products. Food supplies would shrink. People would starve. *War of the Worlds* would be a merry-go-round compared to what happens when the entire planet is fighting for food." He said to himself, "I wish I had a bottle of Benzedrine."

Cricket gave his hand a quick squeeze.

Embarrassed, he cleared his throat. "Does Francis speak Arabic?"

"Of course not."

"At the Sinclair Station, he said that teaching the aliens to speak was part of his plan. Saud speaks Arabic." Lee took *The Times* from his coat pocket and opened it to the World Series article. "But Ike speaks English. If that blowhard, Lakeside, would have given me half-a-cha—"

"He's not the only blowhard," Cricket said.

"Do you want to hear what I have to say or not?"

"I already know. President Eisenhower's going to be in New York, at the same time we are, to toss out the first pitch of the game."

"How'd you know that?"

"Because presidents always toss out the first pitch." Cricket sipped from her strawberry soda. "So what?"

"Did you also know this?" Lee began reading from the article. "And I quote, 'Mr. Eisenhower has a tight schedule. That evening he is appearing at a private fund-raiser hosted by entertainer *Steve Allen.*'"

"Where at?"

"Hold on," Lee skimmed the article out loud. "'Small crowd, music Skitch Henderson, dignitaries. Undisclosed location.'"

"What does it all mean?"

"Beats me." Lee slumped in his seat.

Captain Kravit eased the throttle slightly. "You don't ever want to do it without a Trojan, *especially* if she's from overseas."

Les, the co-pilot, said, "I had an overseas gal once, she was stacked and hotter than a Phoenix sidewalk."

Mr. Duhamel, sitting at his station, behind them, soberly said, "My mother's from overseas."

"Sorry," Captain Kravit said. "I didn't mean anything by it."

"Me, neither," Les added.

"Gotcha," Mr. Duhamel said, laughing.

"One of these days, Alice." Captain Kravit balled his hand. "Bang! Zoom! To the moo—"

The cabin darkened. A large object hovered before them. "What the hell is that?" Captain Kravit asked.

"A giant baseball cap?" Les offered, staring at the brass colored object.

Francis stared at the image of the L-1049 in the flying saucer's transmonitor. He said to the alien puppet, which was perched in his usual spot on Francis' shoulder. "I bet Lakeside's on that plane."

"Validity?" Howdy Doody scratched his wooden elbow.

"Because the time frame fits, and I know that bastard would fly the Super Constellation just so he could spend as much of my dough as he can."

Howdy Doody nodded in agreement with the two aliens standing next to them. One looked like hefty singer, Ethel Merman, and the other looked like the Wizard of Oz's Tin Man. Both of the aliens were scratching their elbows like flea-infested dogs scratching their hindquarters.

"See if he's on board," Francis said.

"Within the bounds of indubitable." Howdy Doody rocked his head back and forth, and at the same time waved his hands at the egg-shaped transmonitor. The image inside the egg jumped from the nose of the L-1049 to a quick shot of TV show *Annie Oakley*. The pig-tailed cowgirl was blazing her twin six-guns into a gang of rough men. The image crackled to a Royal Castle hamburger stand and finally to the interior of the L-1049.

"There he is!" Francis stared at Sam E. staring at his whisky glass. "Transport us on board."

Howdy Doody shook his head. "Energy at present too weeny-teeny."

"Damn it," Francis said. "There goes our fun."

"Fun?" the alien said.

"Yeah. Fun with the airplane."

Howdy Doody looked at the other aliens. They smiled and nodded at each other. "Ho-Ho-*Ho!*" Ethel Merman said, as they waved their hands around the transmonitor.

Tired of staring at his empty glass, Sam E. closed his eyes and counted in his head fresh filled tumblers jumping over a wooden fence. *One, two, three, four, fi——*

The plane lurched as if hooked and jerked upward by a fisherman's line.

Sam E., torn from his seat, felt the whisky glass fly from his hand. It shattered against the plane's interior. Fear swept through him. He sprinted from the lounge toward first class.

Making his way along coach, he heard a stewardess say, "Everyone relax and put on your seatbelts. It's just an air current."

The woman with the child on her lap, patted her hysterical child, and repeated, "Ah, a-ah baby, Ah, a-ah baby," in a nervous, sing-song voice.

"It had to be a hurricane," the sailor who had been sleeping across two seats said, as he picked himself off the floor.

"Ah, a-ah baby," the woman said, "Ah, a-ah baby."

"It was just an air-current," the stewardess repeated.

"A brouhaha!" the old man said.

"It was a colossal baseball cap," the woman said. "A floating hat."

Sam E. stopped. *Son of a bitch!*

"Lady," the old man said, "you got noodles in your noggin."

Sam E. said to him, "Leave her alone. She's upset."

"Ah, a-ah baby," the woman said, crying. "Ah, a-ah baby."

The old man lowered his wire-rims, and said, "She's noodles."

Sam E. said, "Give it a break."

"Take it up the bung hole!" The old man glared at him.

The stewardess, a thin girl with black hair, smiled nervously. "Please calm down, everyone."

Sam E. held up his palm to the old man as a peace offering. He sat next to the lady with the child, and said quietly, "You're right, it was a baseball cap. I've seen it, too." He secured the seatbelt around her and her lapped child.

The woman looked at him, and said, "Ah, a-ah baby."

As he walked back to the aisle, Sam E. said to the others in his best Bette Davis doing her best Margo Channing, "Fasten your seatbelts, it's going to be a bumpy night."

"Hmmf!" The old man gave his *Sports Illustrated* an angry ruffle, as Sam E. entered first class.

"The engines are dead, sir." Les flicked the auxiliary fuel pump switches several times.

The silent plane leaned slightly nose-end down. It was frozen in position.

"Then how come we're still in the air?" Captain Kravit asked in a slow, even voice. His placid demeanor was an over-reaction to the panic pinching his insides.

"I haven't the foggiest," Les said.

Captain Kravit tapped his flattened needle gauges. He tried the radio.

Doreen burst in. "Ty?" she said to the captain. "What the hell is——?"

Captain Kravit held his hand up for silence. "Jim, are you getting any readings?"

"No," Mr. Duhamel said. "By all that's holy, we should be falling."

Doreen gasped. The airliner lollopped downward like an ill-folded paper airplane.

Sam E. tumbled into a seat across the aisle, cattycorner to Cricket and Lee.

Cricket clung to Lee's arm, shivering. Lee was pale, his breath coming in short, beefy strokes. They stared at each other with terror. As the plane rocked downward, Sam E. couldn't take his eyes off their faces. From the other side of the rear partition, in economy, he heard wailing and screaming. And though logic told him it wasn't his fault, he felt overwhelming guilt. He looked up and said as loud as a schoolteacher addressing an auditorium, "Cool it, Francis, I know you're screwing with us. You can't kill us. You need me alive." *What if he has another plan and doesn't need me anymore?*

Doreen burst through the front curtain. "Everyone place your heads down!"

Ignoring her, he said, "If you don't stop the plane from falling, I'll go on *The Allen Show* and say something in my act to piss Steve off so he won't ever step in my dressing room!"

"What the hell's going on?" Doreen asked.

"How about this one?" Sam E. said. "'Steve Allen couldn't ad-lib a fart after a bowl of bean soup'. Or how about, 'What did Steve's wife say after having sex for the first time? 'Are you guys all on the same team?'" His ears popped from the change of cabin pressure. "Allen would never want to see me after that. Hey, saucer-men, there goes your oil!"

The plane slid downward. The earth came closer and closer: haze became panorama became ant-size wheat fields became life-size roadways and cars.

Sam E. looked at Lee and Cricket. Their eyes clung to him as if he were a parachute. He glanced at Doreen, panicked. Shutting his eyes, Sam E. tried to flash his life before him, like he thought it was supposed to happen when you die. What he saw was a mish-mash of scalpel scarred lines and squawking sax notes. He squeezed the armrests until his knuckles hurt. Sam E. waited: Not panicked, not calm. *Lonely.*

"I'm beginning not to like that guy." Francis watched Sam E. through the spacecraft's transmonitor.

"Oil, Francis," Howdy Doody said, scratching his wood ears.

"Oil, Francis," the Tin Man, said, scratching his metallic head so vigorously his funnel-hat clinked forward.

"Don't pay attention to Lakeside," Francis said. "We're gonna *get* fuckin' oil!"

"Oil, Francis," Ethel Merman said.

"Francis, oil," Howdy Doody said.

"Snack on this." Francis slipped a can of 3-IN-ONE from his pocket and handed it to him.

"Oil, Francis!" Howdy Doody heaved the small can back.

"Oil, mother-fucker!" Ethel Merman and Tin Man yelled. They closed in, pointing their index fingers at him.

Two other aliens, who looked like their barnacle-hide selves, crunched forward as if emerging from a dark cavern. They leveled their claw-like fingers at him.

"All right, all right! When we get to New York you're gonna get the first mother lode," Francis said. "I promise."

The aliens eyed each other. They nodded at one another. Ethel Merman and the Tin Man went back to scratching their limbs. The other two disappeared in the shadows.

"Fun. New Ork," Howdy Doody said.

"That's right, fun time in New Ork," Francis replied. "Isn't that right, doll?" he said to Lois, who was strapped to the platform floating in the middle of the room.

She tried to say something angry, but her mouth was muffled by a magnum-colored object resembling wax lips.

Francis laughed at her frustration. He said to Howdy Doody, "Lakeside's boring me. You ready to split?"

The alien nodded. He waved his puppet hand at the transmonitor.
The saucer shot up and away.

The Constellation's propellers spun to life. The plane leveled and droned on. Doreen burst into tears. Cricket kissed Lee with a passion Sam E. had never seen in her before.

Mentally drained, Sam E. passed out…and saw himself in an audience.

He watched his mother on stage, swaying beneath a cobalt spotlight. His mother said to the crowd, "Sammy's second grade teacher asked him, 'What do your parents do for a living?' And Sammy answers, 'Daddy's dead and mommy sells her pussy'."

Sam E. couldn't see anyone in the dark theater, but he knew it was a full house.

His mother laughed, and continued, "The teacher says to Sammy, 'You get your ass to the principal, you foul-mouthed boy!'"

Sam E. pleaded with her to stop, but his voice wouldn't carry.

"Ten minutes later my little Sammy returns," his mother said, loosening her brown terry-cloth robe. "And the teacher says, 'What did the principal say to you?' And Sammy says to the teacher, 'He gave me an apple, and *asked for my mom's phone number!*"

The audience howled. Tony, his mother's pimp, blew a loud wolf whistle and yelled, "Give 'em hell, Judy!" He tapped Sam E.'s shoulder and said to him, "We don't choose our destiny, only how we handle it."

Tony dragged his mother, kicking and pleading, from the stage. Sammy wanted to kill him but he was terrified to move. Sam E. wanted to murder him too, but he couldn't get around Sammy, who was blocking his way.

Lee jumped on stage. "There are bigger things at stake!"

Curley haired, mustached John Wilkes Booth leapt from the balcony and fired Francis' .45 into Lee's skull. Lee collapsed on the floor, drowning in his blood. The deep red turned into gooey thick brown oil.

"Oy-yell, Oy-yell, *Oy-yell!*" The audience sprang to their feet, clapping and stomping. Sam E. grinned. He got it, but just as quickly lost it. He grew solemn. His breathing—short strokes at first—smoothed into steady waves. He heard Captain Kravit say, "Well, ahem, folks, looks like we ran into a bit of a rain cloud. We apologize for the inconvenience. Keep your seat belts on until further notice."

Sam E. forced his eyes open. Lee and Cricket were standing over him. He thought he was in a hospital, before realizing he was lying in the Constellation's sleeping quarters.

"Hi," Cricket said. "Welcome back."

"Is everything okay with the flight?"

"It's fine," Lee said.

He pictured Lee as he saw him in the dream, with a bullet in his brain, drowning in blood, and the blood turning to oil. That was the one thing in the dream that scared him the most, though he didn't know why. "I know how to get back on the spaceship."

"Really?" Lee asked, "How are you gonna do that?"

As the Super Constellation thrummed toward its destination, Sam E. didn't know if it was the ordeal, the visions, or his own demons crushing him, but whatever it was, he felt like his life was draining away. "By following the oil."

Chapter Twenty-Two
PUNCH LINE

Toothy-grilled Imperials bumper-to-bumper with open-mouthed Buicks, stumpy Nash Ramblers, boxy Studebakers, finny Cadillacs, "Taxi-taxi-taxi!," BMT, IND, IRT, crowd flows, crowd retreats, street steam, sirens, jackhammers, "Get 'cha ass outta here!", slumped men, dashing men, stork-necked alabaster-skinned women, huffy bag-toting hags, kraut dogs, tongue on rye, and Münchner on tap. "Yeah? Well yur an idiot!", boxing gyms, ballroom halls, dirt, piss, and *Barbara Bel Geddes in Cat On A Hot Tin Roof.* Brick alleys, cast iron, limestone, pressed terracotta, Italianate, Romanesque, Art Nouveau, Second Empire Baroque, Futurist, and Art Deco skyscrapers too high to look up on.

"Three-oh-one Park Avenue," the cabbie said, pulling up to a tall, brick and limestone building topped with bronze cupolas, "the Waldorf."

Sam E. stepped from the cab and took a deep breath of New York City's wonderful tangle. He entered the gold stanchioned lobby, ornamented in Greek and Egyptian motifs. Two impatient bellhops trotted to him. Despite himself, he crackled with energy.

"Lakeside," he said to a starchy man standing behind a solemn, cherry wood front desk.

"Welcome to the Waldorf-Astoria, Mr. Lakeside," the starchy man said. He removed a globe-handled brass key from its cubby. "Alpin," the starchy man said to one of the bellhops—a wiry young man with sandy hair—standing next to Sam E. "Help them with their luggage."

"Yes, sir."

"We're traveling light," Sam E. said.

The starchy man smiled starchily. "Alpin, show our guests to room 1249."

"This way." Alpin walked the trio to a gated elevator with a large silver-on-gold mural hanging above it.

The starchy man watched them enter. He picked up the desk phone. "Your guests have arrived. Yes, sir, thank you." He hung up the phone and fussed with his jacket sleeve.

S am E. felt uneasy walking down the muffled twelfth floor hallway. It was too quiet, too isolated. He thought maybe they should think about another room, or another hotel. As he was about to say something, Alpin stopped in front of a deep-brown, heavily polished door.

"Room 1249." Alpin lifted his white-gloved hand toward the porcelain doorknob.

Sam E. stuffed a couple of dollars into the bellhop's red jacket. Alpin inserted the key and pushed the door inward. Sam E.'s uneasiness was replaced with dread.

"How was the flight?" Francis asked. He was standing inside the doorway with Howdy Doody on his shoulder. Behind them was a blonde knockout in a strapless, white taffeta evening gown. Alpin's eyes bulged like an over-pumped tetherball. He had seen a lot of actresses at the Waldorf, but never Marilyn Monroe.

He didn't know if he should point out the brown fluid, which he thought was maple syrup, dribbling down her chin.

"As long as you're staring," Francis said, "why don't you snap a picture?"

"Wish I could." Alpin tipped his bellboy cap to Marilyn.

"Take a hike, Sonny, or I'll mash you into Ken-L-Ration."

"Have a marvelous stay," Alpin said, flippantly. He left the room.

"What do you think of the digs?" Francis escorted them down the archway to the living room. Francis plopped himself on a plush ivy-and-rose sofa chair. He removed the alien marionette from his shoulder and placed him on a matching ottoman. Marilyn positioned herself behind the sofa chair. Francis tugged Cricket's arm, jerking her down on his lap. Sam E. and Lee sat on a tufted-back sun-yellow couch facing Francis.

"Review time, Lakeside," Francis said. "Let me hear it."

"Where's Lois?"

"Safe, as long as you do what you're told. Which is?"

"I have to get Allen alone in my dressing room."

"Good dog, Rinty," Francis said. "When do you do it?"

"After the show."

"That's all there is to it," Francis said.

"Then what?"

"Then your girlfriend is released and you go on your merry way."

"How do I know I can trust you?"

"You'll have to take a chance," Francis said. "But to tell you the truth, I don't have any reason to go back on my word. You do your part and I'll do mine."

"I have a question," Lee said.

"Who are you, again?" Francis asked.

"The writer," Lee said.

"That's right." Francis purposely nibbled Cricket's neck.

Sam E. glanced at Lee, whose eyes burned on Cricket. At the same time she lowered her gaze away from Lee's.

"What's your question?" Francis asked, still concentrating on Cricket.

"After you copy Eisenhower and the rest of the world leaders, how are you going to prevent people from noticing the oil is disappearing?"

Francis stopped. He looked Lee in the eyes. "You know all that?"

"Not until you just confirmed it." Lee added, "So, how do you do it?"

"Simple. Once I get Ike and the other world leaders under my control, I tell them to start a new World War to divert attention. Every country will blame the oil loss on the other country." Francis removed Cricket from his lap, stood, and said to Howdy Doody, "Right, partner?"

"How do, partner!"

Francis said to Lee, "You done asking questions?"

Lee nodded.

"Good." Francis slipped his .45 from his shoulder holster. He attached a heavy tube to the barrel. "Know what this is?"

"A silencer."

Francis nodded, tipping the gun into Lee's temple.

Sam E., glaring at the barrel's stem pressing against Lee's skin, felt his heart popping. *It was the vision.*

"Francis," Cricket said. "Let him go."

"You got the hots for him, don't you?" Francis smiled at her. "It's okay, I think it's sexy."

"He's not my type," Cricket said. "He's too dumpy and too full of himself."

Lee grimaced.

"Then why should I let him go?" Francis asked.

Sam E. watched Cricket struggle to find an answer. "Because you need him," he said.

"What the hell does that mean?" Francis asked.

"You got a flaw in your plan," Sam E. said. "Your spacemen can look like Eisenhower but they can't speak like him. The authorities will know it's a fake."

"I'm working on that." He said to the aliens, "Ain't that right?"

"A nat right?" Howdy Doody said.

"A nat right?" Marilyn repeated.

"You need a good writer to make dialogue, like in a movie. Right, Cricket?"

"Bad dialogue will kill you. In *Robot Monster* it was so bad I laughed until my 3-D glasses fell off."

"Lee would convince everyone your guys are legit," Sam E. said. "He uses words I've never heard before. Politician words."

Francis studied Lee. "Tell me a politician word. And it better be good."

"Obsequious," Lee said.

"Hmm, what does that mean?"

"Overly submissive, eager to please. The world will be obsequious to Francis when he displays his prodigious leadership pre-eminence."

"Give me another," Francis said.

"Inimical."

"What's it mean?"

"Hostile," Lee said. "China's inimical aggression has left us no option but to declare a state of war."

"One more," Francis said.

"Ephemeral. It means fleeting. Love, though it may be ephemeral, lingers forever in the heart."

Sam E. caught the glimpse between Cricket and Lee. He figured Francis saw it, too.

"Okay." Francis lowered the pistol. "You're hired. You start tomorrow, after the fund-raiser, which I'm sure you already know about." He said to the aliens, "Let's get back to the room, we have big plans for tomorrow."

"Oil, Francis." Howdy Doody scratched behind his ear.

"Oil, oil, *oil!*" Marilyn Monroe scratched her elbows.

Francis flung his hands in the air. "How many times do I have to *tell* you? Tomorrow we're going on a panty-raid. You'll have enough oil to swim in." He grabbed Cricket by the elbow. "Let's go."

"Where?" Cricket asked.

"With me." Francis smiled. "We're going steady again." He waved his pistol at her. "You got a problem with that?"

"No." Cricket lowered her head.

Francis cupped her chin and pulled her face up. "We've got some catching up to do." He pressed his mouth to hers, deliberately moaning with pleasure.

Lee flushed. He lurched forward. Sam E. gripped his arm and pulled him back. Lee took two sharp breaths and remained still.

Sam E. slipped his hand inside his coat pocket.

Francis whipped his pistol at him. "What are you doing?"

"I want a cigarette. Okay?"

"I'll get it." Francis reached inside Sam E.'s pocket. He felt the revolver stolen from the motorcycle cop. "Nice try." Francis stuck the gun in his own pocket. He reached in again and pulled out Sam E.'s Pall Malls and tossed them to him.

Sam E. patted his chest pockets. "No matches." He reached for Cricket's handbag. "May I?"

"No way." Francis rifled through her purse. He pulled out Cricket's knife, and said to her, "Still playing with toothpicks, I see." He stuck the knife in his pocket and handed Sam E. her matchbook.

He opened the book and struck a flame to his cigarette. "Two women were smoking. It started to rain. One of the women took a rubber from her purse, cut the tip and slipped it over her cigarette. She continued smoking. The other woman, thinking it was a good idea, the next day went into a Rexall and asked the pharmacist for a condom. 'What kind?' the man asked. The woman said, 'One that will fit a Camel'."

The Marilyn Monroe alien tapped Francis on the shoulder. "Play on words. Punch line: Camel cigarette, Camel mammal."

"That's right, you're catching on."

While Francis was speaking to the alien, Sam E., with a quick jerk of his head, motioned for Cricket to keep him occupied.

Cricket turned Francis around, placed her hands on his cheeks, locked his head in place, and French kissed him.

Marilyn, fascinated, moved in closer to the tongue-swabbing couple.

Sam E. nudged Lee, who was fuming. He nudged Lee again. Lee knitted his eyebrows at him as if to ask, "What?" Sam E. moved his hand in a writing movement. Lee nodded. He slipped his pencil from his pocket and handed it to him. He scribbled something on the inside of the matchbook, handed the pencil back to Lee and slipped the book back in the purse. He snapped the bag shut.

At the snap, Francis jerked away and swiveled back to Sam E.

"Thanks for the light," Sam E. said to Cricket. "I put the matches *right* back in your purse," hoping she would catch his real meaning: *write*.

Francis eyed him suspiciously. "There's something I've been working on, tell me what you think." He pointed his diamond-ringed pinky at Sam E.

Howdy Doody, following Francis' lead, did the same with his pine-carved pinky. Francis said to the spaceman, "Ready, partner?" The alien nodded. Francis poked his pinky forward. Howdy Doody did the same with his pinky. The platinum green cloud sprinkled from the puppet's finger and sprayed Sam E.

A lumpy, electric-shock-like pain balled through Sam E.'s spine. He screamed and crumpled on the floor.

Francis lowered his pinky. The marionette-creature stopped the spray.

"You like my act?" Francis asked. "I call it, 'Pulling the puppet strings'."

Sam E. wiped dripping blood from his nose. Lee knelt down beside him. Cricket took a step toward them.

Francis grabbed her arm and pulled her back. He said to Sam E. "That was just in case you or the writer think you're gonna mess with me." He picked up the room key lying on the couch. "Get off the floor. I've ordered you a new wardrobe, toiletries, the works. There's a big T-bone and baked potato dinner on its way."

Sam E. looked up at Francis like he was insane.

Francis smiled. "I want you in tip-top shape for your big debut tomorrow. We'll be next door, so don't get any stupid ideas." He led the aliens and Cricket to the door. "Obsequious," Francis said, as they left the room.

Sam E. heard the door-latch lock with a loud *ka-lick*.

"I hope whatever you wrote in the matchbook was a punch line worth getting zapped over," Lee said, helping him onto the couch.

With a grand flop, Francis fell back on the eiderdown bed. "This is the life, eh?" Cricket was seated on a gold velvet loveseat across from the bed. Marilyn Monroe was sitting next to her. On an ebony nightstand next to the bed, Howdy Doody was sitting cross-legged. Both creatures were sucking on 3-IN-ONE oilcans.

"Yeah," Cricket said. "The life of Riley."

"You betcha, honey-pie." Francis crossed his hands behind his pillowed head. "Maybe we'll just live right here when we take over. Keep a couple spics around for maintenance. Shit. Better yet, I'll get the mayor to do clean-up! That would be a gas."

"Speaking of gas." Cricket crinkled her nose. "Who broke wind?"

"Burroke?" Marilyn Monroe said.

"Push gas from your ass." Francis waffled his hand to disperse the pungent odor.

Cricket took a cigarette and matches from her purse. Walking to the bedroom window, she opened it and took a deep breath, letting the cool wind and the bustling traffic below blanket her. Cricket placed the cigarette between her lips. Striking a match, her eye caught the inside of the matchbook. "You think it's the oil making them smell?"

"Probably. They get like that after they gobble too much."

Returning to the loveseat, Cricket said to the puppet, "You're stinky."

"Stinky, stinky, stinky." He giggled.

"You need to slow down," Francis said. "We got a busy next couple of days."

"There's something dripping from his elbow." She sat next to the Marilyn alien. "Ewww! There's something dripping from hers, too." Cricket pulled a hanky from her bra and wiped the creature's elbow. She smelled the cloth and crinkled her nose. "Jesus, it's like oil and rotten eggs."

"That's it," Francis said to the aliens. "Party's over, lay off the juice for awhile."

"No," Howdy Doody said.

"No," Marilyn repeated.

"Yes," Francis said.

"No!" the aliens said in unison. "No!"

Francis rose from the bed. "No?" He stomped to the door and yanked it open. "Okay, been nice knowin' you. Adios amigos." He motioned them toward the outside hall. Raising his voice loud enough for the aliens to hear, he said to Cricket, "Tomorrow, me and you are going to a refinery and get lots more oil, then we launch a Sputnik satellite into orbit and we find other spacemen who want the stuff."

Marilyn Monroe pointed a threatening finger at Francis. Howdy Doody leaped from the nightstand. He knocked the finger back. "No more hootenanny tonight, Francis."

"What else do you say?" Francis glanced at Cricket, to make sure she was catching this.

They said in chorus, "Sorry."

"Accepted." Francis shut the door and walked back to the bedroom. He took their 3-IN-ONE oilcans from them. "Now get outta here." They left the bedroom.

"Wow, you really are the boss," Cricket said.

"I told ya." Francis closed the bedroom door. "I pull the strings, now."

Cricket smiled and slung her arms around his shoulders. "Were we really going to go to a refinery?"

"I'm taking them there before the show," Francis said, "as a first down payment. It'll keep them happy and out of my hair while me and the fake Steve Allen takes care of business."

"At the fund-raiser?" Cricket pressed against him.

"Yeah, baby." Francis unbuttoned her shirt.

She unbuckled his belt. "Will you have enough time to get the oil?"

"We're going in the morning." Francis nibbled her earlobe.

"I didn't know they had refineries in New York." She unzipped his trousers.

"They don't." Francis buried his lips on her chest. "They're in Jersey."

"Where in Jersey?"

Francis stopped. He eyed her curiously. "What do you want to know that for?"

"I don't," she said with a meek voice. "I was just making conversation."

"The only conversation I want is pillow talk." He placed her on the bed. As he unzipped her skirt, Cricket focused on the three written words in the matchbook: *Follow the oil.*

Chapter Twenty-Three
IN THE STILL OF THE NIGHT

Sam E. picked up the phone, and said, "This is room 1249. Our door's locked from the outside. Send someone to open it... Because I'm telling you it's locked...I don't know how it got locked, just get it open...Look, I need you to send somebody...Are you bullshittin' me?...This is an emer—Hello?" He banged the cradle several times. "Bastard!"

"I told you," Lee said. "The desk clerk is in Francis' palm. Story writing 101."

"How can it be locked from the outside? That's gotta be against the fire code or something?"

"I'm guessing they have a master key that overrides everything, or maybe they purposely put us in a room with a jimmied lock." Lee paused. "Do you think she'll be okay?"

"You don't have to worry about Cricket. She'll do what she has to."

"Do you think her and Francis will, you know?"

"She's doing everything she can to keep us alive."

"I'm sure she is," Lee said, his voice brimming with disdain.

"That was ugly."

"I can't help it."

"Don't you trust *anybody*? What are you so afraid of? That she won't live up to your high and mighty standards?"

"No." Lee sat on the couch and sighed. "I'm afraid that I won't live up to hers."

"Oh." Sam E. sat next to him. "She's in love with you, you know."

"She is?"

"It's obvious."

"Why?" Lee slumped on the couch. "I look bad in swim trunks, and I'm a square."

"Why does Marilyn Monroe love Arthur Miller? He's no Rock Hudson."

Lee shrugged. "He's rich?"

"Yeah, but more important he's a writer. Writing is hip."

"It is?" Lee straightened up.

"Yeah. And you've got to admit this story is a writer's dream; love blooms amid an invasion from outer space."

"Except the invasion is real." Lee slumped again.

Before he could answer, the front door opened. Sam E. spun in time to see a food cart shoved through, followed by a clothes cart with shirts and suits hanging from it. He sprang. The door bolted shut just as he, nearly reaching the entrance, banged into the carts. He rolled the carts into the living room. "You hungry?"

"My stomach's too messed up," Lee said.

"I'm starving. I need to eat." He lifted the tortoise shelled silver plate cover and whiffed the grilled T-bone.

"What if Cricket doesn't read the message in the matchbook?"

"Even if she does read it, I don't know if it'll do any good." Sam E. placed the tray next to the couch and sat down.

"Then what'll we do?"

"You mean for the rest of the night? Or for the rest of the world?"

"Both."

Sam E. sliced a meat chunk and plopped it in his mouth. "You tell me, you're the writer."

"We kill Francis before he sets his plan into motion."

"How do we do that? Have the Batman swing down and bat-punch him to death?"

"That's not funny," Lee replied, "but if it were a comic book, we'd distract him and then we'd grab his gun, and use his own weapon against him in a display of irony."

"Except he's surrounded by spacemen who can take us down with their fingers."

"That's a problem," Lee said.

"I think we should wait until after *The Steve Allen Show* to do it." Sam E. swallowed his steak. "This is good, you want any?"

"*After* the show?"

"Yeah, if we try it before and we fail it'll give them time to come up with something different. After the show, we might catch Francis alone and off guard in the dressing room."

"After the show?" Lee repeated.

"Yeah, after the show. Is there a problem?"

"All actors and comedians care about is their career," Lee said.

Sam E. put his fork down. He backhanded Lee across the face.

Lee, flushed, walked to the door—forgetting it was locked—and twisted the knob. When it refused to open, he turned and walked past Sam E. into the bedroom.

In his head, Sam E. saw Doc and Marge staring at him. He felt an aching hollow. He heard Al Levin, the grocer's son, say, "Your mom sells pussy." He heard the phone ring.

Brrringaa-Brrringaa

He picked up the receiver. "Did you find our goddamn room key?"

"I've only got a minute." Cricket, sitting on the bed in Francis' hotel room, tightened her bathrobe. "Francis is taking the alien Steve Allen to the fund-raiser, but before that—tomorrow morning—he's taking the spacemen to a refinery in New Jersey."

"Which refinery?"

"He wouldn't say." Cricket heard the toilet flush from down the hall. "One other thing, the spacemen are starting to smell bad."

"What does that mean?"

In the background he heard Francis shout, "King bee's comin' for his honey!"

"I don't know. Movies don't make odors." Cricket hung up the phone.

Sam E. rushed to the bedroom, where Lee was lying. "You know about oil. What refineries are in New Jersey?" He waited. No response. "Come on, Lee, this is important!"

"Fuck you." Lee rolled, turning his back to him.

"Yeah, fuck me." Sam E. walked out of the room.

Lowering himself into the bathtub, Sam E. closed his eyes, sunk his head beneath the tepid water, and held his breath. He tried to clear his mind, but his mother floated above him. Lois swam back and forth. Cricket drifted by. Doc and Marge struggled in vain to keep from drowning. Lee stood in a lifeguard stand blowing his whistle and frantically urging them to shore, as blood seeped from his temple.

Sam E. raised his head above the water, and cried...

He dressed and left the bathroom. Seeing a glowing amber dot puncturing the dark living room, he asked, "What time is it?"

"Around eleven," Lee said, from behind his cigarette.

"I'm going to lie down."

"I'll be up for awhile."

"Lee?"

"What?" Lee kicked his feet on the couch and leaned his head against the armrest.

"Don't die."

"What does that mean?"

"Don't do anything stupid, you know? Francis is dangerous.

We need you to write the ending."

"Yeah, okay." Lee sucked on the cigarette.

Sam E. watched the tip brighten. He heard Lee exhale. He waited for Lee to say something, but when he didn't Sam E. entered the bedroom and laid down on the bed closest to the curtains and thought of nothing, not even his debut tomorrow on *The Steve Allen Show*. He closed his eyes and drifted off.

The sun blazed through the red drapes, stinging his eyes. *Oh shit!* Sam E. thought. I'm gonna be late for the show. He bolted up, hopped in-and-out of the bathroom, jumped into his tux, and stormed out of the room, not caring whether he woke Lee, who was sleeping on the couch. Darting through the cavernous lobby, he raised his middle finger at the starchy man, who bowed and smiled. Sam E. hurled through the revolving door to the curbside limo.

"Mr. Lakeside," a spindly chauffer said. "Mr. Allen's waiting."

"Sorry. I overslept."

As they sped off, Sam E. looked up and saw Francis at the hotel window, waving his diamond-ringed pinky at him. Cricket was standing behind him, smiling merrily.

Sam E. popped out of the limo and into the enormously tall, sleek Rockefeller Center. A sport-jacketed young man with a crew cut urged him in the elevator. "Hurry, Mr. Lakeside, they're looking for you!"

Sam E. stepped out of the elevator. The young man rushed him down a crisp, tan-carpeted hallway leading to backstage and a closed black velvet curtain. Sam E. turned to thank the young man, but he had already left.

Standing motionless, he waited for his cue. He stared at the velvet partition, imagining it parting, and the people on the other side. People like Wernher von Braun and Archie Moore, and the female liquor store cashier near his Vegas hotel room who favored pedal pushers. He would make them laugh and they would embrace him like cotton candy around a paper cone. "That would be heaven."

An amber spotlight burst to bright life. The band pounded an ebullient *ba-bump-ba-bum-bump*! He heard the welcoming applause of the audience, and Steve Allen say, "Mr. Sam E. Lakeside!"

Sam E. stepped forward.

Sitting in his dressing room, on a brown-vinyl couch, Sam E. didn't remember his performance so much as the raucous cheers afterward, and the delight he felt when Allen's sidekicks—friendly Bill Dana and petite Imogene Coca—stopped in and congratulated him. He was so happy he scarcely noticed the quiver. When it became a rumble, he stood. When the rumble became plummeting klieg lights, he jumped. Steve Allen peeked in, and yelled, "*Skiiiisshhh*!" The floor cracked. Sam E. ran out of the dressing room. Cameras shattered. Imogene Coca lay in a grisly heap. He plowed through the scrambling audience. Some were crying. Some screaming. Others, beneath chunks of fallen concrete and rebar, were soundless. He slipped on a bloody isthmus as he raced out of the splintered, plate-glass NBC doors onto Rockefeller Center. Next to him, on the sidewalk, a crushed taxi tumbled on its roof: the blackwalls lolloping obliquely. Hydrants spouted like thumb-pressured hoses. In the middle of the plaza, a manhole cover twirled in place, making a *qwo-qwo-qwo* noise, like a turntable needle caught on the inner portion of a spinning 45. The dead were sprawled like autumn leaves along the pavement. A stink, like fetid fish and asparagus-tinged urine, tightened Sam E.'s throat. The back half of a smoking plane angled out of Radio City Music

Hall's roof, causing the baluster of lights smattering the cigar box building to wink erratically.

"Welcome to Planet Francis." Francis leaned against a brown brick building. Cricket had her arm snaked around his shoulder. She smiled deliciously.

"Watch this." Francis waved his pinky upward. A stone gargoyle tumbled from a parapet, splattering to pieces on the street.

Cricket winked at Sam E.

"Where's Lois?"

"Lois?" Francis said. "She's right here."

Lois, whom Sam E. hadn't noticed until now, unbuttoned her buckskin vest and exposed her breasts to him. "What do you think of them?"

"This isn't fair," he said to Francis.

"I know. That's what makes it fun." Francis poked his thumb and index finger in his mouth and blew a siren-sized whistle. He said, "Boys!"

Up from an underground subway entrance marched the spacemen; each one a copy of Lee.

Sam E. wanted to run, but his legs locked like rusty pogo sticks.

"Watch this." Francis took out his pistol. He fired it into the temple of the first Lee.

He fell.

Francis fired again, and the second Lee dropped. Francis fired again. The third Lee dropped. The fourth Lee dropped. The fifth.

"Stop it!" Sam E. screamed. He heard Lois and Cricket laugh.

Francis fired and fired and fired; each bullet blowing a red glow dot in Lee's head.

Sam E.'s heart jack-hammered. A bayonet-like pain pierced his skull. He pliered his palms against his ears and squeezed.

"Sam."

Sam E. opened his eyes. He saw the rosy tip of Lee's cigarette.

He struggled to remember where he was…"What time is it?"

"Around five."

"Oh," Sam E. felt his heartbeat settle. "Did I wake you?"

"Yeah." Lee paused. "You must have been in one hell of a fun house."

Sam E. sat up, pushing back his damp hair. "Look, about earlier, I overreacted."

"We both did." Lee sat on a chair next to the nightstand. "If anyone's held this together, it's been you."

He remained silent, watching Lee's silhouette start to take shape.

"You asked about the Jersey refineries, earlier. I recall there's quite a few, but the biggest, and one of the closest, is Eastside, about twenty miles on the other side of the Hudson River."

"That's probably where they're going."

"Cricket told you?" Lee asked.

"Yes. She also said Francis is taking the fake Steve Allen to the fund-raiser."

"She's a hell of a girl."

Sam E. heard a catch in Lee's throat. It made him think of Lois; he envied Lee for having someone to experience that kind of emotion for. "The saucer-men are going to the refinery this morning. I want to be there."

"We're locked in here, remember?" Lee tugged a chain attached to a Tiffany lamp sitting on the nightstand. The lamp turned on. "And the television show is today."

Sam E. studied Lee's face, more anemic and less meaty. He wondered why he hadn't noticed it before.

"The time frame's off. You can't write it this way. It doesn't give our heroes enough time to rescue—" Lee stopped.

Sam E. finished the sentence in his head. *Lois*. He felt defeated. "One other thing, Cricket said the saucer-men were starting to smell."

168

"That's interesting. Did you notice how they were scratching all the time?"

"Yeah. So what?"

"I think they're either overdosing or developing a reaction to the oil. I had the same kind of thing when I…when I was on bennies."

Sam E. didn't say anything.

Lee looked at him curiously. "Don't you want to know why I took the stuff?"

"I already know. You want to be something better, someone other than yourself and you don't know how." He looked into Lee's eyes, seeing his own reflection. "Now that we know the alien Steve Allen is going to the fund-raiser, how does that help us?"

"Let me ruminate on it." Lee took a long drag on his cigarette. "I'll figure it out."

What happens, Sam E. thought, if one of the heroes, the smart one, gets a bullet in the brain? "There's something else I have to tell you, and you're not going to like it," he said, watching Lee's cigarette smoke minuet through the lasso of lamp light.

Chapter Twenty-Four
TWILIGHT TIME

Reaching his hand over, Francis grabbed Cricket's breast, feeling for the nipple.

Cricket opened her eyes. "What time is it?"

"Sun-up." Francis tweaked the firm flesh. "Nearly party time."

Cricket felt his small, lean frame scoot toward her back, inching his crotch closer to her haunches. She felt his erection against her. She rolled over and faced him. "Promise me that no one will suffer."

"Party doll, I don't want to hurt anyone." Francis slid his hands along her hips. "All I want is to be in charge."

The answer scared Cricket.

He rolled on top of her, lowered himself and imagined she was the veiled Asian woman he saw yesterday afternoon standing near the front desk. He whispered, "You're thinking of him, aren't you?"

Cricket felt Francis' tongue penetrate her mouth. She closed her eyes and imagined Lee—his scent, his intellectual eyes; his flesh. Joy and doom engulfed her.

"So," Lee said, from his perch on the living room couch. "I'm going to die?"

Sitting on a sofa chair across from him, Sam E. said, "I didn't say that. I said I keep seeing it in my dreams."

"Why didn't you tell me earlier?"

"I don't know." Sam E. knew it was a lie. He stared at Lee's bulky silhouette receding into a mauve patina as the rising sun filtered through the laced curtains.

"If I do die," Lee said calmly, as he snuffed his cigarette, "then you go on."

"You're not going to die. I can't do this alone. I'm a certified coward. I go on stage to boost my self-esteem. You don't need a psychoanalyst to figure that one out."

"Maybe you go on stage because you're *not* a coward."

Sam E. stared at his hands folded in his lap. "I lied about why I didn't tell you about the dream." He took a small breath. "I didn't tell you because I'm so fucking frightened I feel like throwing up. You have answers, and all I have are wisecracks. I can't do it by myself."

"Yes, you can," Lee said. "Sometimes a writer has characters killed, and he has others take over. It happens all the time in comic books."

"Why are you so calm about this?"

"I'm not, but there are bigger things at stake."

Sam E. felt even more cowardly. He wanted to ask Lee how it felt to be brave. Instead, he said, "This isn't a comic book and I'm not Captain Midnight." Sam E. walked into the bathroom, bent over the toilet and vomited.

Approximately twenty minutes later the door to the hotel room unlocked. Alpin, the bellboy, standing outside, pushed in a linen-draped cart with coffee, juice, and bagels. "G'morning." His voice was glib. "Enjoying your stay?"

Sam E., combing his hair in a black-framed oval mirror in the hallway, leaped toward him. The bellhop ran outside the door and started to close it.

"Hold on!" Sam E. stopped. "I won't come any closer. I

promise. I just want to talk."

Alpin continued shutting the door. Before it closed completely, Sam E. said, "Hey, kid, how would you like to earn fifty bucks?"

"Doing what?" Alpin peeked his head inside.

"Give us the key."

"Have a pleasant stay." Alpin started to close the door.

"And a private meeting with Marilyn Monroe."

Alpin widened the door. "Yeah? How?"

Sam E. nodded to Lee, who was walking out of the bathroom, toweling shaving cream from his face. "This is Monroe's manager."

"I thought the little guy with the pointy nose was her agent," Alpin said, skeptically.

"Nah, that's her bodyguard. Lee, ah, Goldwirth here, he's her agent, and I'm her publicist."

Alpin raised his chin and stared down at them. "If you're who you say you are, why are you locked in the room?"

"Because," Lee said, "she's preparing for a part; a government agent who ran away from spies by locking them in her room. She's pretending we're the spies."

"Oh," Alpin said. "Lee Strasberg method acting, like Brando in *A Streetcar Named Desire*."

"That's right." Sam E. walked to him. Alpin motioned for him to stay back. Sam E. stopped. "You want to meet her or not?"

"I don't know. I could get in a lot of trouble."

"You know," Sam E. said to Lee, "the kid would make a great rehearsal partner for Marilyn's make-out scene."

"What make-out scene?" Alpin asked.

"I don't know, he's a little young," Lee said, "to be necking with Marilyn."

"Necking?"

"You're right," Sam E. said. "And then there's the unzipping of the dress."

"I can't give you the key," Alpin said. "But I could forget to lock the door. Promise me you won't tell anybody."

"We won't, if you won't." Sam E. held up the fifty dollars. He made his way to Alpin and stuffed the bills into the bellboy's coat pocket. "Do me a favor." He added a ten. "See to it that stiff-assed guy at the front desk is tied up for the next thirty minutes."

"My pleasure." Alpin doffed his bell cap. "What time do you want me back?"

"Back?" Sam E. asked.

"To rehearse with Marilyn."

"Oh yeah, come back tonight."

"What time?"

"After *The Steve Allen Show*. Marilyn loves to watch it, they have great guests, particularly the comics."

"Okay." Alpin turned to leave.

"Hey, kid," Lee said. "What time's the fund-raiser?" He glanced at Sam E., as if to say, 'It's worth a try'.

"What fund-raiser?" Alpin asked.

"The one for Eisenhower."

"That's not here, that's at…Why do you want to know that?"

"Marilyn could use it in her prep work," Sam E. said. "It would be really helpful."

"How helpful?"

"Ten more dollars helpful."

"No one's supposed to know that information," Alpin said.

"Then how come you know it?"

"My cousin Corey's working the tables."

"Really? It might be twenty dollars more helpful." Sam E. fanned two tens in front of him.

"That's F.B.I. stuff." Alpin waved the bills away. "I don't want Hoover and his agents hound dogging me."

"Marilyn could sure use that information. She'd be mighty

grateful." Sam E. added a twenty. "Did you know she's a thirty-eight C and her bra has only two snaps in the back?" He winked.

Alpin snagged the bills. "The Persian Room at The Plaza, but you didn't hear it from me." He darted out the door.

Sam E. and Lee waited. No clunk of the dead bolt. "So?" Sam E. asked.

"They're going to use the fake Steve Allen to get into the fund-raiser and then they're going to take over the president," Lee said. "I'm starting to get my appetite back."

Sam E. grabbed an onion bagel from the breakfast cart, smiled, and tossed it to him.

Chapter Twenty-Five
PLAY BALL

Riordan rubbed his chin and studied the gadrooned edge of the long, mahogany conference table he headed. The board knew the two mannerisms meant he was going to make a command decision. "Gentlemen, we're going to start up T.E.L. production again. America wants to see the USA in their Chevrolet, and we're going to help them do it."

The board, six homogeneous men in brown suits, flanked evenly on each side of the table, sipped their coffee and nodded. That is, all except Jack.

"Jack?" Riordan said to the hefty man. "You want to toss something out?"

Jack took a deep breath. He rubbed his bald head and thought of the surprise sixtieth birthday party Florence planned for him this Sunday. "The state still remembers what happened the last time we produced tetra-ethyl lead."

"Shit," Riordan said. "That was what? 1942? Fourteen years ago. Nobody remembers that." Riordan looked around. The five men shook their heads.

Of course not, Jack thought, you're all in your thirties. Fourteen years ago you were copping feels from debutants. "Seventeen of our people died from the poisoning. Eight others went insane."

"We'll be more careful." Riordan sipped his coffee. "And more generous to our good friends at city hall." He leaned back in his chair with an assertiveness that said the matter was ended.

Jack studied the back of his own plump, liver-spotted hands, and said, without looking up, "Your father would have remembered."

Someone coughed, or gagged; Jack wasn't sure.

Riordan said, "Gentlemen, meeting's over. Jack, would you stay a minute?"

Ernest, the slim, pale man sitting next to Jack, squeezed Jack's arm as he stood. Jack watched the others throw glances at each other as they quietly departed.

Riordan again rubbed his chin and studied the table edge.

Jack stared at the chiseled-faced man. He thought of his surprise party, and how heavy his briefcase seemed these days. Riordan blew a puff of air, looked up and said, "Jack, how would you like your gold watch engraved?"

"Your father didn't retire until he was sixty-seven."

"That was my father."

"I saw them die, Riordan. I knew five of them."

Riordan rested his elbows on the table and steepled his fingers. "How many people work here? How many, Jack?"

"Three hundred and sixty-three."

"Right. And another what? Couple thousand we keep in business from our being in business? If we go down, half of Jersey goes down."

"We're not going down," Jack said.

"You've been with Eastside Refinery since I was in knickers."

Diapers, Jack thought.

"It's a different world. America's moving, Jack. They're leaving the city for the suburbs. You ever been to a shopping center? Or a curbside diner?"

Jack shook his ruddy, jowl-heavy face.

"They're like goddamn quickies, in and out without much satisfaction. The point is, America needs oil to keep moving, they crave it. It's a goddamn drug."

Jack, as he always did when he was gloomy, pressed the outside of his shirt beneath where his Star of David lay.

"First there was Stalin and now that new guy, Khrushchev, egging on the American military complex. They're going at it in overdrive. And you want to know the best news?" Riordan winked. "Whatever happens, we win."

"Your dad worked his ass off, just like I did for this place, but *not* at the expense of others."

"You want to be sanctimonious, fine." Riordan flattened his dark, pinstriped vest. "But don't bullshit a bullshitter."

Jack leaned forward. "What is that supposed to mean?" Who is this prig, who has the same brown hair and eyes as his father, but none of the humanity?

"You think I don't know Dad bribed half the commissioners and blackmailed the rest to get them to play ball? Don't look so surprised, Jack. He bragged about it at the dinner table."

"You're lying." Jack felt his heart pounding beneath the Star of David.

"Am I? You remember that commissioner, about thirty-years ago? The one accused by a prostitute of fathering her child?"

"Lassiter. It was quite a scandal," Jack said.

"Was Lassiter voting yes or no to allow Dad's tanker expansion?"

Jack lowered his eyes.

"About a week later the pregnant girl was found dead in the Hudson. Case closed. The commissioner voted again and this time Lassiter changed his vote to yes."

Jack's throat soured.

"How could I know that? I was only eight at the time. You get the picture? Dad loved to talk at dinner time." Riordan rose, stood behind Jack and gently placed his hands on Jack's shoulders. "Dad loved you. We all love you, Jack."

Jack felt ephemeral, like the time Florence dragged him to see *Peter Pan* at the Winter Garden and he watched Tinker Bell's light dimming.

"What time's your surprise party?"

"Four o'clock, Sunday."

"I'll be fashionably late." Riordan clapped Jack's shoulder. "Enjoy your retirement, you deserve it." He stepped sharply from the room.

Staring at the conference table, Jack wondered which was heavier, the table or his briefcase?

J ack tapped his horn at the sleeping guard as he drove past the guardhouse and entered Eastside Refinery. Because Florence wanted him out of the way to make final arrangements for his surprise party this afternoon, Jack knew she was delighted he wanted to take one last drive around the muscular steel tanks and snaking pipes that folded into and out of each other. Braking his Eldorado near the railroad tracks, he stepped out and breathed the pungent, mucky odor. Most people hated the oil smell, but God, how he loved it. It was the scent of hard work and ingenuity; it smelled like the American dream. He drew another breath as a row of tanker cars screamed to a halt, and a heavy forklift thrummed in the distance. Jack stared at his wide, elongated, morning shadow as he lifted his slipping slacks over his large belly.

He glanced at the sky, losing its morning luster to the rising sun. It reminded him of his son. The brave lad, he thought. Arthur is the sky, and polio is the sun. "How many years, now?" he asked himself. For the first four or five years after young Arthur was buried, Jack succumbed to tears at the very thought. He wanted to cry now, but couldn't. "Arthur."

He stared again at his long, sad shadow, watching in wonderment as it was engulfed by the deeper shadow of a gigantic baseball cap. Jack looked up, but there was nothing. From the tail of his eye, he caught a platinum-green flash. Thinking it might be God sending him a message, he pressed the six-sided star beneath his shirt. He closed his eyes and prayed, prayed for Arthur, prayed for his own soul, prayed his heart would relax and the tingle in his arm would sooth itself.

"What's up, Pops?" Francis asked.

Jack opened his eyes.

"We're looking for oil."

Jack stared at the small, sharp-faced man, not sure if he was the answer to his prayers. "Oil?"

Francis nodded. "My friends and I. Behind you."

Jack turned around and came face-to-face with a cadre of ball-capped men in white-with-navy pinstriped baseball pants and interlocking NY's on their jerseys. Though he was a Brooklyn Dodger's fan, he recognized them immediately.

"They want oil, Pops."

Jack barely heard Francis, so absorbed in the five men; Mickey Mantle with his Oklahoma grin, the fervent Elston Howard, bulbous-face Yogi Berra, fair-haired Whitey Ford, and their bowser-face manager, Casey Stengel. Jack stared at the baseball players; each one resting their bat on their shoulder, and picking at their cheek and elbow with their free hand. Jack felt his armpits sweating. "Why are you here?" he asked the ball players.

Francis clamped Jack's cheeks and jerked his face toward him. "I'm the boss, you talk to me."

"I don't understand."

Francis smiled and released Jack's face. "I'll make this simple. Give us oil, or you die right now."

Jack felt light, lighter than he had in thirty years. So light his feet were lost, his arm no longer tingled, his heart unruffled. *God works in mysterious ways*, he thought. "Any of the tanks has enough crude oil to flood Madison Square Garden."

"You got any refined stuff? My friends prefer that."

"Sure." Jack felt downright ditsy. "The box cars are loaded with barrels of it." He imagined Arthur on his back, gearing his son up for a piggyback ride.

Francis raised his gun to the back of Jack's skull and tightened the trigger. "Well then, oils well that ends well."

Jack, who was sure God was sending him a message, laughed gustily. "Hey, that's a good one. 'Oils well!'"

"You really like it?"

"Funny!" Jack remembered how Arthur giggled as he jogged him around on his back. "Darn funny!"

Francis lowered the gun. He motioned his team toward the railroad tracks.

Watching them walk toward the railcars, Jack said, before he drove off, "I'm having a surprise birthday party this afternoon. You're all invited!"

"Go home, Pops," Francis said, without looking back. "We're throwing our own surprise party."

Chapter Twenty-Six
LIFE COULD BE A DREAM

Sam E. and Lee stepped from the cage elevator and entered the lobby with brisk, but quiet, strides. A sleepy-eyed man in stiff work pants and shirt nodded to them as he guided a vacuum cleaner along the opulent rose weave rug.

Passing the front desk, they eyed a bun-haired woman with glasses, standing behind it. She was filing messages into cubbyholes.

"I don't know how he got rid of tight-ass," Sam E. said to Lee. "But the kid was worth every penny of Francis' money."

Exiting the revolving door, a smiling doorman in top hat, long tails, and riding breeches said to them, "Taxi?"

Sam E. nodded.

The man lifted a whistle hanging from a lanyard around his neck. He blew it and waved his gloved hand.

As the cab pulled up Sam E. glanced at *Gavaghen's Irish Pub*, a homey, stained glass-front bar across the street, tucked between a haberdashery and a delicatessen. A slight fellow in a trench coat tippled out. Sam E. longed for the luxury of a Saturday night blowout. The quick toot of the taxi's horn brought him back to a reality that felt like a Sunday morning come down.

A thickset black man with salt-and-pepper hair and deep-set mahogany eyes stepped out of the cab and opened the back door.

The Waldorf's doorman glanced at the black man, and said quietly, "Would you care for another taxi?" Sam E. smirked at the doorman; ostentatiously ignoring his tip and, along with Lee, entered the vehicle.

The cabbie doffed his cotton newsboy cap and entered the vehicle. "Where to, gents?"

"Eastside Refinery," Sam E. said. "You know where it's at?"

"I know where everything's at. It's in Elizabeth, New Jersey, but I ain't goin'. I work the graveyard shift and you were my last fare. That's too far of a ride. Sorry."

"It's perfect weather for a morning drive." Sam E. leaned forward, waving two twenties over the cabbie's shoulder. "Don't you think?"

The cabbie snatched the bills. "I hadn't noticed how nice it was until now." He clicked on a red transistor radio lying next to him. A breezy doo-wop song floated from the thin speaker. He lowered the meter, singing along with the song.

Sam E. heard him warble something about *sh-boom* and life being a dream. "Yeah, a dream," he said to himself, as the cabbie wheeled onto Park Avenue's bumble of traffic.

Francis tapped the bloody wooden tip against the dead man's protruding brain pulp. The freckle-faced skull the matter oozed from didn't budge. He handed the bat back to the pin-stripe attired alien, and said, "R.B.I."

"Arbeeeeye." Mickey Mantle slung the bat over his shoulder and lugged another oil drum from the near-empty box car.

Francis counted the battered bodies. Nine, just enough to make a team. "The Jersey Oiler-Makers." Not bad, he thought, better than anything that asshole Lakeside could think of. "Shit. I'm letting the prick get to me, again." The worse thing was, he didn't know why. Francis stared at a dead man with a pulverized nose. "Maybe I'm jealous because he's making people laugh, controlling them."

"Maybee I'm jealous," Casey Stengel repeated. The spaceman rolled a barrel along the planked floor.

Naw, that's not it, Francis thought. I'm gonna be World President, nothing can top that. It's because the guy's never had to take it on the chin. He gets applause while I get stepped on. He spit into an encroaching red puddle and ground the heel of his wingtip into the bloody mixture.

"Oil," Casey Stengel said to Francis, as he trundled the final barrel past.

"Yeah. Enough to last you awhile."

"Skiiiisshhh." The alien hopped down the freight car.

"Skeesh." Francis followed him.

The alien set the oil barrel next to a stack of other oil drums gathered near a large cylindrical storage tank. Glancing up at the giant baseball cap peeking out of a strawberry colored morning cloud, Francis noted the storage tank was even larger than the saucer. For a moment he thought of climbing the tank's tall steel ladder to survey the New York skyline, his skyline, a few miles to the east.

"Oil." Casey Stengel motioned to the barrels and to the half-hidden space craft.

"Not yet. Before we load up, the World President is gonna leave his calling card." Francis rubbed his hand along the storage tank's steering wheel sized oil valve. "It's time for my applause." He gripped the valve and twisted it.

As the cab exited the dim, exhaust-heavy, reverb swish of the Lincoln Tunnel into the toasty, New Jersey morning, Sam E said, "A cabbie walks into a bar carrying a piece of asphalt, he says to the bartender—"

"'I'll have two beers. One for me and one for the road'," the cabbie said.

"Everybody's a comedian. What's your name?"

"Fred Greene. And yours?"

"Sam E. Lakeside. I'm a *professional* comic."

"Not with that joke, you ain't," Fred said, unimpressed.

"Is that how cabbies get their tips in New York? By trashing the passenger?"

Lee laughed. "My name's—"

"Lee Beaumont," the driver said.

"Do I know you?"

"No." Fred reached his arm behind him. "But, can I shake your hand?"

"Sure, but why?" Lee gripped the cabbie's hand.

"Because I loved *Horror in the First Degree.*"

"Really?"

"It scared the crap out of me, and made me feel sorry for the poor monster all at the same time."

"Can I get a hint at what's going on?" Sam E. asked.

"That was based on *The Cabinet of Dr. Caligari*," Lee said to Fred.

"I *knew* it!" Fred said, as they approached the tollbooth to the Jersey Turnpike. "I told Josephine—the missus—that."

"You did?" Lee asked in a flattered voice. "Did she like the story?"

"Who's Dr. Caligari?" Sam E. asked. "And what's wrong with his cabinet?"

"She doesn't appreciate comic book literature." Fred handed the tollbooth operator a dime. "The barber shop boys and I think you got a bum wrap with that Kefauver clown."

"They do?"

"We're fans."

"My manager was a barber. He used to cut my hair when we couldn't afford it." The other two, absorbed in their conversation, ignored Sam E.

"How come you don't have any negro characters?"

"It never crossed my mind," Lee said, questioning himself.

"I'm not talking about those simpletons with the googly eyes and eggplant lips who stutter and say silly things. Real negroes, like me."

"A negro protagonist. That's a good idea."

"Damn right." Fred pulled onto the turnpike.

Sam E. watched the ochre New Jersey landside slipping past them. He felt a jealousy gloved in pettiness; like his spotlight was being stolen. His emotions disturbed him, but still, he couldn't help himself.

"Why're you two going to Eastside?" Fred asked. "Some sort of convention?"

"No," Lee said. "We're trying to stop an alien invasion."

"I can't wait to read that one."

"Fred," Sam E. said. "How would you like to be the first negro character in a science fiction story?"

"Don't do that to him," Lee said, quietly. "We need all the help we can get."

"Is he for real?" Fred asked Lee.

"Yeah, but—"

"You got a gun?" Sam E. asked Fred.

"What do *you* think? I work the drunkard shift in New York City."

"Don't listen to him," Lee said.

"Why not?" Fred asked. "And why do I have to have a gun?"

"Tell him the truth, Sam," Lee said. "That's only fair."

Fred eyed them through his rearview mirror.

Sam E. couldn't tell if Fred's scrunched eyebrows were due

to his curiosity, or because he thought the two of them were nuts. "Fred, you're a fan of outer space films, I bet."

Fred nodded. *"Klatuu berata nik-toe."*

"Yeah, yeah, I know," Sam E. said. "I've learned a lot about spacemen movies." He hesitated; feeling the heavy sting—which was coming—of being labeled a lunatic once again. He thought next time he saw Cricket he'd ask her how Miles Bennell handled it in *Invasion of the Body Snatchers*. Sam E. stifled the discomfort by thinking of Lois trapped in the saucer. He took a deep breath. "Here goes."

In a mad jig, Francis hopscotched from storage tank to storage tank, twisting the over-sized faucets. Behind him, single file and duplicating his leaps were the five bogus New York Yankees.

Stopping in front of the guard shack, Francis ignored the sleeping watchman, as he caught his breath. He was exuberant. It reminded him of skipping school and crawling under his house in Ohio and lighting candles. He loved the orange flame. He could snuff it, create it, pass it quickly under his thumb and not burn his skin; or hold it still and singe his flesh. He watched the flickering fire for hours, twirling the candle in his fingertips. He masturbated once to it, but that wasn't as much fun as he thought. No, the pleasure was in the power—the ability to control.

But control never came easy. Not at home, where his old man, 'the smiling milkman', and his two-inch leather belt with the solid brass buckle, ruled. Or at school, where William Farco and the other toadies in that brick-shit grammar school laughed and beat the snot out of him. Fuck them, Francis thought. He was about to turn the last tank valve open when he got an idea.

"Hey!" he shouted to the sleeping guard. "Wake up! You got customers."

The guard, a pyknic man with a gnarl of keys jangling from his side, jogged out of the slant-roofed shed. He stared at the oil oozing around his steel-toed boots. The man pulled a revolver from his holster. He aimed the barrel at Francis' nose. "What's goin' on?"

Control, Francis thought. He pointed at the man's knee and motioned to Mickey Mantle. The space traveler swung his bat with a savagery the real Mantle could only imagine.

The man's kneecap cracked with a sound like Zorro's whip. His gun flew, and his body folded to the ground.

Francis did another quick hopscotch because he had more control than he'd ever had in his life. "Is evv-ery-body," Francis twisted the final tank valve open, "happy?"

The aliens got on their knees and lapped the oozing fluid from the flowing pipe.

"Cut that out." Francis jerked them up by the collar.

"Snack," Whitey Ford said. "Potato Chips."

"No. This is to let 'em know we mean business."

"Business," Yogi Berra said. "Selling oil for profit."

"When I give the word," Francis said. "You guys are gonna zap the oil barrels into the baseball cap and we're gonna haul ass. Can you handle that, team?"

They nodded. "Easy as Swanson TV Dinner," Elston Howard added.

"Bring the saucer down, boys." Francis watched the syrupy liquid creep along the asphalt toward the other oozing slithers. "And get ready to zap." He reached into his pants pocket for his matches.

F red exited the Newark tollgate onto US 99. "Man, either you're a lunatic or you think I'm one dumb nigger," he said to Sam E., as he accelerated onto the divided double-lane highway, which was crowded, but not congested. "I'm just glad you paid me in advance." He looked at Lee through the rearview mirror. "Do you have to hang with nuts like him to write stories like that? I can't wait to tell the boys at the barber shop." Fred laughed. "How about this for the title? *Oily Invaders From Outer Space.*"

"Not bad." Lee penciled the title in his notepad.

"Yeah, cute," Sam E. said. "But it's not a story. It's true."

"Okay, let me ask you something," Fred said. "If the spacemen want to take over the president why don't they just fly the saucer over to the White House and zap everybody?"

"I don't know," Sam E. said. He glanced at Lee. "Why don't they?"

"Simple," Lee said. "They wouldn't get away with it. There's only about six of them and they're not powerful enough to take on the entire Pentagon."

"Yeah," Sam E. said to Fred. "What he said."

Lee continued, "Their plan is to infiltrate and control the government. In order to do that they need to get rid of the real Eisenhower and, at the same time, replace him with the alien replica. They figure the best place to do that without suspicion is at the fund-raiser. And Sam's the key to getting them in there."

"Okay," Fred said. "Let me ask you one more thing. You're supposed to be some sort of comedian going on *The Steve Allen Show*, right?"

"Yeah. So what?"

"But first you're going to stop the aliens at the refinery, right?"

"That's the plan."

"What time is it?" Fred asked.

Sam E. glanced at his Timex. "Nearly nine-thirty."

"And you got to be at The Hudson Theatre, where they broadcast, at what time?"

"Ten-thirty for the first run through." Sam E. sunk, knowing what Fred was leading to.

"Even if I thought you weren't crazy, which I don't, you're telling me you're gonna stop a gang of bug-eyed monsters and make it to the broadcast in an hour?"

Sam E. laughed.

"What's so amusing?" Lee asked.

"Yeah," Fred said. "What's so funny?"

"We're telling you about flying saucers and copy cat spacemen stealing oil, and you don't believe us because you can't put a time frame for me to be on television?"

"Well, it doesn't make sense. It wouldn't hold up." Fred added, to Lee, "Right?"

Lee shrugged. "We were hoping you could get us back in time."

"Whoa, Nellybelle," Fred said. "The forty bucks was for a one-way ticket. As soon as I drop you off, it's splitsville. My shift's over."

"We'll give you more money." Sam E. reached into his pocket.

"How much?" Fred exited US 19 toward Kellogg Park Avenue.

Sam E. counted his bills. "How much you got, Lee?"

"Four dollars." Lee handed him the bills.

"Sixteen dollars?" Sam E. said to Fred, half-pleading.

"Enjoy your stay." Fred entered a two-lane avenue.

Sam E. studied the blue collar, stucco houses lined up on each side of the street like old soldiers. He wondered what it was like to have a home. "You got kids?" he asked Fred.

"Son, seventeen, works at a shoe shop in Harlem. Why?"

Sam E. handed him the sixteen dollars. "Take him and your wife—"

"Josephine." Fred steered the cab onto a shrub enclosed, long gravel road.

"Josephine," Sam E. repeated. "Take them for a nice steak dinner, but do it today, okay?"

"Mister, you're starting to scare me." He drove along the crunchy road, coming closer to a wooden guardhouse, which said Eastside Refinery on it.

Chapter Twenty-Seven
SH-BOOM

Cricket—staring into the saucer's egg-shaped transmonitor—watched an image of Francis and the aliens treading from storage tank to storage tank. The asphalt was covered with oil. She had a bad feeling.

Lois was strapped to the floating platform in the center of the saucer. She was staring wild-eyed up at the Howdy Doody puppet standing straddled over her neck. The alien slanted his freckled face sideways in curiosity at her. He bent down, puckered his lips and pressed them against the restraint covering Lois' mouth. She screamed, but the sound was deadened by the device.

"Kiss-kiss." Howdy Doody kissed her cheek with a loud smack.

Cricket ran to him. "Hey! Stop that!"

"Kiss-kiss," the alien repeated.

"No! That's for humans, not for you."

The puppet frowned. "Heartbreak Hotel."

"That's right." Cricket clutched Lois' chilly hand, strapped at the wrist. Lois tried to say something, but it came out as tears. "Untie her," Cricket said. "She can't hurt you."

The alien shook his head.

"Why not?" Cricket's heart fell at the sight of the pale, trembling girl with the bent feather hanging from her headband.

"Francis say no."

"Well, then how about the mouthpiece? At least let her speak."

The alien shook his head.

"Did Francis say?"

The alien shrugged.

"If you remove it, I'll tell you a joke. It's a funny one that Sam told me."

"Waggish, rib-tickling, a hoot?" Howdy Doody's cherry red, gap tooth smile resembled a quarter moon turned on its curved spine.

"The most! And we won't let Francis know, okay?"

"Baby, you're the greatest!" The alien rubbed his hand over Lois' mouth restraint. The metal-looking strap fell like a silk cloth.

Lois screamed.

Cricket clamped her palm over her mouth. "Can't do that. Okay?" Lois stared at her for a second, panic-stricken, and then nodded. "All right," Cricket said. She lifted her hand.

Lois gagged and took a deep breath. "I'm eleven years old, I'm having my tonsils out and Doctor Koenig just put me under anesthesia, right?"

"No." Cricket rubbed Lois' forehead.

"Tickle my rib, like Sam E.," Howdy Doody said to Cricket.

Cricket held her breath. She thought hard. *What was that thing Sam said about the guy at confessional?*

"Slap my knee," Howdy Doody said.

"A man goes to church. He tells the priest, 'I just had sex with twins'. The priest says, 'Why are you telling me this? You're Jewish'. The guy says, 'I'm telling everybody because I'm happy'." Cricket forced herself to giggle. "You get it? He's confessing because he *wants* everyone to know." Shit, Cricket thought, it was funnier when Sam told it.

The alien's smile sunk. "Stinker." He sat on the toe end of the platform, dangling his tiny, cowboy-booted feet over the edge. His back was to Lois' prone body. He lifted a squeeze can of 3-IN-ONE Oil from his shirt pocket, and sucked the tip.

"You okay?" Cricket asked Lois.

"I know I'm not eleven years old and having my tonsils out, if that's what you mean."

"That's a good start. Did the saucer-men…do anything?"

"I think so." Her blue eyes dulled, highlighting the lavender circles beneath them. "I'm awfully scared."

"Collywobbles, creepy-creeps," Howdy Doody said to himself.

"Where's Sam?" Lois asked.

"At a hotel in New York City."

"Oh," Lois said, her voice sounding disappointed. "Where are *we*?"

"Hovering somewhere above an oil refinery in New Jersey."

"Am I going to die?" Her eyes welled.

"We're all going to die someday." Cricket held in her own tears. "I think he's in love with you, you know."

Lois smiled wanly. "I knew it when we kissed."

"Kiss-kiss?" Howdy Doody spun his wood head backwards to face them.

"No kiss-kiss for you," Cricket said, glaring at him.

"Oooh." The puppet continued his head spin until he again faced away from them.

"No matter what," Cricket squeezed Lois' hand, "you two have each other. That's something to be grateful for."

Lois lowered her face.

"You do love him?"

"He's funny and sweet and…I don't know," Lois said. "I don't know."

"Oooh." Cricket sounded much like the kiss-kiss deprived space alien. She thought of Lee and herself. Sadness pinched her. She was about to say some gibberish about following your heart, when the Doody-alien screamed, "Skiiiisshhh!"

He leapt from the floating platform, skittered to the transmonitor and repeated, "Skiiiisshhh."

Cricket ran over and stared into it.

"What is it?" Lois asked, hysterically.

"It's the refinery." Cricket watched the image of Eastside Refinery in the egg-shaped object. The refinery was ballooning into yellow-and-orange flames smothered in a black smoke cloud. "It's on fire!" She felt her stomach tickle, like she was on a plunging elevator. The image was getting closer. "We're landing." As they drew nearer to the flames, the saucer was growing hotter.

"This is Elysium!" Francis spread his arms like Moses parting the Red Sea; the heady blaze swirling around him and the Yankee lookalikes. A beefy smoke patch pushed into and over them. Francis hacked and loved it. He screamed over the grumbling fire, "Fuck you and your leather belt, Dad! Fuck you, William Farco! Fuck you, Annabeth prick-teaser! Fuck you, Gus Greenbaum!"

"Fuck you! Fuck you! Fuck you!" the aliens chanted, as the saucer drifted like a wet feather to the ground behind them; briefly swishing the inferno, as if the blades of a ceiling fan had blown it. The ship's visor, facing Francis and the aliens, lowered like a ramp. The triangular opening, leading into the ship, appeared.

"Okay, aim your fingers at the oil barrels and get ready to zap them into the saucer." Francis' pulse leaped with the flames.

The aliens pointed their digits at the clump of barrels.

He took one last look at the inferno and rolled his thumb and forefinger together as if they were twirling the candle he used to play with underneath his house in Ohio. "Blast away!" he shouted over the searing blaze. He waited. The barrels remained. "Come on!"

"We are," Whitey Ford said.

"How come they aren't moving?" Francis wiped his heat-soaked brow.

"Doesn't work on not alive things, only us and aliens like you."

"Why didn't you tell me that?"

The aliens looked at each other and shrugged. "We didn't know."

"Jesus effin' Christ. Let's get the hell out of here."

"Oil, effin' oil! Oil, effin' oil!" the aliens chanted.

"You want the stuff, bring it in yourself." Francis felt the hot sweat circle beneath his armpits and belly. "Me and Howdy have to get back to the hotel." He jogged up the ramp into the ship.

"**H**oly shit!" Fred slammed the taxi's brakes in front of the guard gate. He stared through his windshield at the flames and smoke in front of them. He beeped the car's horn for the guard.

"Don't bother. I'm betting he's no longer with us," Sam E. said. The oily black smoke caressed the closed windows. "I'm going out there."

"Me too," Lee said.

"You guys are lunatics," Fred said.

"You're not going, Lee." Sam E. thought of his vision of Lee with a bullet in his brain. If it was going to happen this was going to be the place. "You need to get back and figure out how we get into the fund-raiser."

"Then why the crap did I come here in the first place?" Lee asked.

"I needed a straight man." Sam E. didn't want to admit he was too scared to take the ride by himself. "Now get out of here!" He wanted to add, "Before I change my mind."

"I'm staying."

"Cricket needs you."

Lee said, "I won't leave without you."

"There are bigger things at stake," Sam E. said. "Trust me."

"No." Lee lowered his eyes.

Sam E. gripped his shoulder. "If something happens to me you need to carry on."

"No," Lee repeated.

"You told me a writer has characters killed and he has others take over," Sam E. said. "If that's true then you need to trust me, right Fred?"

"I'm officially off duty, but yeah, trust is important."

Lee's throat clutched. He hesitated. "I'll cover for you back at the hotel."

Sam E. pressed the door handle and pushed it open.

"Here." Fred opened his glove compartment. "Compliments of the house." He pulled out a chrome plated snub nose .38.

"Then you believe us?" Sam E. asked, taking the pistol.

"Let's say I'm willing to trust you," Fred said. "You want this, too?" He reached in his leather jacket and pulled out a switchblade.

Sam E. waved if off. "No. That's Cricket's department." He stepped from the taxi and rushed toward the blaze, taking a nervous potshot at it with the snub nose.

Cricket and the Howdy Doody alien stared into the saucer's transmonitor, watching the image of Francis enter the ship and tap them on the back of their shoulders. They turned.

"Get us back to the hotel," Francis said to Howdy.

"No," the extraterrestrial said. "Oil, effin' oil!"

"You too?" Francis smelled the acrid fumes that followed him inside. He heard a gunshot come from outside. "Cops must be here. I hate to miss the grand finale, but we got no choice."

Lois coughed from the pungent odor.

"Who took her gag off?" he asked.

"Oy-yell! Oy-yell! Oy-*yell*!" The alien said, stomping his wooden leg on each 'yell'.

"They're moving the barrels into the ship." Francis looked into the transmonitor, which only showed the blanket of black smoke smothering the refinery. "It's getting late. We got to get the fuck back to the Waldorf, now." Gesturing to the transmonitor, he said to Howdy Doody, "Can this thing get us there? And don't give me that oy-yell shit."

The puppet eyed him angrily, muttering, "Oy-yell, Oy-yell." He wafted his hands over the transmonitor until the image of *Gavaghen's Irish Pub*, across the street from the Waldorf, appeared.

"No, not there. Take us to the hotel room," Francis said.

Howdy Doody shook his head. "Broadcast interference."

"Fine, that's close enough." Francis pushed Cricket into the egg. She disappeared before she could cry out. "You next," Francis said to Howdy.

"No," the alien puppet said. "Oy-yell! Oy-yell! Oy-yell!" He jumped and flailed his fists above his ears.

"I told you! They're lugging in the barrels. They should be here any minute."

Outside, another gunshot rang. Lois shrieked. Francis eyeballed her. He shouted to the badly behaving alien, "Shut up or no more oil!"

The alien calmed down by degrees.

Francis walked to the frightened girl. He stared at her curvy body squirming on the platform; listening to her cry.

"Francis," the alien said, quietly.

"I know," Francis said. "You want to stay and get your share of the oil. I want to get back to the hotel." He straightened Lois' bent feather, smiling at her. "I've got an idea."

"Kiss-kiss?" the alien asked.

"Not exactly." Francis pressed his hand over Lois' mouth to stifle her whimpers.

Lifting his jacket collar over his nose and mouth as a filter, Sam E. stepped farther into the black smoke, which came and went in swirls. He followed rustling noises inside the churning cloud. As he moved forward the noises grew louder and more frantic. He came to the five New York Yankees and the oil barrels they were carrying two-at-a-time; one on each shoulder. They were marching them up the saucer's ramp and into the ship.

Sam E. knew he had fired Fred's gun twice. He'd seen too many *Lone Ranger* episodes not to know you always counted your bullets. There were six in a chamber. The four bullets left weren't very comforting. He pointed the gun at the aliens and lowered the collar from his mouth. He said to the ball-playing space creatures, "Did you hear about the hundred pound alien with fifty pound testicles?"

The spacemen stopped marching. They turned and faced him. Elston Howard and Yogi Berra cocked their heads in curiosity much like Nipper, the RCA dog who perpetually listens to his master's voice.

As the flame and smoke whirled around him, Sam E. said, "The hundred pound alien with the fifty pound testicles was half nuts." He grabbed his crotch. "Half nuts," he repeated.

The aliens looked at each other and nodded. Sam E. pointed his gun at them and took a step forward.

The aliens glared at him.

"I need to get on the ship." Sam E. approached the ramp.

"Oil, effin' oil," Casey Stengel said.

"I don't want the oil." Sam E. stepped on the landing. "I want the girl." The aliens moved aside. He walked between them, along the ramp, toward the triangular entrance. His heart fluttered. His fingers chilled against the snub nose, though the flames warmed the chrome pistol. He approached the ship's passageway.

Pwapt!

Sam E. jumped. An oil drum slammed down between him and the entrance.

"Claunk!"

Mickey Mantle plunked the second of his barrels on top of the first. "No girl for you."

"Why?" Sam E. asked. "What do you care?"

"Girl for you, no effin' oil for us." Mickey Mantle's blue eyes were replaced by the alien's reflective purple tint.

Sam E. looked at the others: Casey, Whitey, Elston, Yogi. All were staring at him with furious purple eyes. Four bullets and five spacemen, he thought. "Get out of the way," he said to the Mickey Mantle alien. Through the gathering smoke Sam E. saw the alien smile; a joyless upturn of the lips that seemed an imitation of how the alien thought a human should react. The alien pointed his index finger at him. The other aliens dropped their barrels and did the same.

Sam E.'s heart pummeled his chest. He felt like he did the night on the mountain digging his grave, but a thousand times worse. He wanted it to be only about Lois, about his mother, about Doc and Marge, but one mean thought pulled above the rest. *I want my shot on The Steve Allen Show. I earned the goddamn right.* He lowered his pistol and stepped back.

Sam E. sobbed. He heard Al Levin, the grocer's son say, "Your mom sells pussy." Through the burning, acrid petroleum scraping his nostrils raw, he smelled Lois' apricot scented hair. He remembered sitting in Doc's tiny kitchen, getting a free haircut. Heat seared his ears. He raised his pistol and fired it into the air.

"Step aside," he said, walking forward.

Mickey Mantle jiggled, blurred, and re-jiggled; towering over Sam E.'s head. Its body reshaped itself into the locust thing with the crushed Rottweiler face. Its branchy claws reached for Sam E.'s skull. Behind him, he could sense the others doing the same. He fired a bullet into the alien's face. The slug plopped in its hide like a candle in a birthday cake. The alien wiggled his head and the bullet plunked to the ground.

Who's on first? What's on second? I Don't Know is on third. Abbott and Costello's routine jigsawed across his mind. *Two bullets left.* Sam E. felt the alien grip and crush his temples. A high-pitched ringing filled his head. He heard distant sirens. Purplish flecks, like confetti, sprinkled inside his eyes. The other aliens tightened around him. *Why is in left field. Tomorrow's pitching, and Today is catching. Two bullets left.* He aimed and fired.

Francis, from inside the ship, heard the gunshot. By the volume, he knew that whoever fired it was too close for easefulness. He glanced at the fringed-suede figure unstrapped and sitting up on the floating platform. He smiled at the beautiful, haunted-looking sable eyes. "See you in a while, crocodile." He jumped into the transmonitor and disappeared.

Sam E.'s fired bullet punctured its target—the first oil barrel the alien had dropped in front of him.

The alien looked at the seeping liquid. He hesitated, puckered his razor-thin lips and continued squashing Sam E.'s head.

Sam E. fired again. His final bullet hit the alien's second barrel. The other aliens pounced on the leaking fluid. "If you don't let

202

go," Sam E. said in a weak voice to the alien squeezing his skull. "I'll shoot the rest of the barrels open and you'll have no oil for yourself."

The alien eyed the other slurping aliens. He eyed Sam E.

Sam E. aimed his gun at another barrel. "I'm a fast draw. I can shoot every one of the barrels before you can kill me." He hoped the alien wasn't too much of a western fan to know the number of bullets in a chamber.

Like a petulant child making one defiant foot stomp before caving in; the alien squeezed Sam E.'s skull with a final burst before tossing him aside. He growled, "Skiiiisshhh," as he pummeled his way into the alien pile up.

Sam E. ran past the oil-sucking brood. Hearing sirens again, he wasn't sure if they were real or inside his aching head. He entered the ship's portal, which led to a narrow, arched corridor. The passageway—a dimly lit orange—was a gradually curving, inclining hall that changed smells more frequently the deeper he went into it. Some odors he recognized like the faint rose odor of Brylcreem hair tonic, the acerbic pinch of burnt popcorn, and the pine crispness of Spic and Span; other aromas were like nothing he'd ever smelled. If he wanted to turn back he knew he couldn't. The passageway had a dark current of its own: a merciless flow that dragged him deeper and deeper into itself until it flushed him out into the ring-shaped room with the transmonitor.

"Lois!" He ran to the dazed looking figure.

"Sam E.?"

He held her head in his hands. Her body seemed as if it had shriveled. He looked in her eyes. "You're safe now, I promise."

"Promise, Sam E.?"

"Yes. I'll get you out of here." It dawned on him that he hadn't planned on how he was going to do that. He looked for the passageway he had just entered from, but it had vanished. He looked at the transmonitor and it was still showing Gavaghen's Irish Pub. Sam E. recognized it from when he entered Fred's taxi. He gently led Lois to the device. "I'm going to put you inside, but don't worry, it won't hurt you, okay?"

"Promise, Sam E.?"

Her eyes look so sad, he thought. "Yes." His own eyes welled. "I promise. No more hurt."

He placed her in front of the screen. "Ready?" Her eyes looked at him with a gentleness that melted the lonely, harsh years of working flea-bitten, empty clubs.

"Sam E., kiss-kiss?"

"Yes," Sam E. whispered. He closed his eyes, bringing his mouth to hers. He breathed in, anticipating the sweet smell of apricots. He smelled oil: a sour, musty brown stench. He flung open his eyes just as Lois' eyes turned reflective purple. Horrified, he pulled back but the alien's gristly tongue entered his mouth and pulled him to her pulsating lips. Sam E. screamed. The turgid alien flesh squirming inside his mouth stifled the sound.

Sam E. froze; he felt the creature's cold appendage slither down his throat. He tasted something between a soft-boiled egg yolk and engine sludge. His chest filled with a metallic rancidness that reminded him of his mother who sold pussy, and the pimp who beat her, and his father who had the impertinence to die before he ever met him. The weight was too heavy for his comedian-honed shoulders. Sam E. was sinking.

He was sinking to the bottom of a rusty colored lagoon. He looked up at the receding surface, feeling a giddiness and a sadness that he couldn't explain. It felt like he had given up something. Was it something he wanted or didn't want? He closed his eyes.

Drifting lower into the cold water, the lagoon said softly, "Come with me, come with me. You're nearly there. Isn't it nice?"

"Yes."

The lagoon massaged every tendon and muscle in his body. It seeped below his skin and rubbed his fatty tissue, it fingered his corpuscles until his blood no longer pounded in his veins. Sam E. was relieved.

"Reach for it," the water whispered.

The burden was lifting. He was at peace. Sam E. reached.

"No, Sammy. We don't choose our destiny, only how we handle it."

He recognized his mother's voice, even as his heart slowed. He thought hard, remembering what she had asked him never to forget all those years ago in his bedroom. He felt the resolve in her voice, the strength. His limbs tingled and his pulse quickened. He stopped reaching. He was floating to the surface.

A muster of tire squealing black-and-whites roared past the Eastside Refinery guard gate. A fire truck and a bulbous tanker truck trundled in the distance. The patrol cars—each topped with their own fez shaped revolving red beacon—braked and spun in the lubricant. They smacked into each other, gliding to a gooey stop near the smoke-surrounded spaceship.

Pairs of white-shirted cops leapt from the vehicles and stood behind their open doors, aiming guns and rifles at the saucer's dome, which towered above the smoke. A black jacketed captain stepped out of the lead car's passenger side and yelled through a bullhorn, "I don't know how you got that flying son-of-a-bitch in here, but whoever you are, you've got two minutes to come out with your hands up, or you're gonna face an artillery of weapons!"

The aliens, sucking the last of the leaking oil barrels dry, looked at each other. The creatures jiggled, blurred and re-jiggled into their New York Yankee clones. They walked toward the policemen.

The cops alternated their eyes between the space ship and the New York Yankees, surfacing from the fat smoke.

The captain—a mustached, hefty man—said, "Stop right there."

The baseball players stopped.

"Put your hands in the air."

The saucer-men raised up their hands just enough to point their index fingers at the men. Mickey Mantle poked his finger forward. The platinum-green spray flew from his fingertip.

"Take him down!" the captain shouted.

"It's Mickey Mantle, Captain," a policeman said.

"I don't give a damn if it's Ida Lupino."

Bullets whizzed. The platinum-green spray flew from each of the alien's fingers. Policemen fell one by one as they were engulfed in the green mist. The captain, also a volunteer fireman, grabbed his army surplus Rebreather from the back seat. He flung the brass canister over his back, brought the breathing hose to his mouth and turned on the demand valve.

As the flame and smoke flared around him, the captain took his time and aimed his revolver straight at Mickey Mantle's fair-haired scalp. The captain fired. The bullet stormed toward the slugger's face, lodging in his left eye. The Yankee slugger plucked the lead from his pupil and tossed it back to the air-masked Captain. The astounded man had little time to contemplate what had just happened before the first oil tank explosion blew his patrol cars into the air and himself into smithereens.

S am E.'s eyes thundered open with the roar of the blast. He was locked mouth-to-mouth with the Lois-creature, who was staring at him. He slugged the alien in the gut. The space being tumbled backward; its tongue shriveling out of Sam E.'s body. The ship grew hotter. Sam E. heard a shuffling ruckus and knew the other saucer-men were entering, no doubt with their barrels. Lois jiggled, blurred, re-jiggled into its towering, mangle-faced, locust form. It stormed toward Sam E., shooting its platinum-green spray at him. Sam E. took a long, headfirst leap into the transmonitor.

A thin, ruddy-cheeked man in a bowler and a velvet collar Chesterfield downed a shot of whiskey, chasing it with a foamless Guinness. He said to a scrappy rusty hair bartender with a swollen lip and bruised nose, "The trouble with boxers today is you start fighting *after* you're hooked on dames. By the time the broads made my prick bar up, I made damn sure I knew my way in the ring."

The bartender swiped air with his palm. "I don't getchur point."

"That's because you let the broads get to you." The elderly man took another sip of his pint. "Why do you think you fell before the sixth round?"

"Go home, Beaty," the bartender said. "You're drunk."

"I am at that, but I can still fight my way out of Alcoa Wrap, unlike a certain proprietor I know." He flicked his finger against the side of his nose and toward the bartender.

The bartender shook his head, walked to the end of the bar and counted the till.

Beaty said to the empty barstool next to him, "You never give up the fight, right?"

"Right," Sam E. said.

Beaty glanced at Sam E., who was standing behind him. "Hey," Beaty said to the bartender, "there's another one."

"Another what?" the bartender asked.

"Another ghost, only this one ain't like the good looking Jane or the small guy. This one's kind of goofy looking."

"That isn't nice." The bartender walked over to them. "What can I getcha?" he asked Sam E.

Sam E. waved him off. "Just passing through." He walked toward the door.

"Stay away from dames if you want to put up a real fight," Beaty shouted to him, as Sam E. exited the dark bar and entered the bright, noisy sidewalk. He looked around, thinking it would have been a nice day except for the oil-black smoke fanning upward from the western horizon. He headed across the street to the Waldorf-Astoria.

As he was nearing the hotel's entrance, a taxi parked along the curb honked. "Hey, you made it!"

Sam E. looked back. Fred Greene stuck his head out the cab's window, and waved him over.

"I thought you had to go home?" Sam E. asked.

Fred shrugged. "I told Josephine I was working overtime. Lee asked me to stick around in case he needed transportation."

Sam E. smirked. "How much did he have to pay you?"

"Hey, man, I'm trying to help out here. You haven't got a big posse. You should try and keep what you have."

"You're right," Sam E. said. "I'm sorry."

"I saw the black smoke coming from Elizabeth. I thought you were burnt toast. What happened?"

"You and your barbershop pals wouldn't believe me." Sam E. took Fred's snub nose from his jacket and tossed it in the cab. "It's empty."

"I'm not surprised." Fred slipped the pistol into the glove compartment and took out a small paper sack. "Give this to Lee." He handed Sam E. the bag.

Sam E. glanced inside. The sack contained two 3-IN-ONE squeeze cans.

"He asked me to pick it up for him. He said it was snacks."

Sam E. took one of the cans from the bag and handed it to Fred. "Keep this one, just in case."

"Why? It's not on my diet."

"It might be." Sam E. walked toward the Waldorf's revolving glass doors.

Francis again slammed his gun's butt in Lee's ear. Cricket clamped her hand over her mouth to stifle her groan.

An electric shock-like pain plummeted through Lee's skull and down his spine.

"Where's Lakeside?"

Lee, a sock stuffed in his mouth, shook his head. He tried to jerk his rope-burned wrists free from the tall-back art-deco chair he was bound to.

Francis slammed him again. Blood fell from Lee's ear.

"That's enough. You'll kill him!" Cricket said.

He smiled at her. "What's the matter? You don't get a charge out of this kind of stuff anymore, party doll?"

"Leave him alone. He doesn't have the information."

"Right after he tells me what I want to know. And if that doesn't work I'll go after *her*." He motioned to Lois, slumped on the couch. "If that doesn't work, you're next on the list." He raised his gun, ready to slam it against Lee.

The door swung open. Sam E. entered.

Francis aimed the gun at him. "Where the hell have you been?"

"At a bonfire in Elizabeth."

"You were at the refinery? How'd you know about that?" Francis glared at Cricket.

"It wasn't Cricket. It was your stiff-ass desk clerk, downstairs."

"I don't believe you."

"I paid him a hundred bucks to let me out of the room and another fifty to tell me the fund-raiser was at the Park Plaza. Who else would know that?"

"The son-of-a-bitch," Francis said. "I'll take care of him."

"And the punch line is it came from the cash you gave us." Sam E. walked over to Lee. "Let him go."

"Why not," Francis said. "He wouldn't tell me anything, anyway."

"He couldn't. I did it all on my own." Sam E. loosened his binds. Francis shoved the gun in the nape of his neck. He froze.

"One other thing, don't let it happen again," Francis said.

"Sure," Sam E. said. "Sure."

"Because if you do, your sweetie's gonna get the bullet, not you."

Sam E. glanced at the slumped figure on the couch. "How do I know that's the real Lois?"

"Because I said so." Francis pushed the revolver harder into Sam E.'s neck. "Who are you to question me, anyway?"

"I want to talk to her. To make sure she's human."

"Go ahead. Touch her if you want."

Sam E. sat next to the frightened girl. "How are you doing?"

"Okay, I guess."

"You sure?" Sam E. asked.

Lois smiled weakly. She nodded.

He touched her hand. It felt human, but he was fooled before. "Do you remember what song came over the radio when we first met at Indian Joe's Cafe?"

She nodded. "Sixty Minute Man."

"Do you remember what I said to you?"

"Sugar, I have the LP version, 'Ninety-Minute Man'," she said. "It was funny."

"It *is* you." He reached in to kiss her. She pulled back for an instant before allowing Sam E. to press his mouth against hers. A primordial uncertainty crept over him. Does she love me? Before he could bring the feeling to rational thought, Francis burst out laughing.

"Now I get it!" he said, busting a gut. "You thought the Lois back at the ship was *this* Lois!" Tears streamed down his eyes. "You didn't kiss the saucer-man, did you?"

"Go to hell, Francis."

Francis started laughing again, "You *did!* How was it?"

Sam E. said nothing. He saw revulsion in Cricket and Lee's eyes. He avoided Lois' look.

Francis walked over to him, still laughing. He rammed his knee in Sam E.'s gut with a ferocity that caused Francis to grunt.

Sam E. tumbled from the couch, losing his wind. Lois knelt beside him, gathering him in her arms. He struggled for breath.

"That's for sneaking off." Francis jerked Lois away from him. "Get ready for your TV appearance, Lakeside." He clutched Cricket and Lois by the arm and led them to the door. "Me and the girls will be back in thirty minutes." He wiggled the door key. "And Lakeside, in case you get any more ideas about running off again and making-out with outer space creatures—don't—the door will be locked."

Desperately gasping for air, Sam E. glanced up at Lee, struggling to help him to the couch. The *ka-lick* of the door being locked from the outside filled the room, but neither man heard it.

Chapter Twenty-Eight
THIS COULD BE THE START OF SOMETHING

In muscle Tee and slacks, Sam E. rinsed his Gillette in the bathroom sink and wiped the remainder of shaving cream from beneath his ears. He slapped the top of his hand several times against the puffiness below his chin. Jack La Lanne, on his exercise show, bestowed the virtues of this procedure for removing fatty deposits, and Sam E. thought it was worth a try. He felt okay, but...something inside hurt. He knew exactly what it was.

"Butterflies?" Lee rubbed the rope-burn marks on his wrists. They were raw from being tied to the chair.

Sam E. jumped. He watched Lee's image standing at the bathroom entrance, in the gold-cased mirror above the sink. "Not butterflies, conscience," he said to the mirror image. "Lee, is it wrong to want to go on *The Steve Allen Show* and bring the house down?"

Sam E. could tell by Lee's troubled expression that he was struggling for the right words.

"Your heart's in the right place, isn't it?" Lee finally asked.

"I think so. I owe it to Doc and Marge...and my mother."

"I think they'd be proud of you."

Sam E., stunned, turned and faced Lee. He had never had the word 'proud' associated with him. "We're gonna take care of the rest afterwards, I swear."

Lee stuck his palm out. "It's been a while since I've had faith in anyone." They shook hands. The gloomy portent of Lee dying from a bullet to the brain encumbered Sam E. again. "Stay out of trouble, okay? Don't get close to gun barrels."

"I'll play it cool," Lee said. "I promise."

Sam E. headed to the closet to retrieve his evening shirt. He felt uneasy despite Lee's assurance. The front door banged open. "Show time!" Sam E. heard Francis say. Sam E. hurriedly buttoned up and tucked in the shirt.

"Let's get a move on." Francis waved his gun as he and Cricket walked into the room.

"Where's Lois?" Sam E. asked, slipping his tux jacket on.

"Now, is that nice? You didn't welcome your kiss-kiss partner back." Francis patted Howdy Doody, who was perched on his shoulder, wobbling.

"Kiss-kiss." The alien puckered his lips at Sam E.

"He's sloshed," Sam E. said. "And he smells like rotten eggs."

"That's not your concern." Francis took Sam E.'s bottle of Old Spice from the bathroom counter and sprinkled the cinnamon scented aftershave on the puppet.

"My concern is Lois," Sam E. said.

"She's back at the room being guarded by Ozzie and Harriet Nelson," Francis said. "They'll be watching you on television. If anything goes wrong they have orders to scalp your Indian squaw."

Sam E. glanced at Cricket, as if to say, "Is he telling the truth?"

Cricket nodded.

"Any other questions?" Francis asked.

"Just one. How could he," motioning to the alien puppet, "duplicate Lois if she wasn't on television?"

"She was on television," Lee said, entering the room. "We saw her on the news in Kingman, after we traded in the car. Remember?"

"Which reminds me." Francis sat Howdy Doody on the floor.

"Okay," he said to the space puppet, "Presto, change-o."

The alien, still wobbly, jiggled, blurred, and re-jiggled into a nondescript looking man in a gray suit.

"Who's he? I don't recognize him," Sam E. said.

"You're not supposed to, smart guy," Francis said. "He's a losing contestant from the game show *Beat the Clock*."

"A normal person," Lee said. "So he doesn't create a disturbance like the puppet would have."

"That's the idea," Francis said. "Now, he's going to be the assistant to Lakeside's manager, which is me."

Lee said, "And later he becomes the Steve Allen lookalike."

"And nobody'll miss him when he makes the change." Francis said to Sam E., "Let me hear the plan one more time."

"Again?"

Francis aimed his .45 at him.

"After the show I get Steve Allen in my dressing room, alone, so you can replace him with 'your assistant', and then you and the alien Steve Allen go to the fund-raiser where he takes over Eisenhower."

"After you do your part," Francis said, "I'll give you the key to my room and you and your girlfriend can ride off into the sunset."

"What's going to happen to them?" Sam E. nodded to Cricket and Lee.

"Nothing." Francis wrapped his arm around Cricket. "She's with me, and he's my speechwriter."

Cricket lowered her head. Francis pecked her cheek.

Sam E. saw Lee's face flair with anger. He knew Francis saw the same thing.

"Oh, and they're both coming to the show." Francis smiled.

"They'll only get in the way," Sam E. said. "Let them stay here."

"No way. They're extra insurance in case you get any stupid ideas."

Sam E. watched him gloat. "You finally get to be the puppeteer, don't you?"

"After tonight, funny man, I *own* the strings," Francis said. "Now, let's go fuck the world."

"Skiiiisshhh!" the contestant-spaceman said.

"Skiish," Sam E. said. He wondered how the human race would look after Francis made love to it.

The Waldorf-Astoria's doorman again hailed a taxi. Fred pulled up. Sam E. glowered at the doorman, as if to say, "Keep your opinions to yourself." The doorman smirked. He raised his nose and ushered the group to the cab.

Francis motioned for Lee to sit up front. He gestured for Sam E., Cricket, and the contestant-alien to slide in the back, where he squeezed in. "Hudson Theatre, you know where it's at?"

"Yes, sir." Fred steered the cab away from the hotel. He nodded tacitly to Lee and Sam E. "You look familiar," Fred said to Francis. "You someone famous?"

"Not yet." Francis lazily eyed the hubbub of people; some gripping twine-handled shopping bags, others rushing down into, and up out of, underground subway stations, and still others loitering around newsstands, smoking.

Fred looked inquisitively at Sam E. through his rearview mirror. Figuring Fred was curious about whom the spaceman was, Sam E. motioned to the contestant-alien sitting next to him. The alien was scratching his elbow.

Fred nodded lightly. He turned a corner, and said, "This is it. One-forty-one west forty-fourth street."

Sam E. stared in awe at the four-story Hudson Theatre, a plain building except for its bronze-lined canopy and Italian Renaissance box office.

Fred drove past the front and into a small lot located in the rear. "Congratulations, you've arrived."

Sam E. smiled. Despite his troubles he was excited. The taxi glided to a perfect stop in front of the backstage entrance.

Fred stepped out and opened the doors.

Francis, leaving the cab, handed him a five. "See ya around."

"You just might at that." Fred stole a quick look at Sam E. and Lee. "I'm working a long shift today." He doffed his newsboy cap and drove away.

ector, Sr., looked at the fifty-dollar bill. He glanced at the small, pointy-faced man holding it out to him. The gray-haired, bony stage door manager studied the group he would have to let in to earn it; a bland, gray-suited man who smelled like Old Spice and hard-boiled eggs; a hefty man with tortoiseshell glasses, bushy-topped hair, red bowtie and blue dinner jacket; and a redhead with a petite nose and supple breasts beautifully profiled in a strapless, olive sheath dress. Hector, Sr., glanced at his clipboard and said to Francis, "I don't know if I can let them in. The only ones on the list are Mr. Lakeside and his manager, Mr. Ronco, which is you."

"Look," Francis said. "There's a mix-up. I told them I was bringing my girlfriend and my business associates."

"I don't know. Who did you tell?"

"Who do you think?" Francis asked, his voice sounding annoyed.

"Miss Cofresi?" Hector, Sr., corner-eyed Cricket's bust line.

She turned slightly away.

"That's right," Francis said, quickly. "Miss Cofresi."

"I don't know." Hector, Sr., snuck another peek at Cricket's breasts. "We're pretty tight because Presley's performing."

"Look, buddy, we're already late. Either you let us in or we figure something else out." He slipped his hand inside his jacket and gripped his shoulder-holstered weapon.

Sam E. nudged Cricket, motioning her to wiggle her chest.

Cricket smiled at the doorman, bent forward and scrunched her shoulders, emphasizing her cleavage for the man's appreciative eyes. "I'd really be grateful," she said. Reading the doorman's name, *Hector, Sr.*, stitched on his shirt pocket, she added with a wink, "Why, Hector, you're too young to be a senior."

Hector, Sr., took a large breath and snatched the fifty. "Go on." As Cricket passed him, he bowed and added, "Ma'am."

All of Sam E.'s years on the road hadn't prepared him for the cavernous backstage of the Hudson Theatre. The room, so tall it looked ceiling-less, was shouldered with a labyrinth of corridors, overhangs, backdrops, wardrobe, make-up, and writer rooms. The floor stage was ant-farmed by grips, camera operators, stagehands, gaffers, sound engineers, and others who Sam E. wasn't sure what they did. He noticed two things the people had in common: a sense of urgency and a cigarette between their lips. "Hey," Sam E. said to a pear-shaped man hoisting a scoop light up a pulley-rope. "Do you know where Sam E. Lakeside's dressing room is?"

"Never heard of him," the man said, without stopping, "but all the dressing rooms are to your left."

Sam E. headed to his left.

Francis grabbed his arm. "Remember, I'm in charge." He said to the contestant-alien, "If either of them tries anything clever, hit 'em hard with the zap." He glanced at Sam E., Lee and Cricket.

The contestant-alien nodded, took a 3-IN-ONE oilcan from

his pocket and squeezed the fluid in his mouth.

"I told you to knock off the juice." Francis led him, and the rest, down a slim hallway to the left.

A small woman, forty-ish, with large glasses and a larger cup of coffee, knocked, and at the same time, steamrolled into Sam E.'s dressing room. "I'm Jen Cofresi, the producer. I don't know how they do it in Vegas, but in New York City when call time is 10:30, it's 10:30, not noon."

"I'm sorry," Sam E. said. "This is my first time on television and I didn't know how things worked."

She curtly handed him the rehearsal schedule. "Your manager should have been on top of that."

"That would be me," Francis said, sitting on a square-cushioned, broccoli-green couch. He motioned for Cricket, Lee and the contestant-alien to do the same. "I'm Doc Ronco." He rested his foot on a coffee table in front of the couch. The table held a small TV.

Jen, noticing him and the others for the first time, said to Sam E., "Who are those three?"

"Contestant," the alien said.

"What? We don't broadcast quiz shows at this studio."

"Consultants," Francis said. "They're my business consultants."

Jen peered over her glasses and scrutinized them. She frowned at the alien. Francis signaled the creature by raising his diamond-ringed pinky. The alien followed by raising its own finger at her.

Jen leaned forward. "You got coffee on your cheek." She pointed to an oil splotch on the alien's chin.

Francis lowered his pinky, whisked out his pocket hanky and quickly wiped it away.

"You can watch the dress rehearsal. No one's allowed backstage during the actual show, but you can view it on TV." She motioned to the tabletop television.

"Sure." Francis tucked his hanky away. "We don't want to cause any problems."

Pushing her glasses up her nose, she said to Sam E., who was studying the rehearsal sheet, "As you see, at 8:30 Steve did a run-through of his opening bit, at 9 a.m. Steve and guests Imogene Coca and Elvis Presley did their comedy skit, Louie Nye at 10, you were supposed to do your routine at 10:30, at 11a.m. Presley did a run through of 'Hound Dog', at 11:30 Steve did his closing. We're currently on lunch break while engineering, sound, and the band key up. Lunch ends at one and then everyone goes into make-up and wardrobe. From there, we do the dress rehearsal. At eight o'clock we go live."

"I feel terrible about being late," Sam E. said. "Would you tell Mr. Allen that?"

"Better yet," Francis said, "Jen could have Steve come here after the show and you can tell him personally." He added, to Jen, "How about it?"

Jen rolled her eyes. "If you need anything, ask for Henry or Mark." She waved her hand. Two clean-cut, clipboard-carrying young men in navy-blue slacks and white broadcloth shirts appeared at the doorway. "Break a leg," she added, leaving as quickly and as strongly as she entered.

Sam E. slipped the rehearsal sheet through his mirror frame. Itching to perform, he twiddled his thumbs, eyeing impatiently the large round dressing room wall clock. It seemed to labor from 12:32 to 1 p.m., the end of lunch and the beginning of rehearsal.

Chapter Twenty-Nine
BREAK A LEG

"**S**even twenty-seven," Sam E. said, watching the second hand skim the dressing room wall clock. He was pleased with the dress rehearsal. Though rushed, he did well, and he didn't sense any lingering animosity in Steve Allen. He straightened his collar, and thought, thirty-three more minutes until Sam E. Lakeside makes his mark in the world.

The dressing room door slapped opened. "You looked pretty good out there," Francis said, entering with the others.

Lee nodded.

Cricket threw a smile at Sam E.

He studied Cricket. Her face had changed. The cheeks were thinner, but more steadfast. The cynicism in her gray-green eyes was overtaken by a sad, iron resolve. She didn't look prettier, Sam E. thought, but she looked more beautiful. She deserved someone good. He was glad that Lee loved her.

Francis and the alien plopped on the couch.

Sam E. closed his eyes. Slowly, quietly, meticulously, he said, "Red-lea-ther-yel-low-lea-ther, rub-ber-bay-bee-bug-gie-bum-per."

"Come again?" Francis asked.

"Shhhhh, I think he's warming up." Cricket leaned against the pastel green dressing room wall, next to Lee.

Sam E. repeated the phrase, faster and louder each time. Not only did this loosen and prime his mouth muscles, but also calmed him; though calm wasn't quite the right sentiment. Homeostasis was closer to the feeling. He opened his eyes and stared at the soft-white bulbs surrounding the make-up mirror. Knowing he couldn't perform without removing the pressure from his shoulders, he buried everything inside the grave he dug for himself on the Nevada mountainside: Lois, Doc and Marge, his mother's prostitution, the bullet puncturing Lee's skull, Cricket, Francis and the space-creatures, and an oil-less world. For a fleeting moment the hazy bulbs resembled their ghosts reaching up for him from the craggy pit, but he buried that, too, and he again saw the makeup mirror.

Knickety-knock-knock. "Five minutes, Mr. Lakeside. Showtime."

"I'm on my way," Sam E. shouted to the voice behind the door. He stood, slipped his jacket on and glanced at himself one last time in the mirror; running his fingers along his eyebrows to make sure nothing was out of place.

Lee clutched Sam E.'s shoulder. "Break a leg."

"Break a leg," Cricket repeated.

"Yeah, break it." Francis turned on the television. "But bring back Allen when the show's over."

"Rabbit's foot, horse shoe, four leaf clover," the alien said.

Sam E. walked to the door, hearing nothing. *No matter what happens, I have this one moment on television.* He was in his zone. His reward for everything he's been through had arrived. If ever he believed in God, this would be the thing he would look upon as an offering from Him. Sam E. took a deep, deep breath—corking up yesterday, ignoring tomorrow, concentrating on now—and exhaled. His time had come—Sam E. Lakeside's time had come.

Chapter Thirty
HI HO STEVERINO

Elvis crooned to the morose basset hound sitting on a tabletop in front of him that the canine was supposed to be high class but it was all a lie, that the animal never caught a rabbit, and he wasn't a friend of Presley's.

When Presley ended the last refrain, his combo banged a Bb chord, shoved it down a half-step to the song's A root and made the chord scream until the singer swung his arm down and straightened his crooked knee; signaling the song to come to a sledge hammer ending. Ponytailed teenage girls smattering the audience exploded in high-pitched, orgasmic squeals resembling air raid warnings. Steve Allen, adjusting his horn-rimmed glasses, pumped the singer's hand several times. Presley, in top hat, long tails and white bowtie, walked off stage. He said to Sam E., who was standing in the wings, "This outfit's all wrong. And Mr. Allen's got me singin' to a *dog*. Have you seen Colonel Parker?"

Smoking and concentrating on his cue, Sam E. mumbled, "Try the dressing rooms."

Presley nodded and walked away as Steve Allen said, from center stage, "Straight from Las Vegas we have a *new find* that's creating quite a *stir*." Steve rubbed his Vaseline-shiny, eight ball black hair.

Bug-eyed, pixie-faced Imogene Coca, in an ill fitting chef's hat covering her brown pageboy hair, tootled on stage waving a ladle. "Chef Boy-o-boy-o-boy!"

Sam E., caterpillar-stomached, waited for the setup and his signal to go on.

"Where's the stew wine?" Imogene air-stirred the ladle.

"I'd say about half-way down your throat," Steve said, cackling. "I said, we have a *new find*, Chef, not a *stew wine*." The tall entertainer—who bore an uncanny resemblance to Superman's alter ego, Clark Kent—laughed along with the audience.

"Oh." She looked into the camera. "Anybody seen the rum balls?" The audience cheered. Jaunting off-stage, she winked at Sam E. as she passed him.

Adjusting his glasses, Steve Allen said, "Ladies and Gentlemen let's have a warm welcome for Sam E. Lakeside!" The brass-heavy house band, led by leader Skitch Henderson, played a snappy intro.

Sam E. waited, snuffing his cigarette as the band came to an unsure halt.

Steve Allen, cackling nervously, looked toward the band. "Is Sam E. here?"

Skitch Henderson nervously stroked his goatee. He looked inquiringly at his sax section. They all shrugged.

"No?" Steve asked, perplexed.

Sam E. jogged on stage and shook Steve's hand. "Sorry I'm late, Steve. I had a fight with my wife."

"Is everything okay?"

Sam E. nodded. "Oh, yeah. She came to me on her hands and knees." He pulled a fresh cigarette from his tux pocket.

"You must be a tough cookie," Steve said. "What'd she say?"

Sam E., torching his cigarette, shrugged. "'Get out from under that bed, you little chicken liver'."

The audience howled.

"He-*hee*-huhee!" Steve howled, as he trotted off stage.

"This is my first visit to New York," Sam E. said, as a man behind a boxy camera with a glowing red light rolled it to Sam E.'s left. "I knew I was in the city because my middle finger got cramps from over-use."

The studio audience cheered.

"I'm from Las Vegas, I'm not used to how forward New Yorkers are." His jitters loosened up. "I was at the theater last night and a lady in the audience shouted, 'Is there a doctor in the house?'" Like a long distance runner, he felt his body settle in. "The lights came on and several doctors stood up." Jen Cofresi, watching from a monitor in the wings, was smiling and nodding. "After the lights came on, the lady stood, pulled her daughter—who was about twenty—up with her, and said, '*Good! Now are any of you doctors single and interested in a nice Jewish girl?*'" Cheers echoed through the aisles and Renaissance style balconies.

Sam E. stepped forward. "The one thing New York has is cars; I drive a lot myself. My wife came up to me the other day, and said, 'I think there's water in the carburetor'. 'How would you know?' I asked. 'You don't even know what a carburetor is'." Nothing mattered but the jokes, the laughter, and the embrace. "'I'm telling you', she insisted, 'there's water in the carburetor!'" And the embrace was everything. "I said to her, 'I'll check the carburetor for water. Where's the car?'" He took a drag off the cigarette to let the question settle in. "She says to me, '*In the lake*'." Sam E. smiled playfully. He scrunched his shoulders and spread his hands, palms out, as if sharing a joke on himself with his best friends. The audience—even the gum snapping teenagers—whooped heartily. He heard Steve Allen cackle somewhere off stage. Jen Cofresi looked up from her monitor, raised her hand and formed a circle with her thumb and forefinger, flashing him the OK sign.

"Did you know," Sam E. said, "I was the guy who painted the stripes down the middle of the highway?" The audience laughed. "No really, that was my first job, but it only lasted a few days. I got fired because the foreman said my work was slowing down." This was his heaven. His God. "But I couldn't help it," he said, "*I kept getting farther away from the paint can.*" Skitch Henderson's band struck a zesty motif. The audience slapped and slapped their jubilant palms together. Sam E.'s elbows floated. His cheeks flamed. His toes prickled. He bowed and blew a kiss to the crowd. Like an incoming wave, the sea of claps renewed its smacking.

A pair of bright spotlights sailed over the audience as a camera operator whipped his camera around to catch everyone laughing and nodding at each other. The teenage girls stood and twirled their hands like gyroscopes above their flushed faces. Steve Allen whisked on stage and pumped Sam E.'s hand even more energetically than he pumped Presley's. He said into the center camera, "Sam E. Lakeside! Ladies and Gentlemen, Sam E. Lakeside!" Sam E., no longer a complex thinking human burdened by death and destruction and invasions, was a single-cell amoeba made up of one emotion—joy. He raised his hand to the audience and trotted off as a white-booted woman with bare, marble-carved legs, wearing a torso-sized Old Gold cigarette carton, two-stepped past him onto the stage.

In the wings, Sam E. bent forward and placed his hands on his knees, staring at the black, scuffled plank floor. He took a series of deep breaths, feeling the amoeba of joy slipping away and the burdened human being creeping back in.

S am E. stood outside his dressing room, hesitant. Normally, after a performance like this he would whisk the door open as if it was blown by a windstorm, and burst forward with a wide grin on his face. Doc and Marge, and a perfumy girl with sparkling eyes and maroon-painted fleshy lips begging for a laugh, and dressed in a bare shouldered, deep cleavage cocktail dress would be standing inside. In one continuous motion he would kiss Marge on the cheek and the girl on the lips, feel Doc's strong open hand smack his shoulder blade, pour himself a whiskey, flip the make-up table's chafed, wooden chair backward, straddle it, spread his arms, and say, "What'd you think?" knowing damn well the answers would include at least one or two of the following: knock-out, terrific, sexy, the sky's the limit, the most!, let's celebrate, and, pour me another.

Then after another drink, Sam E. and his date, and Doc and Marge would grab a sirloin and mashed potato dinner at the corner table of The Chez When, while listening to *Nick Scratch and his Devil's Four* jazz combo. Afterwards, he would again kiss Marge on the cheek, shake Doc's hand and he and the girl would exit Doc's Buick Roadmaster.

Sam E. would key his apartment door open as he and the girl listened to Doc's engine shrink in the distance. Inside, he would say something amusing. As she giggled, he would nibble her shoulder, unzip her bodice and to the *click-click-click* of the kitchen's Kit Cat Clock, he would lead her into his bedroom.

Tonight, Sam E. stood outside his dressing room not knowing what to expect behind the brown door with his name taped to it. Doc and Marge were gone. There were no more girls. In the room there could be two dead bodies, Lee and Cricket's.

He could run. He could call the cops. He could bully his way back on stage and tell the world of the invasion. He could stop pretending that Lois turned away from him because she was traumatized and not because she didn't love him. He could do any of those things, but he wouldn't. He was afraid. He would do the one thing that required the least courage: he would open the door.

Lee, the contestant-alien, Cricket and Francis were squeezed together on the couch, their backs to the entrance. They were watching Steve Allen on the TV. He was pretending to be a reporter interviewing an extremely nervous Don Knotts, who was quivering like a poked square of Jell-O. He was pretending to be a dynamite maker. As Sam E. opened the door a wave of audience laughter flowed into the room and muffled out as he shut it.

As if pulled by a linked chain, the four whipped their heads back in unison. Cricket ran to him and wrapped her arms around him. "You were the most!" and for a second he thought he saw Doc and Marge.

Lee started to rise, but Francis motioned him to stay put. "You were damn good," Lee said.

The contestant-alien hopped in his seat. "Funny, funny, funny!" Francis pulled his .45 from his shoulder holster and as he tightened the silencer attached to the barrel, said, "You know, Lakeside, that was pretty good. You play your cards right and I might keep you around."

"Doing what?"

"Doing your own show." He slipped the gun back in his jacket, and said to the alien, "You like that idea?"

The alien nodded vigorously. "Funny, funny, funny!"

"On television?" Sam E. asked.

"Sure," Francis said. "How's this for a title, *The Sam E. Lakeside Cavalcade of Comedy*."

"Why?"

"Because, when I take over I want entertainment and you're funny. So, what do you say?"

"You're serious?"

"Yeah. No tricks."

Sam E. wasn't prepared for this. He knew he should give an indignant '*Fuck you!*' He thought he should feel ashamed for not uttering the epithet, but he wasn't. What he thought, was, *Is this the destiny I get to choose?* As Cricket gripped his hand and led him into the room, he thought, just as much as Cricket earned the right to a good life, he earned the right to do what he did best—make people laugh.

"What do you say?" Francis repeated. "Want to be part of the team?"

"I don't know," he heard himself say. He felt Cricket's hand release his with a gruff sharpness. He watched Lee studying him, as if he was making up his mind whether he—Sam E.—was being clever or not.

Sam E. sat in the chair next to the make-up table. "What about Lee and Cricket?"

"What about them? I already told you she's my girl and he's my speechwriter. They're not going anywhere."

"What if she isn't your girl anymore?" Sam E. thought of Cricket and Lee being together.

"Why, you want her?" Francis asked. "Did you finally figure out the waitress wasn't in love with you?"

"That's not true."

"Lois told Cricket she didn't love you." Francis glanced at Cricket. "Didn't she?"

Sam E. looked at Cricket.

She stared at him stone-faced, giving not one hint of confirmation.

In that lack of confirmation, Sam E. got his proof. "She said she was unsure," Cricket whispered.

"Sure she was," Francis said, his voice sounding smug. "But to answer your question, Lakeside, I promised you Lois, you can have Lois. So what do you say? You want your own television show?"

Knock-Knock. Jen Cofresi barged in. "Someone wants to see you!" She stepped aside. A beaming Steve Allen shuffled past her.

"Sam!" Steve said. "You were terrific! That bit about being late was a knock-out."

"Thanks, Mr. Allen." Sam E. stood. "I—"

"Call me Steve." Steve loosened his tie. "I can't stay long. I'm hosting a fund-raiser." He turned to Jen. "Has the limo arrived?"

"I'll check." Jen scuttled away.

A Jen Cofresi—someone with loyalty, skill, and devotion—all geared to one person, impressed Sam E. He was envious of Steve Allen for being that person, and not himself.

"I can't stay," Steve said to Sam E., "but I told Jen to set up something for you in September, if you're available?"

"You bet I am!"

"Great." Steve removed his tie. "There's a bar set up down the hall, I know Louie Nye, and Don, and Imogene will be——" Allen's brown pupils fluttered up, leaving a pool of white, his knees crooked. In a half turn, he collapsed on himself.

Sam E., his mouth gaping, stared at the contestant-alien, who, unseen by Sam E., had snuck up behind Steve. Remnants of the platinum-green cloud waffled from the spaceman's finger. The alien jiggled, blurred, and re-jiggled into a clone of Steve Allen.

Francis looked the clone over. "Perfect." He slid his .45 from the leather strap beneath his armpit. He bent over the real Steve Allen and cocked the trigger.

"Hold it," Sam E. said. "Don't kill him. He's going to be part of my television show."

Francis eyed him suspiciously.

"You don't think I can do a whole hour by myself, do you?" Sam E. tapped the unconscious entertainer with the tip of his black oxford. "Why do you think Allen has sidekicks like Louie Nye and Don Knotts?"

Francis narrowed his eyelids into twin slots of black. His slender face seemed to harden like a shrunken head. Contemplating, he tongue-clicked the roof of his mouth.

"Do you want a funny show or not?"

"Funny, funny, funny!" the alien Steve Allen said.

Francis glanced from Sam E. to the alien, to Steve Allen and back to Sam E. After the second go-round, he said to the alien, "You got enough zap to get Allen back to the ship?"

The alien shook his head. "No. Hotel room."

Francis said to Sam E., "Put him on the chair." He looked at Lee and Cricket. "You two stay on the couch or I'll get a new writer and girlfriend. Got it?"

Cricket nodded. Lee said, "Got it."

Grabbing the tie that had fallen from Allen's hand, Francis tossed it to Sam E. "Tie him up."

Sam E. roped Allen's hands behind his back in a stiff, tight knot.

Francis slipped his gun back in his holster. He took a makeup-stained sponge from the makeup table, lifted Allen's slouched head and stuffed his mouth with it. He took a towel, also from the table, and tied it around Allen's packed mouth. "Okay, when he wakes he'll be no problem." Francis said to the alien, "Zap him to the room. Make sure it's 1251."

The alien pointed each of his index fingers at the unconscious entertainer. Platinum-green rays, like nozzled water from a garden hose, streamed from each finger and attached themselves to Steve Allen. The rays wriggled around the chair-shackled man like a pair of intertwining caterpillars, lifting him off the floor until his greasy, tousled hair nearly rubbed the ceiling.

Knock-knock. Jen Cofresi surged in clutching a dinner jacket and bowtie.

Everyone froze except Francis, who wrapped his hand around his holstered revolver.

The alien turned toward her, and said, "Skiiiisshhh!"

Jen hurried past Francis to the Steve Allen clone. "What's up with the weirdo talk, you practicing a beatnik sketch?"

Sam E. glanced at the ceiling. The chair and the real Steve Allen were gone.

"There's been a slight change," Jen said, not waiting for an answer to the sketch inquiry. She handed the alien Steve Allen the bowtie and jacket. "Someone slashed the limo driver's tires. Because of the time, we called you a taxi. The cab's waiting at the backstage entrance."

Francis, still gripping the holstered gun, said to her, "Steve invited us along with him. Wasn't that nice?"

She looked skeptically at the Steve Allen-alien. "You did?" Unseen by Jen, Francis nodded at the space creature.

The alien, in imitation, nodded. "I like Ike," he said.

Jen shrugged. "Okay, I'll let them know you have guests. Shall I tell the driver you'll be down in ten minutes?"

Francis nodded. The alien nodded.

"Very good." As she left, she repeated, "Ten minutes."

After Jen shut the door, Francis said, "When we leave here, this is how it's gonna work." He motioned to Cricket, "You're my girl. You're in my arms the whole time." He said to the alien, "Steve Allen is my best buddy, he's beside me the whole time." He gestured to Sam E. and Lee. "You two are in front of me the whole time. If either one of you so much as farts wrong, you're gonna have a zap induced heart attack." He nodded to the alien, who pointed his finger at them. "Got it?"

Sam E. and Lee nodded.

"That includes you too, party doll."

Cricket lowered her eyes and nodded.

"Good girl. Help Mr. Allen with his bowtie and dinner jacket so we can split."

My own television show...My own television show, Sam E. thought. He couldn't get the thought out of his head. And why should he? Doc and Marge would have wanted that for him. His mother would have wanted that for him. His father, though he never knew him, would have wanted that for him—any father would want that for their son. Whether she loved him or not, Lois would want that for him. Maybe after he got his own show she would see him in a different light. Watching Cricket slip the jacket on the spaceman, he thought having the power to decide your destiny isn't such a bad thing, after all.

"You know," Francis said to Cricket as she clipped the bowtie to the alien's collar, "like I said the other night, I think I'll make New York City my headquarters. I can broadcast my commands from this studio and Lakeside can do his show here, too." He turned to Sam E., "You like that idea?"

Cricket patted the bowtie into place. She glared at Sam E., and he could feel the weight of her eyes. He didn't have to look at Lee to feel his anger. "I like it a lot."

"Then it's settled." Francis held out his bent elbow to Cricket. She intertwined her arm with it. The alien Steve Allen took his place on the other side of Francis, and Lee and Sam E. took their places in front of them, facing ahead.

Walking to the door, Lee whispered, "All actors and comedians care about is their goddamn career."

Ignoring him, Sam E. gripped the doorknob and gave it a twist.

He defiantly swung the door open.

Chapter Thirty-One
THE PLAZA

S am E. and Lee slipped into the cab's front seat. Cricket and Steve Allen slid in the back. As Francis was sliding in the back he glanced at the cabbie, who was holding open the door. "Don't I know you?"

"Yeah." Fred doffed his newsboy cap. "You're somebody famous, right?"

"Not yet. But very soon."

Fred shut Francis' door and stepped into the driver's seat. He said to Steve Allen, "Your producer said you're going to The Persian Room at the Plaza, right?"

"That's right," Francis said. "You know where it's at?"

"I know where everything's at." Fred lowered his meter, smiled at Sam E. and Lee, and drove the cab northbound onto the nightly rabble of Sixth Avenue traffic. "We're only about five minutes away. How come you're not taking a limo?"

"Someone slashed the limo's tires." Sam E. pretty much figured out who the culprit was.

"Ewww, that's too bad." Fred glanced at Sam E. and again smiled. "What's going on at the Persian?"

"A fund-raiser," Sam E. said.

"For who?"

"For Kukla, Fran, and Ollie," Francis said with fire. "Why are you so curious?"

"Just makin' conversation." Fred weaved through the crowded, double-wide road.

"Well don't," Francis said.

Fred shrugged. He turned the cab right onto Fifty-Ninth Street, pulling next to a nineteen-story building. It resembled a medieval French chateau with coned steeples on each end. The stately towers looked like two guards standing watch over the aristocracy.

Fred hopped out of the cab. He opened the front and rear passenger-side doors for Sam E. and Lee, and Francis and Steve Allen. He scooted to the driver-side rear door and opened it for Cricket. As she stepped out, he slipped his switchblade from his jacket. "I hear this is your department," he whispered, as he handed it to her. Cricket, in one motion, opened her clutch bag, tucked the knife in it, and as a cover pulled her compact out.

"Do that later," Francis said, as she powdered her nose. "We're in a hurry."

"Okay." Cricket put the powder away. She took her place next to him.

As the others gathered themselves in position, Francis eyed Fred, who was entering his cab. "Just a minute." His voice was laced with suspicion.

"Yeah?" Fred asked.

"What do you think you're doing?"

"What do you mean?" Fred glanced nervously at Cricket's handbag.

"You want to get paid?"

Fred grinned. "Damn straight I do. Can't believe I forgot. It's been a long shift." He hustled over to Francis, who gave him a five.

"Thanks," Fred said. "I'm taking my wife and son out to a nice steak dinner." He threw a quick wink at Sam E. and hopped inside his taxi.

Sam E. watched the cab enter Fifty-Sixth Street and evaporate into the throng of headlights. He wondered where Fred and his family would be a year from now. Where anyone would be a year from now?

"Let's go," Francis said, pushing him onward.

Sam E. stepped toward the gleaming glass doors. He wasn't sure if he was incredibly happy, depressed, angry, or relieved. As the lobby doors parted the only thing he was certain of was that the gold-heavy archways and pillars would lead them to the elevator that would carry them to the only place that mattered—The Persian Room.

Chapter Thirty-Two
THE PERSIAN ROOM

"**M**r. Allen, we've been anxiously waiting for you," said the shorter of two strong-set, square-faced men. The pair was dressed in three-button black suits with white shirts and black ties. They were standing in front of the tufted, red-leather swinging doors leading to The Persian Room.

Sam E. knew you didn't have to be an Einstein to see by the men's austere demeanor and the way their eyes focused on 'Steve Allen', and at the same time focused on the rest of them, that they were government agents.

"These are the four guests Jen Cofresi phoned us about?" the shorter man asked, formally eyeing the rest of them. At the same time the taller man ran a pen along a clipboard with a list of guest names.

"Friends," Steve Allen said.

"I'm Doc Ronco," Francis said, "this is my girlfriend Cricket McSouly, my assistant Lee Beaumont, and—"

"I know him," the taller agent said, looking at Sam E. "You were funny tonight, Mr. Lakeside."

The shorter agent quickly added, "Not as funny as Mr. Allen, of course."

"Of course not," the taller agent said. He checked off everyone's name from his list.

"Hey," Sam E. said to the taller agent. "Did you hear about the communist who was convicted of spying? His attorney told him, 'I have bad news and good news. The bad news is you got the electric chair. The good news is I got the voltage lowered'."

The taller agent, unsmiling, said, "You mind if I use that?"

"Compliments of Sam E. Lakeside."

The shorter agent said, "Mr. Allen, your manager inquired about a photo with you and the president. After the dinner ceremonies the president will see you privately in his hotel room. He would personally like to thank you for hosting this event and to present you with a token of appreciation. The meeting will last no more than seven minutes. Afterwards, a photographer will be on hand to take a picture."

Francis nudged the alien.

"Friends?" the alien asked the agents.

"Sorry," the shorter agent said. "The invitation is for you, only. Security reasons. I hope you understand."

"Steverino!" A blue-eyed, sandy-haired man with a mustache and goatee scuttled out of the elevator and rushed to Steve Allen.

Sam E. recognized Allen's bandleader—Skitch Henderson—who with his facial hair and paisley sport coat looked like a friendly, hip Lucifer.

"Maestro, conductor," Steve Allen said to the agents. "Skitch Hen-der-son."

"Performing dinner music. Sorry. I'm late," Skitch said.

"For the music, or the dinner?" Sam E. asked.

"You still have time for both," the taller government agent said to Skitch, as he scratched *Skitch Henderson* from his guest list. The shorter agent pushed open The Persian Room's swinging doors and motioned the group inside.

Sam E. was surprised how unimposing the place was. About fifteen white-linen draped round tables, each with two pairs of white china place settings and a glowing candle in the center dotted the entrance side of the dimly lit room. In the middle of the room was a mosaic-patterned wooden dance floor. On the far side of the dance floor, a raised platform, about eighteen inches tall, stretched width-wise like an airplane wing. The platform held a long table that faced the smaller tables. The platform-raised table held twelve place settings—six on each side—and was separated in the middle by an oak dais with a microphone attached to it. In a lonesome corner of the room a gleaming-brown piano rested. Skitch Henderson made his way there. He sat on the bench, took sheet music from his jacket, and thumbed through it.

Seated at the tables were formally attired couples. Most had a quiet, effete manner; noiselessly slicing beef Wellington with thick-handled silver forks and knives. White-clothed waiters with black hand towels draped across their forearms unobtrusively tipped terracotta-colored wine into the guest's stemmed, crystal glasses.

A smiling *maitre d'* in a double-breasted gold jacket guided Sam E. and the rest to a circular table near the side of the long table. Sam E. marveled how everyone in the room pretended not to notice the thin-lipped, white-haired bald man with silver-rimmed glasses who was sitting to the left of the dais. He was dressed in a black tuxedo, munching a dinner roll and sipping wine.

Not caring about the dispassionate attitude of the others, Sam E. gawked at Eisenhower. The president glanced up, smiled, and waved in Sam E.'s direction. He waved back before he realized the president was waving to the alien Steve Allen, who was sitting between him and Francis. Embarrassed, Sam E. took a sip of wine.

"Okay," Francis said to the alien. "You know what you're gonna do?"

"Tell jokes, go to hotel room, zap Ike," Steve Allen said.

"That's it in a thimble."

"You've got some problems," Lee said.

"Like what?"

"Your spaceman doesn't know how to tell jokes, for one. Secondly, if your Steve Allen zaps Eisenhower away and then takes Eisenhower's place, who's going to take the place of the fake Steve Allen?"

"You think you're smart, don't you wise ass?"

Lee shrugged.

"Well, I got somethin' better." Francis eyed him between the table candle's feathering yellow flame.

"What's that?"

"Horse sense. How do you think I got this far? You think you could have done what I did?"

Sam E. studied Lee. He could tell by the way Lee lowered his eyes that he knew the answer, and it wasn't comforting.

"My horse sense spooks the hell out of you, don't it?" Francis smiled. "Sure it does, I can see it in your face."

Francis is right, Sam E. thought. It's one thing to reason out actions, but another to outguess instincts. Lee's smart, but he bases his ideas on logical assumptions. Lee looked at him and he could tell Lee was thinking the same thing. Sam E. glanced at Cricket, but her eyes, more experienced with Francis' horse sense, gave no clue to what she was thinking.

"As far as replacing Steve Allen after he takes over Eisenhower, that's my problem, not yours," Francis said to Lee. He passed his thumb over the candle's fire. His face glowed with the power he felt in doing that. "You just worry about making my guy sound presidential." He said to Sam E., "And you just worry about your career."

A high-pitched squelch, like the shriek from a kicked cat, sliced the room. A bespectacled, thick-skinned man with thinning hair, who had been sitting to the right of President Eisenhower, was at the podium tapping the microphone. Sam E. recognized the man from the newspapers, Secretary of State John Foster Dulles. After the squelching noise stopped, Dulles said, "Thank you for supporting the re-election of the man who led us to victory in World War II, and one of the greatest Republican presidents to serve this great Nation under God. With your help and President

Eisenhower's, we will hold back the tyranny of The Soviet Union, Red China, and the beatniks."

Polite chuckles speckled the room.

Dulles said, "I'll leave the humor to the professionals. And with that, let's welcome the brilliant entertainer and humorist, Mr. Steve Allen." The guests applauded as Dulles took his seat next to Eisenhower.

The alien ascended to the dais. The room quieted. He faced the mic, looking awkwardly at the hushed crowd.

Sam E. shook his head. "This is going to be a disaster," he whispered to Francis.

"Horse sense," Francis said in a calm voice.

The alien scratched his elbows. He waited. The crowd waited. Eisenhower waited. With each wait the discomfort increased.

"Disaster," Sam E. again whispered.

Finally, the alien said, "Sam E. Lakeside."

"What?" Sam E. asked.

Francis smiled. "Consider it a warm-up for your new TV show."

"Sam E. Lakeside," the alien repeated. "Friend." He waved for Sam E. to come up. Francis pushed him from his seat. Skitch Henderson hit a strange chord as if to propel the surprised comedian forward.

As he made his way to the dais, President Eisenhower looked at John Foster Dulles. The two men shrugged at each other.

The alien said into the mic, "I like Ike!" The crowd applauded.

The alien ushered Sam E. to the microphone. Staring across the room, Sam E. saw a light from a chink in the swinging doors and the two government agents stick their heads in, appraising the situation. Sam E. lit a cigarette, smiled at the seated couples, and said, "Show me where Lenin is buried and I'll show you a communist plot." The crowd laughed. He removed the microphone from the podium and walked to the dance floor. "A busload of Democratic senators was speeding along a back road when the bus smashed against a tree and overturned in a farmer's field. The old farmer comes along, digs a huge hole with his tractor and buries all the men." He turned to President Eisenhower, and said, "I bet you didn't know that, did you Mr. President?" The crowd laughed. Eisenhower, playing along, smiled and shook his head. Sam E. again addressed the crowd. "A few days after the farmer buried everyone, the police chief drives past and sees the wrecked bus." Sam E., winking at an elderly lady, grabbed a glass of wine from her table. "He asks the farmer what happened. 'There was a horrible wreck and I buried them all', the farmer says. 'Were they *all* dead?' the chief asked. 'Well', the farmer said, 'some of them said they were alive, *but you know how them Democrats lie.'*"

The crowd burst into applause. Eisenhower laughed and waved to the partisan attendees. The two agents smiled at each other. They let the doors swing shut as they resumed their watch outside.

The alien stepped to the podium and proclaimed loudly, "I like Ike!" and Skitch Henderson hit another avant-garde sounding chord.

Sam E. sipped his wine. He was once again high-spirited as he waited for the cheers to crest.

Francis attracted Sam E.'s attention. He smiled and tapped his finger against his temple, and mouthed the words, "Horse sense."

Sam E. closed his eyes. Horse sense, he thought. His mother's determination, Doc and Marge's kindness, Lois' gentleness, Cricket and Lee's love, the cheering crowd—all swirled around him. It was the embrace. He reached out and squeezed it; swallowing the euphoria like a man eating his final home-cooked meal. As the cheering faded, Sam E. opened his eyes and stared into Francis' triumphant, self-satisfied, dark eyes. Francis is right about horse sense, Sam E. thought, except he hadn't counted on the horse sense of someone else: me. He glanced at Cricket and Lee, who were slumped and emotionless.

Sam E. took another sip of his wine for courage, and thought, at least I had my moment. He made his way back to the podium. "I walked into the optometrist's office the other day and told the receptionist, 'I keep seeing spacemen in front of my eyes', and she said, 'Have you seen a doctor?' I said, 'No, just spacemen'." The crowd chuckled. He took another drink. "What do you do if you see a space, man?" Sam E. said, puffing his cigarette. "Park your car in it, man." He stared hard at Francis, whose smug expression froze into an uncertain grin. "Seriously," Sam E. said, "I've been seeing space creatures for a while." This is it, he thought, feeling the world tumble as he placed the mic back on the podium. Standing next to the alien Steve Allen, he said into the microphone, "Steve, here, is an alien." He turned to the alien. "Isn't that right, Steve?"

The crowd tittered nervously. Eisenhower whispered something to John Foster Dulles, who nodded to a man sitting at the end of the table. The man quickly walked to the swinging doors.

The alien stepped to the mic, and said, "I like Ike!" The crowd applauded.

The two agents rushed through the swinging doors with the man who was at the end of the table. The agents had their hands in their jackets beneath the armpit, where a shoulder holster would be holding a revolver.

"The real Steve Allen is in room 1251 of the Waldorf, along with a sweet girl named Lois and a pair of spacemen who look like Ozzie and Harriet Nelson from the TV show." Sam E. gulped the remainder of his wine.

The crowd groaned. Sam E. saw Cricket lower her head and shake it in disbelief, as if to say, "I told you they wouldn't believe it."

The two agents grabbed Sam E. The man who had been at the end of the table approached Eisenhower and whispered in his ear.

"It's true!" Sam E. struggled to break the agents hold. His wine glass flew from his hand. "He's a space creature. A copy of the real Steve Allen!" Sam E. thought he was going to throw up. His eyes bulged like a dumb beast. "They're coming after you," he said to Eisenhower, "so they can steal our oil!"

The crowd booed. Francis relaxed. His smile returned.

From the corner of his vision, as he was being manhandled, Sam E. saw the pity in Eisenhower's eyes, and worse yet, the revulsion in the others' eyes. He thought of Miles Bennell, the poor schnook from *Invasion of the Body Snatchers* who was branded a loony. He felt himself crying as he was being dragged away from the alien, who cambered his neck in curiosity at the spectacle; felt the ting of salty snot drifting into his lips as he was dragged near the table where Francis, Cricket, and Lee were sitting; felt like he'd been pummeled in the gut by Rocky Marciano when he saw Francis laughing hysterically, Cricket sobbing, and Lee reaching into his coat pocket as if looking for a cigarette.

As he was hauled past them, he heard Lee yell, "He's telling the truth. I can prove it."

"Listen to him!" Sam E. screamed to the unresponsive agents. He managed to turn his head back in time to see Lee pull a can of 3-IN-ONE from the pocket he had reached into. Lee stepped forward. He jerked away the spout tip with his mouth and cocked his arm back, ready to fling the can at the alien like a grenade.

Bolting up, Francis shouted, "He's trying to kill the president!" as he whipped his .45 out and aimed it at Lee's temple.

The premonition flashed like a camera bulb in Sam E's brain. "No!" he hollered, elbowing the stunned agents. Sam E. ran toward Lee, marveling how everything slowed and grew silent. It was almost corny, he thought, as he followed the floating bullet waffling from the silencer, and the blue smoke-puff sluggishly tagging behind it. From the corner of his eye—as he watched the bullet gracefully drill forward—he saw Cricket toss Fred's switchblade. The shiny knife drifted with care from her fingertips, cartwheelling toward Francis. Sam E. again focused on the bullet's steel hull and copper tail drifting forward like a feather blown by the breath of a child from her tiny palm. He sprung elegantly forward, oddly opposite how he imagined he would. He thought he heard the muffle of his heartbeat as he watched the soft-tipped shell inch onward, as if it had no other place in the world to be except in Lee's temple...

Then the movie sped, like the old piano-pumping Keystone Kop flicks, only speedier and much funnier. Sam E. knocked Lee aside. The alien Steve Allen sprayed his platinum-green mist over the stunned crowd. The agents fired their weapons at the creature. John Foster Dulles threw his body over Eisenhower. Skitch Henderson stood and screamed, *"Skiiiisshhh!"* His eyes flared purple. He sprayed the same platinum-green rays that earlier transported the real Steve Allen to the hotel. The rays tightened around Francis, Lee, Cricket and Sam E. like a pair of intertwining mittens. Sam E.'s body chilled. His breath flew from him. Because things were moving so rapidly he had no time to catch up with his thoughts, other than to think, *What did the Tommy gun say to the .45?* as he felt the impact of Francis' bullet puncture his chest.

Chapter Thirty-Three
VOX DEI

*Y*ou're not such a big shot.

"Hey, that's pretty good." Doc ruffled a white-with-gray pin-stripe barber's cape.

"I just made it up," Sam E. said.

Doc plucked a cloth-clip from his powder-blue barber's jacket, and with it pinned the cape around Sam E.'s neck.

"How come you're cutting my hair?" he asked, as Doc foot-pumped upward the cushy, red-leather and chrome barber chair Sam E. was sitting on. "You gave that up when we started making money."

"Tonight's special, Sam." Doc slid a tall, black comb from the straw-holder shaped Barbicide jar behind him. Slipping his hand in his jacket's waist pocket, he said, "This is a Gustav Kaiser, hand-forged in Germany," as he pulled out steel-blue scissors. He fanned the blades—*whizzz-whizzz-whizzz*—like hummingbird wings, near Sam E.'s ear.

"Not too close."

"Don't you worry, it'll be perfect. You've got a show to do," Doc said, his plump, ruddy cheeks beaming.

"I do?" Sam E. relaxed. He stared at the black velvet curtain in front of him, as the cutting blade's *whiit-whiit-whiit* clipped his hair. Watching his curled locks tumble past the chair's cast-iron footrest to the waxed wooden floor, he realized they were on the stage he often dreamt about. He heard voices coming from the other side of the curtain.

"What kind of crowd we got tonight?"

"A full house."

"No kiddin'?" He thought he heard his mother on the other side of the curtain, laughing. Not the spent, bitter laugh that ate her alive, but a young, hopeful, lilting sound. Her laugh seemed to bring about a man's laughter. Sam E. didn't know how, but he knew the man was young like her. He was brash, kind, and they were in love. He knew the man was his father. He wondered if Lee and Cricket were in the crowd.

The aliens must have transported all of us here from the fund-raiser, Cricket thought, as she stood in Francis' hotel room trying to make sense of what happened. Standing beside her were the Steve Allen and Skitch Henderson aliens. Henderson, she assumed, was the other spaceman Francis was using in his scheme to take over the president. In front of her, strapped to their seats, unconscious, were Lois and the human Steve Allen. The alien Ozzie and Harriet, who were guarding them, were lying lifeless on the floor, an empty oil drum next to their bodies. Their faces were crinkled inward and oil was oozing from their elbows, knees, and ears. Their hair had hardened, like uncooked angel hair pasta, and had splintered from their heads. The creatures had a putrid, mucky-brown odor, like swamp mud.

Cricket felt a chilled hand grab her calf. Francis, on his knees, was reaching up to her. She heard him wheeze an ugly, scratchy sound that resembled, *"Contrawl."* She watched his hand sink and his body fall backward along with Fred's switchblade handle, which stuck out of one side of his neck, and the blade's tip, which stuck out of the other side like Frankenstein's neck bolts. She stared stoically at his body until she felt Lee, who was standing behind her, push past her. Cricket watched Lee drop the 3-IN-ONE oilcan that he was still holding from the fund-raiser and rush to Sam E.

He was slumped in the middle of the floor, bleeding. "Sam," Lee said, kneeling beside him.

"Sam," Cricket whispered. For the first time since leaving home she was frozen with fear.

"Can you hear me?" Lee felt for Sam E.'s pulse.

"**H**ave you seen Lee?" Sam E. asked Doc. "I was afraid he was going to die."

"You did a marvelous thing." Doc rubbed warm shaving cream along the nape of Sam E.'s neck, below his hairline. "You saved Lee's life."

"Is he in the audience?"

"No, he's staying in New York. I hear he's starting his own comic book company. Comes up with a super-hero who makes his living as a stand-up comic. He turns it into a movie franchise in about thirty years."

"Really? Maybe I could write some jokes for him."

"Ya know, I bet you could." Doc flipped open a tortoiseshell handled straight razor; massaging the blade vigorously along a broad, leather strop.

"And what about Cricket?" Sam E. asked.

Cricket hadn't cried real tears in so long she wasn't sure what they were until she rubbed them between her fingertips. She felt incredibly lonely and ashamed, but didn't know why; *because of Sam? Lee? Her dad laughing in her face because she screwed her life up?*

"Get over here," Lee said to her.

Cricket, unmoving, watched Lee humped over Sam E. She couldn't stop the tears.

"God*damn* it!" Lee shouted, "I need you!"

She stopped crying. Just like that. Another thing she didn't know why. She raced over, bent down and Lee pressed her left hand over the bloody hole in Sam E.'s side.

"Keep it there while I get help."

Cricket nodded.

She whispered to Sam E., "It'll be all right. I promise." Looking up at Lee, she added, "Won't it?"

Lee stood. "I don't know."

"It'll be alright, Sam," Cricket whispered again, as she rubbed his clammy brow.

"**C**ricket's going to go through a terrible spell," Doc said, as he scraped the warm razor behind Sam E.'s ear. "But if she gets herself through it, she'll hook up with Lee and they'll have a couple of top-notch kids."

"I hope so. They're meant for each other."

"Marge says the same thing." Doc shifted the razor to Sam E.'s other ear.

"Doc?"

"Yeah?"

"Where is Marge?"

Doc stopped his shaving for a moment, staring at nothing in particular. He smiled. "She's in the audience."

"I like her a lot."

"She loves you, too." Doc picked up his keen stroke.

"Doc, did we beat them?"

Lee took a step toward the door, keeping his eye on the aliens. Skitch Henderson stepped in front of him. "Oil."

"No," Lee said. "It's over."

Henderson flashed scalpel-like teeth, repeating in a harsh voice, "Oil!" The creature pointed its spray-emitting finger at Lee.

"Go ahead. But that won't change anything. The oil is toxic. I know because I was hooked on something just as bad. It's like poison."

"Poysuun," the alien Steve Allen said, cocking his head. "Toxic."

"You're overdosing. You'll die." Lee nodded to Francis, "Dead, like him." He pointed to the shriveled Ozzie and Harriet. "Dead like them. Bye-bye, gone. It's lousy merchandise."

"Lousy," Henderson said. "Dreadful, egregious, shit, ropy."

"Yes. Your customers will get sick and they will die. You'll go out of business. Bankrupt."

"Bankrupt?"

"Insolvent, impecunious, belly-up," Lee said. "You'll lose all your money, or whatever it is you get when you sell the oil. Francis lied to you. It won't make you rich. It'll only kill you."

They stared at Francis' blue-cold face and the crimson blood coagulating around the blade slices in his neck, and his twisted body, which resembled a puppet with its strings cut.

"It's lethal goods," Lee said. "You'll end up like your friends."

The aliens studied the fallen Ozzie and Harriet; hairless, faces crumpled inward, their joints secreting oil. Skitch Henderson picked up the 3-IN-ONE can that Lee had dropped. About to take a sip, he again studied the disfigured Ozzie and Harriet, and instead handed the oil to Steve Allen, who tossed it back on the floor. They nodded in unison at each other.

"Fucked up." Skitch Henderson swept his platinum-green ray over the fallen aliens, the Steve Allen alien and himself. He looked at

Lee, and said "Skiiiisshhh," as he and the other extraterrestrials vanished upward.

Lee raced out of the hotel room.

"**T**hanks to you saving Lee, the spacemen saw the light and called it quits," Doc said. "You didn't think God was going to let earth go to hell, did you?"

"I don't believe in God."

"That's okay. God doesn't mind."

A muffled rumble came from the reverse side of the curtain. "Listen," Doc said. "They're starting to chant your name."

In hushed, excited unison the crowd repeated, "Sam-*mee*, Sam-*mee*, Sam-*mee*."

"Do you know Al Levin, the grocer's son? I think I hear him," Sam E. said.

"He's out there," Doc said. "I think he wants to apologize to you for some bad things he said about your mother."

Sam E. smiled. He hesitated. "Is Lois there?"

Cricket, keeping her eyes on Sam E., and the blood seeping between her fingers, said, "Stay with us, stay with us."

"Lois, is that you?" he whispered.

"**N**o," Doc said to him. "Lois couldn't make it." He removed the aluminum cloth clip, flipped the barber cape from behind Sam E.'s neck and wafted the cloak twice, forming a twin wave like the tracks of a double-dip roller coaster.

"Oh," Sam E. said, staring down at his lapped hands. "That's too bad."

254

"Don't take it personal." Doc turned behind him to an alabaster countertop lined with rainbow hued Bay Rums and Lavender waters. "She's awfully fond of you."

"I don't think she was in love with me."

"I know. She wanted to tell you things like she was so young and so confused and she wasn't ready to fall in love, but she was afraid to hurt your feelings." Doc clutched a whiskey-shaped bottle from the counter. It had a proud, black-striped Bengal Tiger on its label and the words *Lucky Tiger Hair Tonic* printed above it.

"I'll never forget her, Doc. She wants to be a teacher."

He squeezed Sam E.'s bicep. "She's going to think about you her entire life."

"I hope she's not sad."

"She's going to have a nice marriage and a good teaching career. Her first child, a girl, she insists on naming Samantha."

"Sammie for short," Sam E. said, smiling.

"That's right." Doc splashed a generous amount of *Lucky Tiger* over Sam E.'s hair.

"Chances are it wouldn't have worked out, her and I. I'm always on the road and that's no life for a teacher."

"You're probably right." Doc fingered the caramel-colored tonic into Sam E.'s scalp. "This stuff is a real lady killer. The men in my unit swore by it."

"Yeah?"

"Guaranteed."

The overhead lights flashed on like a row of awakening giants.

Sam E. chanted, "Red-lea-ther-yel-low-lea-ther, rub-ber-bay-bee—

bug-gie-bump-er, Red-lea-ther—"

"What?" Cricket asked, placing her ear to Sam E.'s lips.

Lee burst through the door with Alpin, who was gripping a metal first-aid kit. Lee raced to Cricket. Alpin froze. He stared at Francis lying face up with the knife sticking out of each side of his neck, oozing blood.

"We need the kit!" Lee bent over Sam E.

Alpin took a deep breath. He stepped over the dead body and kneeled next to Lee, unclasping the box's snaps.

"What's he saying?" Lee asked Cricket, as he tore open gauze pads.

"It's his vocal warm-up."

Alpin handed Lee an alcohol bottle from the kit. Lee gently removed Cricket's hand. "Sam, this may hurt." He poured the liquid over the wound.

Sam E. didn't moan, so much as whimper once. His lips moved a second time but nothing came out. Cricket's eyes welled.

"Here." Lee handed her a sack of gauze rolls. "We're going to need a lot." Cricket tore it open and handed some to Lee. He applied them to the fleshy bullet hole.

The door flung back. Two white-smocked medics rushed in with a gurney, knocking Francis' head with the rubber wheels.

Alpin instinctively moved to give the medics room, but Lee and Cricket remained next to the limp body.

"What about those two?" one of the medics, a squat, double-chinned bullfrog of a man asked, motioning to Lois and Steve Allen.

"They're shook up, but okay," Lee said. "Go check on them, kid," Lee said to Alpin.

As Alpin went to them, the bullfrog of a man felt Sam E.'s carotid artery. The other medic, a taller, muscular fellow, out of habit quickly rubbed his stethoscope plate on his pants to warm it. He shuffled the plate inside Sam E.'s red-soaked shirt. The two medics felt and listened for several seconds. The bullfrog of a man glanced at the taller fellow. Each one knew the other's look—a tightening of the jaws and a twitch of the lips—and what it meant.

The taller man removed his stethoscope. He said to Lee and Cricket, "Would you like to say anything to him before we transport?"

"No," Cricket said, her voice stern. "I want to wait till later." She started crying.

"Tell him now," Lee said in a soft voice. He placed his arm around her shoulder, but she jerked it away.

She wiped her eyes, gently kissed Sam E. and whispered in his ear. The only thing Lee caught was, "...that they wouldn't believe you, didn't I?" She brushed Sam E.'s cheek with the back of her slim, trembling hand, walked away and sat, balled up like a punctured inner tube, on the couch.

Lee smiled warmly at Sam E. for a few moments, as if Sam E. was telling him a favorite joke. He leaned in, straightened Sam E.'s ruffled collar, and said, "Break a leg, Sam." Lee stood, nodded at the medics and sat next to Cricket.

The medics lifted him, more gently than urgently, on the gurney. Cricket leaned into Lee, watching the medics roll his body away.

"**B**reak a leg!"

"Thanks, Lee," Sam E. said.

"That was me," Doc said. He lifted a tobacco-brown framed hand mirror in front of Sam E.'s face. "I said that."

"Oh. Must be opening night jitters." Sam E. angled his head, scrutinizing the front and back receding images reflected between the hand mirror and the large counter mirror behind him. He smiled. "Perfect."

"I told ya!" Doc pressed his tasseled loafer against the hydraulic release pedal. The boomy chair huffed down.

The chanting grew louder from the other side of the curtain. The packed crowd stamped their feet and clapped their hands. Louder and louder, the noise grew.

"It's time." Doc stood behind Sam E., brushing hair from his shoulders with a fine-bristled brush.

Sam E. stood. "The curtain never opens because this is where I always wake up."

"You don't have to worry about it this time," Doc said, still behind him.

"Are you sure?" He looked back, but Doc and his barber chair were gone. He knew, though he couldn't explain why, that Doc was in the audience next to Marge, stomping and clapping with the others. Sam E. turned and faced the closed curtains in front of him. *We don't choose our destiny, only how we handle it.* He took a huge breath. The scallop bottom, black cloth parted slowly, gloriously.

Someone said, as she pointed to the stage, "There he is!"

The room hushed.

Sam E. stepped into an amber spotlight surrounding a single, gleaming mic stand. Atop the stand was a tractor-grilled silver microphone. He approached it, gazed into the crowd for a moment, and said, "I couldn't trust my wife, that's why we got a divorce." The audience cheered. He thought of his mother and his childhood. He didn't smell, or see the putrid musky-brown. He saw a woman surviving, and a child surviving. He felt their spirit, not their miserable existence. For the first time, Sam E. celebrated their will to overcome. His torso was without weight and his limbs tingled with this feeling. How terrific it is to make people laugh and how lucky I am to be able to do it, he thought, as he glanced at the velvet curtains parted majestically on each side of the stage like twin angels awaiting his arrival.

258